THE KILLERS' TERMS

THE KILLERS' TERMS

A
COLE HUEBSCH
NOVEL

KEVIN KLUESNER

First published by Level Best Books 2024

Author Photo Credit: Cole Kluesner

First edition

ISBN: 978-1-68512-749-7

Cover art by Cole Kluesner

This book was professionally typeset on Reedsy.
Find out more at reedsy.com

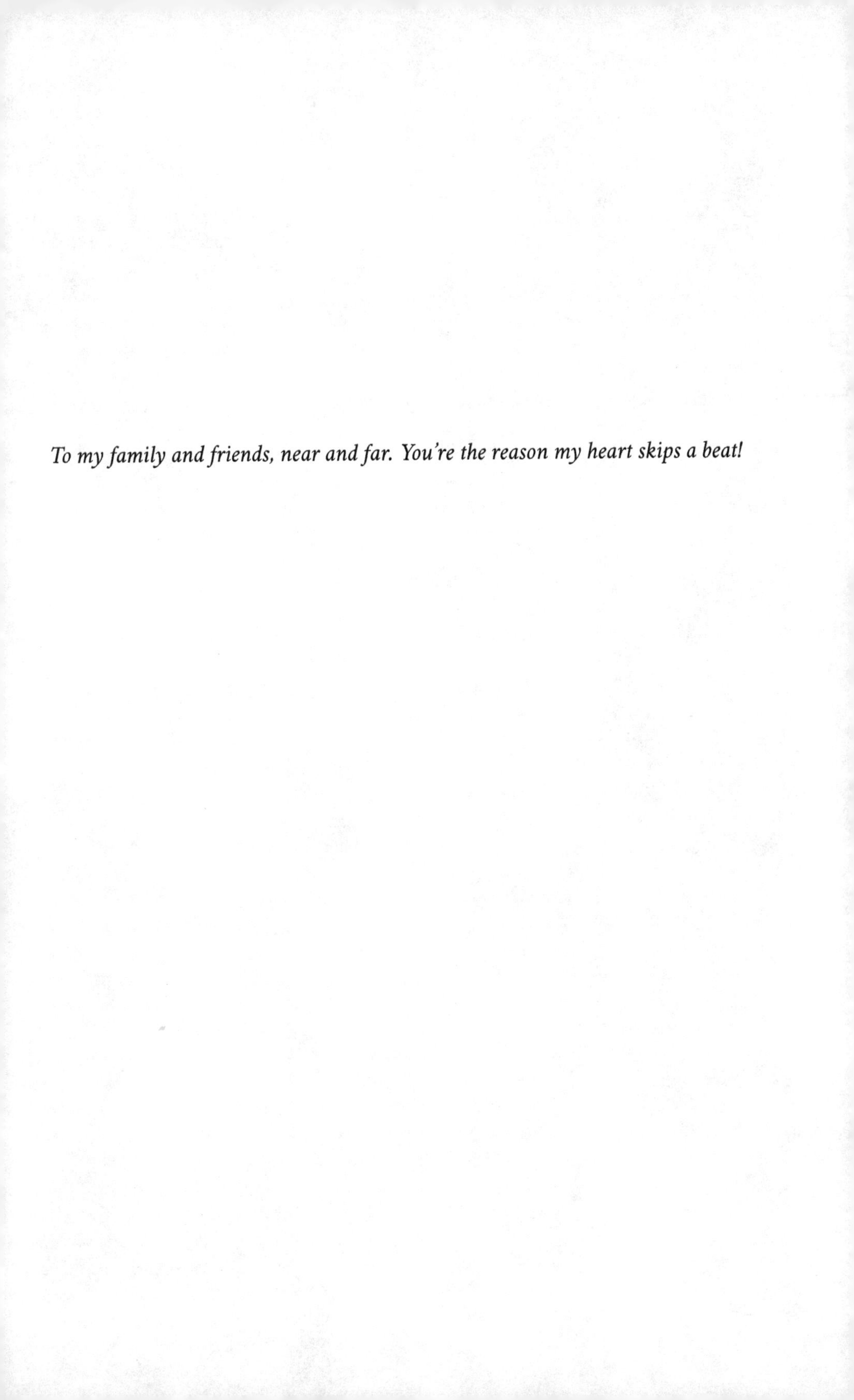

To my family and friends, near and far. You're the reason my heart skips a beat!

Praise for the Cole Huebsch Thriller Series

"It's a joy to follow Special Agent Cole Huebsch through the streets of Milwaukee in this fast-paced thriller. Kluesner exceeds the high standard he set with *The Killer Sermon* to deliver an exciting, humorous, and thought-provoking story with a phenomenal sense of place."—Archer Parquette, *Milwaukee Magazine*

"In quick strokes, Kevin Kluesner vividly sets the scene—present-day Milwaukee—and introduces the protagonist, FBI agent Cole Huebsch, and the attempted political assassination he is tasked with investigating. The prose is strong and rhythmic, guiding the reader page to page as the story rapidly unfolds. Cole Huebsch is a character readers will want to meet again and again."—David Luhrssen, *Shepherd Express*

"Kevin Kluesner's second novel, *The Killer Speech*, intertwines politics, a complex murder investigation, and deftly written prose to create a must-read mystery."—Melissa Collum, *Morris Newspaper Corp*

Chapter One

"Power tends to corrupt; absolute power corrupts absolutely." — Lord John Dalberg-Acton

Michele Fields pulled into a parking space on Milwaukee's Eighth Street, just outside the central library's Centennial Hall entrance. She shut off the car and closed her eyes, savoring the moment. It was five p.m., and she wasn't scheduled to deliver her author talk in the hall for another hour. She exited the car, locked it, and fed the meter before walking to the corner of Wisconsin Avenue. The street was named Grand Avenue up until one hundred years ago, and Michele thought it still seemed pretty grand. St. James, a towering gothic-styled Episcopal Church built in 1867, faced her from across the street, while a larger-than-life bronze of George Washington stood tall on a concrete pillar in the boulevard between the library and church, looking past Michele to the bustling heart of the city to the east, and further toward Lake Michigan. Slight movement in the recessed doorway of St. James caught her attention, and she noticed a large person in the shadows there. She felt a sudden, irrational chill of fear and dismissed it as quickly as it came to her. Anyone could forgive her a little paranoia, given what she'd experienced the past few months, but she wasn't going to let nerves ruin her big evening.

She took a deep breath and held the warm September air in her lungs, feeling the kiss of the early Autumn sun on her face. She smiled when she turned to look up at the main entrance of the library, which spanned the entire city block. Its stoic, gray Bedford limestone walls rose three stories above a raised basement. It was a far cry from her hometown library. She'd grown up on her parents' dairy farm outside Wabeno, Wisconsin, an hour and a half north of Green Bay and over three hours away from where she currently stood. The Wabeno Public Library was a tiny log cabin built in 1897 and converted into the town library nearly one hundred years ago. Her mom drove her to the library every week until Michele was old enough to ride her bike into town, the white, plastic wicker handlebar basket filled with stories to broaden the mind and imagination of a young girl. She looked at the mammoth building in front of her again. This was a different library altogether.

Less than a year ago, Michele was a general assignment reporter for the *Milwaukee Journal Sentinel*. It was exciting work when she first started right out of college, but by the time she turned thirty-five, she felt like she was still writing stories that nobody would remember beyond the next day. That all changed when she covered the murders of reproductive health physicians, and the killer reached out to her repeatedly via email. Michele helped the FBI track down the killer. After he died in a shootout with law enforcement, Michele took a sabbatical from her reporting duties to write a true crime thriller about the murders. She received a large advance, and now the widely anticipated book sat atop the *New York Times* and other bestseller lists a week after its release. Michele smiled. Heady stuff for a Wabeno farm girl.

She pushed through the middle set of large wooden double doors and entered the library's three-story marble, pillared atrium. It took her breath away. To her right was the Wisconsin writers' "wall of fame," and she marveled at the list of names, including legends like Aldo Leopold, John Muir, Carl Sandburg, Laura Ingalls Wilder, Thorton Wilder, and Orson Wells. She also recognized David Marannis, the Pulitzer-prize-winning journalist who grew up in Madison before going on to a long and legendary career with the *Washington Post*. Meeting him in high school had helped steer Michele to her own career in journalism and to the place she stood right now. And there was no place else she'd rather be.

Chapter Two

Cole Huebsch stood away from the podium set up on the steps in front of the FBI field offices on the shore of Lake Michigan. His denim blue eyes squinted into the sun, and he felt a pleasant breeze tousle his hair. The Special Agent in Charge of the FBI's Milwaukee Field Office in the suburb of St. Francis was more than happy to put the spotlight on his friend, Ty Igou, the Milwaukee Police Department Captain and head of the MPD's Sensitive Crimes Division, as he updated local media on recent progress made by the regional joint human trafficking task force. The innovative task force's core team included MPD, the United States Attorney's Office, and the Sojourner Family Peace Center. The task force investigated and prosecuted human trafficking at the state, local, tribal, and federal levels, all while addressing the individual needs of the victims. The FBI was hosting the press conference to remind both the general public and the perpetrators of the crimes that the task force had the support of *all* levels of law enforcement.

Ty walked through a number of criminal convictions the team had won against the mostly men who recruited, transported, and pedaled minors in the state for prostitution. He also described cases of forced labor they were prosecuting, where hopeful immigrants were strongarmed to work for little to no wages in Wisconsin businesses as diverse as restaurants and farms, under the constant threat of being turned in to the authorities for deportation. Modern-day slavery.

As Ty wrapped up and leadership from the Task Force began to take questions from the media, Cole couldn't help wondering if they were making enough progress. It seemed like for every case they solved and convicted, three more tips about new cases came into their hotline. And how many more would they never hear about? He shook his head and then started to worry about the time. He had fallen in love with Michele Fields while working closely with her to catch a killer, and he knew he had to leave soon if he was going to make her event. It was a big night for Michele, and Cole was getting sweaty palms thinking about meeting her parents for the first time. She knew where he was and that he couldn't leave the press conference early, but it didn't stop him from wanting to race across the city to see her. The questions kept coming, with a few echoing Cole's concern about the growth of human trafficking despite the task force's best efforts, and Cole's discomfort grew. Distracted, he noticed a brief flash of light from across the street. A charcoal-colored sedan idled there, but it was too far away for Cole to see the driver or much of anything else. The glint could have been caused by the sun sliding out from behind a cloud and catching the windshield or a mirror, or maybe someone in the car had pointed a lens at him. *Preferably a camera lens and not a rifle scope,* Cole thought to himself, which was funny until he thought it through. He didn't like either option. And he had been a target in his career more often than he wanted to admit. The car was gone when he looked back across the street, and Ty had answered the last question. Ty turned back to Cole with a big smile. "Get out of here. I'll see you at the library!"

"You're coming? And not just for the after-party at Café Hollander?" Cole asked.

Ty laughed. "Wouldn't miss it, buddy. Should be exciting!"

Chapter Three

Michele stepped up to the podium after a welcome from the head librarian and a warm introduction from Daniel Goldin, owner of the area's largest independent bookstore. Daniel and his team at Boswell Books had worked with her publisher to make the night possible. Michele scanned the crowd as she waited for the initial wave of applause to fade. She saw her parents in the front row, and her smile widened. Her mom looked beautiful in a simple yellow dress and a cream-colored sweater, and her dad looked handsome in tan khakis and a hunter-green button-down shirt. Michele shook her head in amusement as she gave them a little wave, knowing her mom had likely bought her dad's outfit from Lands' End with zero input from him. He was a strong man with his own independent streak, but what he wore in public was dictated by his wife, despite his half-hearted protests. Michele didn't see Cole in the crowd yet, which she guessed must be over two hundred strong. But she knew he would be there as soon as he could. She wanted to share as much of this moment with him as possible.

"Thank you! Thank you all for coming inside on a beautiful Wisconsin evening to join me on this author journey I've embarked upon," Michele said, launching into her prepared remarks. She went on to describe her life growing up in Wabeno, taking the time to introduce her parents and giving them credit for providing her with acres upon acres of love, support, and opportunity. She talked about the excitement and nervousness of leaving home at seventeen to study in Columbia, Missouri, at the University of Missouri's prestigious journalism school. She told the crowd about her pride in returning to her home state after landing a job at the largest, most widely read daily newspaper in Wisconsin. She came out from behind the podium as she grew more comfortable, freed by the wireless microphone pinned to her shirt collar, feeling the warm acceptance of the people seated in front of her. She saw their smiles, heard their laughter at the right moments, and felt their concern and empathy when she shared her fears and aspirations.

The entire auditorium grew tense when Michele walked them through that bitter cold January morning when the killer shot a reproductive health physician with a high-powered rifle. The murder took place in Milwaukee, just a few blocks away from the *Journal Sentinel* offices where Michele worked. She described getting to the scene early and shared the words of the clinic staff she had interviewed, capturing their fear, shock, grief, and even anger in the raw moments immediately after the shooting.

Michele was a natural storyteller, whether writing or speaking, and she could feel the audience hanging on her every word. The otherwise quiet auditorium crackled with a current of electric tension and suspense when she described being alone in the dimly lit, cavernous newsroom when the killer's first email chimed in her inbox. Michele paused and bit her lower lip as if months hadn't passed…as if she was sitting in front of her computer monitor reading the killer's words for the first time. The audience squirmed, sharing the very real confusion and fear they read on Michele's face. She swallowed hard and looked up, catching sight of Cole for the first time. He was in the back of the room, standing just inside the main doors. He had a broad smile on his face, and he gave her a nod that told her clearly that he was right there with her now, as he'd been throughout.

Her confidence returned with her smile, and she continued, noticing for the first time that she recognized as many as a fourth of those in attendance. Reporters and editors from her paper and local media outlets, and men and women from the law enforcement community, FBI and MPD mostly, that she'd come to know while working the case with Cole. As she talked, her eyes kept coming back almost involuntarily to a large gentleman seated in the first row. Unlike the rest of the crowd, he never made eye contact with her. Whenever she glanced his way, his head was lowered, and his right knee bobbed up and down soundlessly like a piston. It wasn't particularly hot in the room, but the man was sweating through his blue dress shirt. She wondered absently if he was ill.

She strolled along the front of the raised stage as she talked, the soft clicking of her heels hitting the glossy hardwood planks carrying through the room. She walked the audience through law enforcement's final showdown with the killer in the small Wisconsin river town of Prairie du Chien, where Cole tried in vain to talk the killer into surrendering while surrounded by armed sheriff's deputies, as well as local and state police. "Milwaukee FBI Special Agent in Charge Cole Huebsch was shot in the shoulder that day, and the other officers present shot the killer to death. I see Agent Huebsch in the back of the room tonight," she continued, waving to him. "He's the handsome gentleman in the navy suit standing just inside the main doors. Please join me in recognizing the bravery and service of Agent Huebsch and all law enforcement who helped end the nightmare that started with that killer sermon."

Michele couldn't see Cole blush, but she could see him shaking his head at her as he waved off the applause from the crowd. Michele was about to take questions when the big man in the front row got up stiffly, stepped to the front of the stage, and pulled himself up onto it. The smile left her face, replaced by a mask of confusion, but Cole was already sprinting down the main aisle toward them. The guy didn't appear to be heavily muscled, but he was at least six foot two and weighed two hundred and sixty pounds or more. He pulled a meaty hand out of his pocket and fumbled with something. It was a folding knife, and it was now fully open. He stepped forward, lifting the knife over his head and driving it down hard, aiming for Michele's center mass. She'd been frozen in place but lifted her left arm to block the blade. She succeeded, but the knife cut through muscle and tendons to the bone. Michele's scream of pain and shock echoed Cole's scream of futility and rage as he raced to the stage.

Michele stumbled back a step, her eyes wide, looking at the blood pouring from her arm. The large man rushed her, knocking her backward into the podium, and Cole could almost feel the crack of her head against the hardwood as he hurdled up onto the stage and onto the back of Michele's attacker. He grabbed the man's right wrist with both hands and ripped backward, resisting the overwhelming urge to hammer his fist into the guy's face as he whirled the bigger man around like a rag doll. He looked at the man's right hand, his knife hand, ready to disarm him by breaking his wrist. But the wildly shaking hand was empty.

Ty had raced right behind Cole onto the stage, and he put a hand on Cole's trembling shoulder. "I've got him, brother." He clicked a cuff on the attacker's wrist that Cole was holding, turned the man, and finished cuffing him. Cole watched numbly before turning toward Michele. It was then he saw the knife handle, buried to the hilt in her chest, a flower of crimson blossoming on her white shirt. Her eyes were mercifully closed, unable to accuse him of failing her.

Chapter Four

A big hand rested on Cole's shoulder, and he turned into the reassuring brown eyes of Alan Anderson. Alan was a close friend of Cole's and the administrator of a local hospital. Dr. A. J. Berg, a general surgeon, had attended Michele's author talk with him, and he put pressure on the gash in Michele's arm with his jacket. "The paramedics are already en route. It shouldn't be long, and Dr. Berg will do his best to stabilize Michele until they get here. It's going to be okay."

Ty led the attacker off the stage with his hands cuffed behind his back. Cole looked at Alan again, helpless and scared. He was used to taking charge in the most chaotic situations, but all he could do was quietly ask his friend, "What can I do?"

Berg called over, "I need something to use as a tourniquet to stop the bleeding in her forearm. It might be her least bothersome injury long-term, but right now, she can't afford much more blood loss." Cole took off his jacket and tie, ripping off his white dress shirt. He held it out to Dr. Berg. "Will this work?"

Berg nodded. "I'll use the tie for the tourniquet, but I can use the shirt as a towel. Thanks." As he worked on Michele's arm, he said, "I'm going to leave the knife in place until we get her to the hospital. It's acting as a kind of plug in her wound right now. It's not perfect, but it seems to be staunching the bleeding somewhat."

Cole and Alan turned when they heard a commotion behind them and were relieved to see EMS personnel almost running as they pushed a gurney down the aisle. They wrestled it onto the stage and gently slid Michele onto it with the help of Dr. Berg. Cole stood and helped lower the gurney off the stage. "Are you taking her to St. Joe's?" he called as the EMS started pushing Michele up the aisle."

"Yes," Dr. Berg called back.

Cole stood on the stage in his dress slacks and white t-shirt, confused and in shock, fumbling for his jacket.

"Here," Alan said, holding out the jacket to him. Then he nodded to the front of the stage. "And there's a couple nice folks that could use your strength right now."

Cole turned and looked into the frightened faces of Jim and Debbie Fields. He swallowed hard and went to them, sliding off the front of the stage and offering his hand to Michele's father. "I'm Cole Huebsch. I'm a, ah, friend of Michele's," he said. Jim looked down at the hand and shook his head, coming out of his daze. He took Cole's hand. "Sorry, I…I'm at a loss here. I'm Jim Fields, Shelly's father. And this is my wife, Debbie. Is Shelly going to be okay?"

Cole shook Debbie's small hand, "All I know is that she's in good hands right now."

"We don't even know where she's being taken," Debbie said, tears flowing freely down her cheeks.

Cole put his arm around her, feeling her shoulders quake with fear. "Come with me. I'll take you there."

Cole drove them straight to the Emergency Department at St. Joseph Hospital. After checking in to make sure Michele was being treated there and gathering their visitor badges, Cole and her parents huddled together in a corner. Cole got each of them a cup of coffee, and they settled in for what they all knew could be a long night.

The waiting area was large, but some of the chairs were bunched in clusters to provide at least an illusion of privacy. The lighting was bright but not harsh, and it was quiet. Cole knew from his friend, Alan, that this ED could treat more than two hundred patients in a day, but it was early evening at the beginning of the week, so they mostly had the place to themselves. They were around the corner from the only television, so they only heard it as background noise.

Debbie's kind face was still streaked with tears, but it softened a bit, with a faint smile tugging at her lips. "We were looking forward to meeting you, Cole, but under different circumstances. Shelly has talked so much about you and how you've helped her these past months."

Cole shook his head. "She's the one who's been helping me, both in solving important cases and just growing as a human being." He looked at them both, "You two must have done something right in raising her, because she's an amazing woman."

They waited together mostly in silence, each in turn caught up in their own thoughts and prayers. Cole couldn't help notice how Jim held Debbie's delicate hand in his own calloused one, involuntarily squeezing once in a while in a reassuring way. They'd been married forty-five years, and Cole figured that Jim's gentle touch told her more than words ever could.

A nurse checked in on them from time to time, but after more than two hours, all they really knew was that Michele was being evaluated and treated in a trauma bay and that the team was doing everything they could to take care of her. They knew she was still alive, but not much else. Cole was close to panic and was thinking about calling Alan to intervene when his friend approached with Dr. Berg. It was highly unusual for a hospital administrator to sit in when a physician briefed a family, and it reinforced Cole's opinion both that Alan was a true friend and that Michele's injuries were life-threatening.

Berg was dressed in blue hospital scrubs and had a surgical mask pulled under his chin. It was hard for Cole and Michele's parents not to notice the dried blood on his top. After introducing himself to Jim and Debbie, Berg described Michele's injuries and the team's plan to address them.

"Your daughter's a fighter, but her case is complex, because she has multiple injuries competing for immediate attention. The first thing we needed to do was stop the loss of blood and then run tests to find out how serious her injuries are. We've already called in a number of specialists to review the case with us, and a plan of treatment is in process. The injury to your daughter's forearm is severe. The four-inch blade cut through tendons and nerves as well as muscle. That needs to be repaired by a hand surgeon, or she'll experience loss of function in her left hand. We've been able to stabilize the arm, but that's all we can do at this point until we get the more life-threatening injuries under control."

Cole looked at Debbie and Jim, and their eyes were wide, mirroring the fear he felt. They had dressed up and traveled to the big city to share one of their daughter's shining moments, and now they were hearing that losing the function in her arm might be the least of her worries. They sat in numb shock as Berg continued.

"If there's any good news, it's that the knife in Michele's chest slid through her ribs and punctured her lung. It missed her heart by inches, which would have been catastrophic. It also missed her abdominal cavity, avoiding injury to her critical organs, including her intestines. Your daughter's right lung collapsed, but we've already been able to successfully insert a chest tube to help re-expand it."

Berg paused. He knew that in a situation like this, most loved ones were in some degree of shock and couldn't understand the most basic explanations, let alone complex medical jargon. He slowed down to avoid losing them completely.

"The chest tube is a plastic tube that we inserted through your daughter's chest wall. The drain was placed to suction fluids; it keeps the lung inflated and doesn't allow air back into the wound. So, her chest wound is stabilized at this point. We don't think it will cause any additional short- or long-term issues."

He made eye contact with all three of them before continuing. "We were also concerned that Michele might have a brain injury."

That caught them by surprise. Jim's head cocked to the side, "Brain injury? What?"

"During her attack, Michele was knocked backward, and the back of her head slammed into the wooden podium. She may have hit that same area of her head when she then fell to the stage's hardwood floor. She hasn't been conscious since she went down, not at the scene, not in the ambulance, and not in the hours she's been at the hospital. She no doubt has a concussion, but we've already run an initial cranial CT scan that was normal. So that's good news, at least for now."

"What's next?" Jim asked.

"We've started a blood transfusion, and we'll get her through the night. If everything looks good tomorrow morning, we'll call in a hand surgeon to fix her arm."

"Is she out of the woods yet?" Debbie asked.

Berg considered his response carefully. He didn't want to overpromise but did want to give them hope. "Let's just say she's on the path that should lead her out of the woods," Berg said before excusing himself and leaving. Alan had been quiet during the surgeon's visit, but he stood up and addressed Cole and Michele's parents. "We won't learn anything else tonight. You'll be better prepared for tomorrow and the days ahead if you go home and get some sleep. I have Cole's number, and I'll make sure you know if there's any change in Michele's condition."

The three exchanged glances and, almost in unison, said, "We're not going anywhere."

Alan shook his head and shrugged in resignation. "I thought as much. Michele is going to be moved to a room in our intensive care unit shortly. I'll help you get situated up there."

Chapter Five

When Michele's eyelids fluttered open the next morning, it seemed like they pulled the pins on flash-bang grenades. Harsh light stabbed her eyes, and her head pounded with pain. She closed her eyes immediately, but Debbie caught the flicker of life.

She held Michele's hand and leaned close, whispering, "Honey, it's Mom. You're okay."

Michele kept her eyes shut tight against the light but squeezed her mom's hand. Her eyes began to water, and tears flowed down her cheeks. "I hurt Mom, and I don't understand what's happening to me."

"You were attacked last night while you gave your author talk at the library. But you're going to be okay."

Michele cried out loud, "But I don't remember any of it." Her eyes opened into slits, and she tried to sit up before the pain from her chest and arm created a chorus with the drums beating in her head. She sagged back into the bed, defeated. "I don't understand what's happening or why."

Jim stood next to his wife and dried Michele's tears with a tissue. "This is Dad, hon. For now, just know that your mom and I are here and that you're being taken good care of. Cole was here, too. He left the room just now to get a doctor or a nurse to let them know you're awake."

"I can tell I'm in a hospital, but what's wrong with me?"

Debbie answered, "You were stabbed in the chest and arm last night. The team here patched up your chest wound and put in some kind of tube so they could reinflate your lung. That seems to be doing okay. The doctors said you need 'pretty extensive' surgery on your arm; they need to reattach nerves and tendons, and that will take several hours. You also have a bad concussion from hitting your head when you fell during the attack, but they did a CT scan that showed no internal bleeding. They want to take you to surgery soon, and when you wake up you can begin your recovery." She still held Michele's hand and now reached for her husband's hand with the other. Debbie worked to keep her voice from cracking as she tried to console her only child. "We'll work through this together like we've done any time life's put an obstacle in front of us. It'll be okay."

Michele nodded. She tried to take a deep, calming breath, but the pain in her chest checked that. She was hurting and frustrated but steeled herself as she squeezed her mom's hand once more. *You've been through harder times,* she told herself.

Chapter Six

Cole said his goodbyes to Debbie and Jim as soon as the nurse wheeled Michele out of the room to take her to surgery. Before leaving, he told them he would see what he could find out about Michele's attack and reassured them that the team at St. Joseph Hospital was as good as they came. After stopping at home for a quick shower and to put on a new suit and tie, he raced to his office in nearby St. Francis. He hopped on I-794 South and slowed as he hit the Hoan. The nearly two-mile-long tiered-arch bridge usually offered great views of Milwaukee's harbor, but this morning, the bridge was shrouded in low-hanging clouds and fog. Yesterday's sunny brilliance had been replaced sometime during the past twenty hours by a pall of grey. The scene he drove through might've been painted by an impressionist on their worst day, with nothing more than damp soot and coal dust on their palette. Whispers of mist drifted over the bridge's railings, shadows of the fog in his head. Cole drove on numbly, his headlamps virtually useless, then pounded one hand on the dash as he screamed to remind himself that Michele was still alive and that he had something worth fighting for.

Arriving at the office, he settled in behind his desk, rubbed his eyes, and took a moment to center himself. The hot shower had washed away some of his exhaustion, but he still felt grit behind his eyelids. He called Ty on his cell and asked the MPD Captain if he had anything yet regarding Michele's attack, and Cole didn't say no when Ty volunteered to drive over to the FBI's offices to share what he could.

He groaned when he turned on his computer and began scrolling through emails; over two hundred had flooded his inbox since he'd left the office the day before to attend the press conference. He always had a heavy stream of emails, but this was a torrent, extreme for one overnight. He responded to the emails as rapidly as possible, realizing the bulk of them that came in after ten p.m. were people writing to offer their condolences or help with Michele's attack. Cole grew more frustrated as new emails piled into his inbox faster than he could answer the old. The shrill chirp of his desk phone caught him off guard and he hit the speakerphone button to answer, frustration in his voice as he picked up, "Yes!"

"Ouch! Cole, it's Gene Olson, one of the good guys!" Olson's deep, booming voice filled the room and lifted Cole's spirits. Olson was ten years older than Cole and had been one of his earliest instructors at Quantico. He was calling from FBI Headquarters, the J. Edgar Hoover Building in Washington DC, as a Deputy Director, two spots below the agency's top position.

When Cole didn't respond immediately, Gene said, "I'm guessing you had a rough night. I'm calling to see how Michele's doing and to check up on you, too."

Cole took a deep breath before answering. "Thanks, Gene. Michele's prognosis is mostly good, though she's got months of rehab in front of her if she wants to regain the full use of her left hand. She was also stabbed in the chest, and the blade just missed her heart." His voice caught in his throat. "I could have lost her, Gene."

"That's true, Cole. You could have, but you didn't. Thank God and keep moving. It's all we can do. I'm assuming MPD has the lead on Michele's attack and that it's a clear case of a stalker gone mad."

"My friend Ty is leading the investigation. You might remember him; he's an MPD captain now, but he helped us on a big case earlier this year. You probably heard that the guy who attacked Michele is in custody. I don't know anything beyond that yet. But Ty is coming over within the hour to bring me up to speed on what they've got so far."

"Sounds good. I sent flowers to Michele at St. Joe's, but give her my best and tell her she's in my prayers."

"Will do."

"And one more thing," Gene asked, stretching the moment. "Did Michele's parents like you? You've got some rough edges and all, but you're also a fine figure of a man."

Cole laughed out loud for the first time since Michele had been stabbed. "Fine figure of a man? Who talks that way? And I hope they like me. It's hard for a guy to make a good first impression when their daughter is being attacked by a madman with a knife."

Gene chuckled. "So that's your excuse then. If you need someone to vouch for you, give them my number and have them call me."

"Not in this lifetime. But thanks for checking in, Gene. See you soon."

Cole punched the button to end the call and laid his head down on his desk, figuring he had thirty minutes or so until Ty arrived. An irregular sound caught his ear, *scritch, scritch, scritch,* and a tired smile reached his face. He looked up at the round wall clock as its hands limped spastically around. Everyone, including the maintenance crew, wanted Cole to let them replace the clock, but Cole held on to things with a desperate grip sometimes, because he'd already lost too much in his life.

Cole turned forty-five this past March. He'd lost both parents in a car accident when he was twenty-two, just before graduating with his BA in English and Philosophy from Marquette University. He went into banking and earned his MBA from the same school, but was fired from the bank for taking down a serial bank robber and killer. The FBI recruited him, and he was sworn in after earning top marks on the Bureau's physical and written exams. He took a post in Milwaukee and married his college sweetheart, Janet Stone, a local television reporter at the time. The demands of their jobs and inability to conceive a child pulled them apart; Janet was now his ex-wife and a Fox News anchor in New York, while Cole had risen through the ranks, taking charge of the Milwaukee FBI Field Office six years ago. He'd fallen hard for the reporter, Michele Fields, in the past year. And now he faced the real possibility of losing her.

He looked around his office, where he'd spent too many hours of his life. He could see Lake Michigan through his blinds, and the dull gray skies and water reflected his mood. A flat-screen television and an autographed poster of Olympic wrestling champion Dan Gable adorned two of his walls. A wildly colorful two-foot by three-foot painting hung alone on another wall, a gift from a mostly harmless reformed Baltimore gang member named Weezy, who helped Cole on an important case before going straight and opening a tavern. The painting looked like a mosh pit of garish gang graffiti at first glance, but upon further reflection, it revealed a portrait of Cole that captured him perfectly. The only other thing besides electrical outlets on his walls was a fist-sized hole in the drywall, created when the former head of the Chicago FBI field office threw a chair a few months ago. Cole hung a small silver frame over it and named the 'piece' *Leadership*. He crafted the title out of label tape and stuck it below the frame. He wondered absently how the "artist," special agent Collin Jeffers, was doing since he'd been stripped of his SAC title and sent to the Anchorage field office in a last-ditch chance at redemption. On second thought, Cole realized he didn't give two shits about Jeffers. Not even one.

A pair of Cole's old wrestling shoes hung from a peg behind his desk. He'd worn them when he won his own NCAA wrestling championship and had them autographed right after the meet by Cael Sanderson, a U.S. Olympic wrestling champ and the only Division 1 wrestler to win every one of his collegiate matches. Cole spent much of his youth chasing Gable and Sanderson's legends, and he could use their inspiration now.

He sighed and closed his eyes as exhaustion, and the feeling of impending dread pulled his head back down to his desk.

The sharp rap of knuckles on wood jolted Cole awake. Ty Igou stood in the doorway in his blue MPD Captain's uniform. He held a travel mug in one hand and saluted Cole with a ceramic one, steaming with coffee. "Good morning, Cole!"

"Hardly," Cole grunted, wiping his mouth with the back of his hand in case he'd drooled while out.

Ty handed the cup of coffee to Cole and moved to sit in the guest chair, but Cole redirected him with a wave to a small round table. By the time Cole joined him there, Li Song and Lane Becwar had entered the office. They greeted Ty and Cole before taking the last two seats.

Li was Cole's most trusted analyst, and at her request he was helping her transition into the role of agent. She had recently turned thirty-five and had worked as an attorney at a large Milwaukee firm before joining the Bureau. She was slender yet strong, and her speed and training allowed her to more than hold her own in fights against men three times her size. Her long black hair fell in front of her beautiful face as she settled in at the table. She tucked it behind her ears, revealing the turquoise tortoiseshell glasses that framed her eyes, one chestnut and one sky blue. Most people never noticed, but once you did, it was hard not to stare; her eyes pulled you in and kept you there. Cole would never forget his first introduction to Li, when she told him, "The condition's called heterochromia, and it's the only thing hetero about me."

Lane Becwar was thirty and stood six feet tall, athletic in a rangy kind of way. He'd worked full-time in the local offices of one of the "Big Four" accounting firms before joining the Bureau as an analyst a year ago. He had short but thick black hair, deep brown eyes, and a nose a little big for his strong, oval face. Cole found him smart and funny, both attributes he admired.

"How's Michele?" Li asked after a pregnant moment. She knew Cole typically kept calm and steady no matter how crazy and weird things got around the office, but she also knew what it was like to see someone you love attacked. She understood better than most what he was going through.

"It was a long and sleepless night, but we're hopeful she's going to be okay. They patched up her chest wound last night and took her to surgery this morning to fix her arm. They said it'll take four hours or more to reattach the tendons, nerves, and such. She'll have weeks and even months of rehab ahead of her with the hope she'll get the feeling and strength back in her hand."

"Jesus," Lane whispered.

"Yeah," Cole said. "One minute, you have the world by the tail, and the next, you're flat on your back in a hospital bed fighting for your life. She also got concussed when the guy knocked her head into the podium. But they did a brain scan and didn't see any internal bleeding. I guess we should count that as a blessing." He lost focus for a moment before he went on, "She was in excruciating pain the few moments I saw her awake this morning, and she's asking both what happened and why. We need to find answers for her."

Li tried to lighten the mood, nodding at Ty. "I see you brought your big travel mug. Did you, by any chance, help yourself to a free refill from the FBI kitchen? Those MPD decanters filled with reheated motor oil not up to your high standards these days?"

Lane jumped in. "Decanter? I think the word you're looking for is carafe."

This was a tight-knit group, and the back-and-forth banter helped tamp down stress levels. Cole saw what they were trying to do and said, "We're Americans, and this is America, for Christ's sake. The vessels that house the MPD reheated motor oil aren't decanters. They're not carafes. They are not urns for the love of God. No. Here on this hallowed soil, we call them coffee pots, and proudly, I might add. Ty can't stomach the MPD sludge, so he stole some from us. We forgive him and go on. Now, what do you have for us, Captain Igou?"

"Right," Ty said, slipping his phone out of his pocket and pulling up notes from the case. "This file is fat already, and we're adding to it every minute." He looked directly at Cole. "Everybody wants to make sure we do this right."

Cole nodded in appreciation, and Ty began reading aloud. "The man who attacked Michele is named Albert DeMario. He's fifty-eight years old and hails from Pittsburgh. As you saw, he's a rather large gentleman, six foot three and two hundred and sixty pounds. He's an accountant by trade. Does taxes for people out of his house for a living. He got married when he was closing in on forty to a twenty-five-year-old woman he met online. He and his wife had a baby girl, Megan. The wife left Al and his daughter when the little girl was two, moved to Las Vegas after realizing she didn't much like being a wife, or a mother for that matter. That little girl's now seventeen, and from all appearances, it looks like Al was doing a pretty good job of holding things together until two years ago when the girl developed a rare and deadly form of leukemia. DeMario seems to have devoted himself to saving his daughter. He hasn't worked much since she was first diagnosed, and he's mortgaged his house to the hilt and spent his life savings trying to find her a cure. But the drugs currently on the market haven't done much other than slow the cancer and drain his accounts."

"So, what?" Lane asked. "You just told us a tragic story, but what does it mean? After two years of living every parent's worst nightmare, this guy snaps, flies across the country, and stabs a debut author? Not likely!"

"How did Michele become his target?" Cole added. "I wanted to rip this guy's head from his neck until a moment ago. Now, I'm confused instead of mad. And that pisses me off all over again. How did Michele get on his radar?"

"Everyone take a deep breath," Ty said, surveying the other three. "We've just started digging. But there's more if you'll listen."

All three nodded. Cole took a big slug of his coffee and held the warm mug close to his chin, feeling the moist steam caress his face. "The best part of waking up is coffee in my cup," he said, settling back in his chair and letting out a big sigh. He gestured to Ty, "Go on."

"DeMario didn't grab a knife from his kitchen drawer. He used a four-inch folding blade called the Strider SMF. Easy to carry and conceal, but lethal." He winced and looked at Cole when he said *lethal*, but Cole gave him a *no worries* look, and Ty continued. "The Strider SMF was designed specifically for the U.S. Marines back in 2003. The civilian version costs $600 minimum. Our guy is in debt over his head, completely underwater, and he somehow gets his hands on a Strider."

Li broke in. "Did he buy the knife recently? Any record of its purchase on his credit card or bank statements?"

"No," Ty answered. "We ran those checks and found nothing. Each of those Strider knives has a serial number on it too, just like a firearm, but the number on DeMario's blade was filed off."

Cole shook his head. "This wasn't his idea. If he snaps one day in Pittsburgh, he doesn't fly to Milwaukee and try to murder an author. It just wouldn't happen that way."

"It was premeditated, planned a bit at least if not well," Ty said. "We reached out to the FBI Field Office in Pittsburgh, and they've already grabbed the guy's personal computer. He bought tickets to Michele's event two days ago; at the same time he bought his airline tickets to Milwaukee. He also Googled images of the library's Centennial Hall. They don't have schematics easily available to the public, but he would have been able to get a feel for the aisles, stage height, typical podium location for events, etc."

Cole cocked his head. "Michele was stabbed around dinner time yesterday. I can't believe how much you've gotten done already."

"Thanks," Ty said. "You've got a lot of friends and admirers in MPD and throughout the Bureau. Michele's stabbing has been all over the local and even national news, and as word has gotten out, I've had offers from all over to help."

"Same here, boss," Li said. "There aren't many secrets in law enforcement these days and our colleagues know the story of Michele helping us out on a couple of big cases and how the two of you fell in love. Lane and I have fielded calls from all over the country this morning from fellow officers of the law who want to help. Your sheriff buddy from Prairie du Chien, Fwam Vang, left a message on my machine before I even got in the office. And I heard from another sheriff down in Baton Rouge. I couldn't understand every word he said, but it was clear he wanted to help."

Cole couldn't help but smile, remembering. "Sheriff Beau La Bauve, from East Baton Rouge Parish down in gator country." He sighed, "I suppose it's not fair that this case is getting special treatment, but I'm glad for any help we can get."

"That's about all we have right now, though," Ty said. "We agree with your assessment that someone put DeMario up to this. Whoever it was gave him the money for the airline tickets, the perfect knife for the job, and an extra one hundred thousand dollars."

"What?" All three asked Ty.

"Just before DeMario bought his airline tickets, one hundred thousand dollars showed up in his checking account. No subtlety involved. Your guys in DC are trying to trace where it came from as we speak."

"What did you get from DeMario himself," Cole asked.

Ty shook his head. "Nothing. He hasn't uttered a single word since we pulled him off the stage last night, much less answered any of our detectives' questions. He hasn't talked to his court-appointed attorney either.

"Huh." Cole rubbed the stubble on his cheeks as he pondered that. He had spiked a fiery rage as he stood at the back of the hall and saw the woman he loved being attacked. It had morphed into a hard knot of anger and loathing in the hours since. And as Ty described DeMario and his daughter's plight, it had begun to dissolve, melting into a slurry of confusion and frustration. It was easier to believe in a bad guy, someone pure evil that you could go after with righteous fury and vengeance. Now Cole's motivation and even his next steps felt muddled.

Chapter Seven

Cole checked his phone for a message from Michele's parents or the hospital as he walked down a bright white corridor in the Milwaukee County Jail. He didn't see any notifications and assumed Michele was still in surgery. He said a silent prayer for her as he wound his way through the familiar building; his footfalls echoed and amplified by the hard, sterile flooring. All MPD violent offenders ended up at the County Jail after going through MPD's holding facility and being interviewed by its detectives. It was another good example of agencies collaborating where it made sense both financially and procedurally. But Cole knew things were tense at the jail. Like most jails across the country, it had a shortage of qualified staff and an overabundance of bad guys. There had been a riot at the jail a month ago, where thirty violent offenders barricaded themselves in the library for hours before a team dug them out by breaking a window and using a liberal amount of pepper spray. Conditions in the jail weren't ideal, but Cole felt worse for the guards than the inmates. *Don't do the crime if you don't want to do the time.*

Cole was buzzed through to one of the jail's cell blocks and stood as casually as he could by the raised area where several guards sat, surveying the scene. The area was a large square, with two levels of individual cells ringing three-quarters of the room. All the cells opened up onto the common area Cole was observing. Cole stood out in his suit and tie, but he adopted an easy attitude and looked around. He quickly counted 16 white-topped square tables, each with four cranberry-colored plastic-molded chairs set up around them. Colors were picked carefully and with purpose in correctional facilities, and Cole wondered what the hell mood cranberry was supposed to instill in the inmates. A couple of extra-large brown sectionals completed the room's furniture. African Americans and Hispanics made up forty-three percent of the county's residents, but closer to three-fourths of its prison population. It was an injustice the community had mostly admitted and was trying to address, but it was a complex and persistent issue that Cole didn't see going away any time soon. It did make his job identifying DeMario that much easier. While other inmates were clustered in groups of twos, threes, and fours around the tables, DeMario was seated at a more remote table by himself. All the inmates were in orange, not jumpsuits, but instead baggy, two-piece numbers. They reminded Cole of blaze-orange hospital scrubs. DeMario stood out, not just because of his pasty-white coloring or the fact that he was seated by himself, but even more so by his posture and demeanor. He couldn't have looked more like a human target if someone had painted a large bullseye or *KICK ME* sign on his back. He sat with his arms crossed on the table, shoulders slumped, and his head hanging down. He was oblivious to his surroundings and in a completely defenseless position. Cole knew that big, soft guys attracted the worst kind of attention in lockups almost as much as small, physically weak guys.

That thought had barely left Cole's brain when another large, white male decked out in orange made his way to DeMario. He stood to the left of the accountant and rested his hands on the table. The man's short sleeves revealed blue-inked tattoos running up and down his heavily muscled arms. Cole was no more than twenty feet from the table, standing behind a thick red line on the floor that indicated areas off-limits to the prisoners. Cole didn't think the red line would be much of a deterrent if someone with ill intent decided to cross it. The tattooed man said something to DeMario that Cole couldn't make out. DeMario looked up at the other inmate but said nothing in return. After a pause, the tattooed man's face turned hard, and he said something else that came out as a snarl. Cole couldn't hear the words, but he made them out easily enough by reading the guy's lips and posture. "Answer me, you dumb son of a bitch!" A heartbeat later, the guy reached back and threw a hard right fist that caught DeMario on the left side of his face, knocking him out of his chair and onto the floor.

Cole reacted before any of the guards could, and he was nearly on the attacker before he could follow up with another punch or kick at DeMario. He turned on Cole then, and Cole knew instinctively that a big right hand was coming his way. The thinking was the tactic had just worked on his fellow inmate, so it would likely work just as well on the dumbass in a suit. But Cole knocked the fist away before it connected with his face, then ducked and grabbed the inside of his attacker's left elbow with his left hand. He jerked the guy's arm over his shoulder as he shot his right arm roughly between the guy's legs. Cole heard the guy's "oof" as he stood up quickly, arching his back. He had his attacker in a fireman's carry now, nearly defenseless. The accountant had made it back up onto his knees and watched Cole with his eyes wide. Cole stepped away from DeMario and began to turn in circles, slowly at first but picking up speed until the inmate's long, stringy hair was straight out from his head and whipping around. Then Cole stopped abruptly, bent over, and set the man on his feet again. The guy's face looked green, like a kid who'd just gone one too many rounds with a Tilt-a-Whirl. He wobbled and would have gone down hard, but Cole reached out and steadied him with a strong hand on his shoulder. Cole leaned in close and said something to the guy that no one else could hear, and then steered him to a nearby table and helped him slump into a chair.

Cole heard a few inmates clapping and whooping it up as he walked over to DeMario and helped him to his feet. Someone yelled, "Fucking helicoptered the dude!" Another shouted, "That's fucking old school, man." He looked over his shoulder at Ty and could see him and the guards shaking their heads and rolling their eyes. But they were relieved. If it didn't escalate, everything was cool. Cole knew he'd stepped in when he probably should have let the guards do their thing, but he wanted to establish some kind of connection with Michele's attacker, and he'd taken advantage of the opportunity as it had presented itself. He looked at the man now and saw redness and swelling above the accountant's left eye, but he looked to be otherwise okay. When the guards came over, Cole asked if they would get DeMario checked out and then put him in an interview room. As they led him away, Ty leaned in and asked Cole quietly what he had said to the guy who'd clocked DeMario. Cole looked at his friend and said, "I told him if he ever attacked anyone in the jail again, I would throw him through a window. I also told him if DeMario so much as stubbed his toe while they were locked up together, that I would hold him personally responsible. But I said it nicely." They both laughed and headed down the hall to wait for DeMario.

Cole was well-known and widely respected among the MPD ranks. Everybody knew he was too close to the DeMario case to have a heart-to-heart with him, but they also felt he wouldn't cross the line with Michele's attacker, no matter how strong his feelings. And nobody but the Chief of Police herself would call out Captain Igou for allowing it in the first place.

Cole and Ty stepped into the small interview room and took seats opposite DeMario in the spartan room, knowing that County jailers were watching through the large one-way mirror behind them. DeMario didn't make eye contact, instead looked down at his hands. A cold pack sat unused on the table. "You should press that ice pack above your eye. It'll keep the swelling down and ease the pain a bit," Cole said. "I've got some experience getting hit in the face myself, so I say that with first-hand knowledge."

DeMario didn't respond, and Cole considered his options. Ty had filled him in on the interrogation at MPD. They'd tried every trick to get the accountant to open up, including being friendly, trying to scare him with the threat of a long stretch in jail, and more. But he never said a word. Never showed any emotion at all. So, Cole decided to lay his cards on the table and see what came of it.

He leaned forward so that his face was closer to the level of the guy he was interviewing. "Mr. DeMario. My name is Cole Huebsch, and I'm the Special Agent in Charge of the FBI's field office here in Milwaukee. You are in this jail because you attacked a reporter and author with a knife last night. That woman you attacked is in surgery right now, where a team of health professionals is working to save her left arm, which you damn near cut off. They've already patched up the wound in her chest, where you missed her heart by inches. She's lucky to be alive right now. I was with her and her parents before she was taken to surgery this morning, and you should know that she was in horrendous pain." He paused to let that sink in. "And did I mention that she was concussed when you slammed her into the podium?"

DeMario's eyes pinched, and he winced, so Cole continued. "This seems out of character for you. We've looked into your background and found no evidence of you being violent in the past. Even when your wife left you with a toddler, you just let her go. You accepted it quietly and moved on with your life."

The accountant looked up at Cole, and his eyes filled quickly with tears. His body seemed to tremble slightly.

"You raised your little girl with no help from anyone, and from what we've learned so far, you've done a fine job of it. Megan has grown into an incredible young woman, well-liked by her peers, good in school. A bright future if she can beat her cancer."

DeMario's defenses were overwhelmed, and his body quaked as he began to sob. Cole let him get it out. He sat back in his chair while the man keened and wailed, mourning his life, the losses behind and ahead of him, and the dark turn it had taken. "I would have taken her back," he blubbered.

His first words! "What?" Cole asked. "Who?"

"Jane! My wife." He wiped his nose with his shirt. "When she left Megan and me, I didn't just accept it. I called her and wrote to her, but she ignored me. After a few months, I finally found a sitter for Megan, and I flew out to Vegas to track her down. I found her with the help of a private investigator. She was working as a whore at a ranch in Pahrump, about an hour from the strip. I tried to talk to her, but the bouncers there threw me out. I loved her. I would have done anything to have her come with me. I would have taken her back with the seeds of a thousand men in her belly, but she didn't want anything to do with Megan or me anymore."

Cole shook his head, pushing the thought of the seeds of a thousand men from his mind. "We don't believe attacking Michele Fields was your idea," Cole continued. "You used a particular and expensive knife for the job, and one hundred thousand dollars just appeared in your bank account. Tell me about that."

DeMario looked at Cole with wet, sad eyes. "I can't. I was told in no uncertain terms that my Megan and I would be killed if I didn't kill the reporter. I would prefer to die than hurt somebody the way that I did, but I would do anything to protect Megan!"

Cole slammed his fist down on the metal table, and a resounding boom echoed through the little room. "And I would do anything to protect those I love, including that reporter who's in surgery right now!" Cole shouted. He caught himself and spoke quietly again, but his breathing was tight and ragged. "And keep in mind that you failed. If they were paying you to kill Michele Fields, you failed miserably. If someone told you they would kill your daughter and you if you didn't murder the reporter, then they are likely plotting to kill her right now. And maybe that guy I kept off you a few minutes ago was paid by those same people to kill you!"

DeMario's eyes went wild. "You need to help us! I don't care about me, but you need to protect my Megan!"

Cole leaned in, looking the broken accountant squarely in the eyes. "You tell me everything, and I'll do whatever I possibly can to protect and help Megan. I know those are just words right now, but I mean them."

Cole's phone vibrated inside his jacket pocket, and when he pulled it out, he saw a text from Debbie Fields: *Shelly is in recovery. She'll be back in her room within the hour.* Cole showed the message to Ty and then addressed DeMario a final time as he stood up to leave. "You tell Captain Igou your story, every detail of how and why you attacked Michele. I'm on my way to see her right now. You tell us everything, and I'll call my counterparts in Pittsburgh right now and have them watch over your daughter. Do we have a deal?"

"Yes," DeMario said, grateful relief flooding his face as they shook hands. Cole left the room in a hurry.

Chapter Eight

Michele was sitting up in bed by the time Cole walked into her hospital room. Her mom and dad were seated near her. The blinds were open, but the gloomy gray skies on the other side of the window couldn't dim Michele's bright smile when she first saw Cole. He had brought her a dozen mixed roses, and he set them on the windowsill. Michele looked tired, but otherwise upbeat for someone who'd recently woken up after a long surgery. Her left arm was in a splint, and she had an I.V. line running out of her right hand. After Cole said, "Good afternoon" to her parents, he stepped up to Michele's bedside and asked, "How are you?"

Michele smiled again, "I'm doing okay. If you had asked me earlier this morning, I would have answered differently." She pointed to a laminated pain rating scale taped to the near wall that featured six cartoonish faces, ranging from zero for the happy face on the left to ten for the crying face on the right. "I would have said my pain was a twenty-five and a new little face would be exploding into tiny pieces. But I feel better. They gave me a nerve block in surgery, so I can't even feel my left arm, and whatever else they're giving me for pain is working now, too." She took his hand in her right hand, careful not to tug the I.V. "Thanks for being here."

"I hope you know I would have been here sooner, or better yet, never left your side, but I had a chance to get debriefed by Ty and then to have a word with the guy who attacked you."

"You talked to the man who stabbed Shelly?" Debbie asked.

"Yes. His name's Albert DeMario, and he isn't some random stalker. He's an accountant from Pittsburgh. The single parent of a seventeen-year-old girl who has a horrific form of cancer. He's bankrupted himself trying to find her a cure, but nothing's worked. It looks like someone paid him money that he could potentially use to buy his daughter into a clinical trial. It was her only chance, and he was desperate. He has no history of violence. So, we know DeMario's motive for attacking Michele, but we don't know who put him up to it or what they were hoping to gain by having her wounded or worse. Until we know more, we'll have protection on Michele 'round the clock at the hospital. We can't rule out that whoever paid DeMario to attack Michele won't try to get to her again since she survived. We want to be cautious."

Cole saw the worried looks on Debbie and Jim's faces, and he thought he saw a flash of fear or panic cross Michele's. But it was replaced just as quickly by a look of resolve. Her inner strength, especially in the face of adversity, was one of the many things that had drawn him to her.

Cole leaned in close to Michele, and his eyes were moist as he whispered, "There's so much about you I still need to learn." He gestured with his head to the roses on the sill. "When I walked into the flower shop a few minutes ago, the counter person asked me what she could help me with. And I realized I don't even know your favorite flowers yet. So, I pulled out my phone and Googled *best flowers to bring to a hospital patient*. It suggested hypoallergenic flowers and listed roses first, so there you are. Pretty weak, right?"

Michele smiled and wiped a tear from his cheek. "I don't think I've ever heard a more romantic story."

Cole laughed. "I'm just saying there is so much I have to learn about you, and I can't wait to do that." He straightened up, and his smile grew bigger. Michele cocked her head. She had seen that look on his face numerous times when he thought he was being clever. He held Michele's hand and turned to her parents. "So, does everyone in the family call this beautiful young woman Shelly?"

"That's all we've ever called her," Jim said, reflecting Cole's smile back at him. "She even had a nickname when she was little…"

"No, Dad," Michele tried to cut him off, but she was laughing.

"We called her *Shelly Belly*."

Michele tried to punch Cole but snagged her I.V. tubing in the covers and caught herself before it could yank out. "You're not helping, Dad!" But all four of them laughed.

She turned serious then, reflecting. "Nobody knew me when I went off to college, so I introduced myself to everyone as Michele. Same thing when I moved to Milwaukee and started my career. It's part of my byline, so that's how I'm known to everyone outside of Wabeno, which includes these two yokels here and a few livestock."

"Hah!" Debbie said. "Don't go all city slicker on us. You think you shook the manure and wholesomeness off your boots when you left our little town, but you can never get it off all the way. You're a Wabeno girl at heart."

Michele smiled at that. "And you know I wouldn't have it any other way. I love Wabeno, and I wouldn't change a thing about how I was raised." Then she looked at Cole and squeezed his hand. "And I wouldn't change anything about my life today, other than to get well and out of this damn hospital gown."

"I think it looks kinda sexy," Cole said, blushing as he remembered Michele's parents behind him. "Oops!"

But they laughed with him until Michele's face grew stern. "And one more thing. Nobody ever…and I repeat, ever…breathes the words 'Shelly Belly' ever again!" Which caused the laughter to begin anew.

Chapter Nine

Michele's eyes were heavy after another thirty minutes of small talk. Cole explained his living arrangements and asked Jim and Debbie if they'd like to stay with him. Cole convinced them they wouldn't be imposing, and after protesting, they agreed to use the "Castle Mansion," as Cole referred to it, as their base of operations while they were in town. They were committed to having at least one of them at Michele's bedside at all times, day and night, but they would need a place to shower and sleep at some point. Cole assured them his landlord and friend, Frau Newhouse, would welcome them with open arms, the same way she did with Michele not so long ago. He gave them a key to his floor and the code for the garage before he headed out. It was almost six p.m. when he settled into his car in the parking lot, and he realized he hadn't had a thing to eat since lunch the previous day. The realization made him even hungrier, and he texted Li and Lane to see if they'd be open to meeting up for dinner at Merriment Social, a restaurant located in Milwaukee's Harbor View neighborhood. It was a contradiction of sorts, modern comfort food served in an industrial-chic atmosphere. But Cole had never been disappointed in a meal there, and he thought he could eat the entire menu.

He arrived first at the restaurant and ordered a Rectifier IPA from Eagle Park, which had a brewery just two miles due north of where he sat. It was a California-style IPA with a friendly Midwest personality all its own, and Cole took a big gulp of the hoppy goodness as soon as the waiter set it in front of him. It took the edge off his hunger, but he ordered appetizers as soon as he received a text from Li telling him they were five minutes out. Two large plates, each, of the spicy cheese curds and the fried Brussels sprouts. The dishes were served just as Li and Lane arrived and hung their coats over the back of their chairs.

Without a hello, Lane grabbed one of the plates and began to fill it. "And to think I hated sprouts growing up."

"Me too," Li said, taking the sprouts plate from Lane and scraping it clean. When I came home from school and smelled the scent of moldy sweat socks in the air, I knew my mom was roasting sprouts. I used to hide in my room until she'd come and drag me down to the dinner table."

Cole was looking over the menu. "It says here they make them with pie crust, pecans, wildflower honey, and something called thyme-creme fraiche," whatever the hell that is."

"Whatever the hell that is, is heaven," Lane said, finishing his first helping and going for the second plate of sprouts. Cole beat him to it and filled his own plate. "I asked you here so that we could talk about Michele's case, not so you'd pack on weight. Any more thoughts since I left you two at the office?"

"So, you're expensing this then? I don't have to worry about spending too much of my meager paycheck tonight?" Lane asked around bites of warm cheese curds.

"It's on me," Cole said. "So, what else have you guys come up with?"

Cole caught Li's sidelong glance at Lane. "You're thinking something, Li, and you don't think I'll like it. Just spill it. The truth shall set you free."

The waiter gave Li a brief reprieve when he came back to the table. All three ordered the double Wagyu butter burgers. When the waiter retreated, Li said, "We've been wondering why someone would want to hurt and likely kill Michele. Is there a story she wrote or was planning to write that someone wanted to quash? Michele picked up on that kind of thing with the case involving big pharma we worked on just weeks ago, where she pointed out the suspicious deaths of journalists who were writing about things powerful people didn't want to see the light of day. But there's another possibility…" She stalled, wiping the corner of her mouth with her napkin. Then her eyebrows arched. "Actually, Lane came up with this angle, so maybe he should run with it." She picked up the glass of white wine she'd ordered and took a big sip while Cole's attention turned to Lane, who had just plopped a large curd in his mouth.

"Um, well, what if someone wanted to hurt you, Cole?" he asked. "Wouldn't hurting Michele hurt you just as much as if they attacked you directly? Plus, she is a softer target, both literally and figuratively, than you are."

"Where are you going here, Lane?"

"I'm saying, you've made a lot of righteous busts over the course of your career, put hundreds of really bad people behind bars. Is it inconceivable that one of those people has been holding a grudge? It's no secret that you and Michele are an item. And this wouldn't be the first time a bad guy hurt or killed a rival's loved one."

"Think about it," Li said. "You were the face and force behind putting gang bangers, bad cops, and organized crime bosses behind bars. Hell, you've killed and maimed a few in the line of duty. What if someone attacked Michele to hurt you? Revenge is as plausible a motive as any. We need to look into that possibility."

Cole sat back, his hunger all but gone, replaced by marrow-deep exhaustion. In the madness of the past twenty-four hours, it never occurred to him that Michele's pain and suffering could have been caused by him, that his relationship with her had made her a target. He swallowed hard.

He was used to people coming after him. It happened several times in his career when he was closing in on the bad guys. At some point, they turned on him. He had the scars to prove it. But nobody had ever tried to get to him by hurting someone he loved. They couldn't have because he didn't have anyone...at least not since his divorce a decade ago. He'd lost his parents before he'd graduated college; they'd died together in a winter car accident his senior year. No brothers. No sisters. And he'd turned his back on his hometown for a long time after he'd lost his parents. He had to admit that Michele might have been attacked by someone trying to hurt him. And, in some way, whoever was behind it made a good play, because hurting Michele hurt Cole far more than hurting him ever could. He felt her pain more than he would feel that pain in his own body, and he felt the oppressive guilt that came from not protecting her...from not anticipating someone would target her, and for not thwarting the attack.

Li interrupted Cole's thoughts. "It's not your fault that there are evil people out there. That's why we do what we do, to find the sickos and get them off the street...one way or the other."

He looked at her when she said the last words; he was pretty sure she had acted outside the law to stop a killer recently. But he hadn't confronted her with his suspicions then and wasn't about to now, especially with Lane at the table. "Okay. Unfortunately, I agree that this is worth pursuing. I'll put together a list of the people I think would like some payback against me, and you can chase them down and see if you can find any connection to the attack on Michele."

"There's one other thing," Lane said. "The number one suspect right now seems pretty obvious to me."

Cole sipped his IPA. "Okay, Sherlock, let's hear your early hypothesis."

"A month ago, you and Li were shaking the tree of one of the most powerful industries in the world, big pharma. We couldn't prove it, but all the evidence we found showed that APAG, the American Pharmaceutical Advocacy Group, was killing journalists who were trying to expose some of the inconvenient truths about how they make their profits. Hell, they even had Senator Eric Rhodes shot. Luckily, he survived. But the point I'm making is they killed people who came after them with pen or politics by proxy, intermediaries. They hired killers to take out their oppo."

Cole chuckled. "Pen or politics by proxy? Oppo? What are you reading in your spare time these days, Lane? Thrillers? Literary fiction?"

"He's got a point, even though he's embellishing it," Li said. "I mean, this guy was paid a lot of money and given a professional blade to kill Michele. And he took the money to try to pay for a clinical trial of a pharmaceutical."

Cole thought about it. "It does kinda point to APAG." He picked at his food and looked over a flickering candle at Li. "But we never put anyone at APAG behind bars. We took down the shooters they paid to kill journalists and attack Eric, but we walked away from APAG's CEO. We didn't have enough to tie her to the attacks, and we didn't have the support of the Bureau or the executive branch, for that matter."

Li popped a warm cheese curd in her mouth, considering her next words. Then she looked back at Cole. "But we were the ones poking the hornet's nest. We took out the head of security that was orchestrating the hits and most of the goons who were carrying them out. We also challenged its CEO directly."

"And then we walked away. Nothing more to do, right?"

"But the CEO, Nichole Sebastian, was murdered in a robbery. What if the APAG leadership, its new CEO, or its board thinks that's more than an unfortunate coincidence?"

Cole blew out a long breath. "You referred to APAG's hit men as goons, but they were professionals, former Marines, or special ops guys who turned bad. DeMario is the opposite. If a trained mercenary had attacked Michele at the hall the way he did, we'd be planning her service right now."

That morbid thought hung over the table as the waitress returned with their entrees. They quietly ate their burgers and fries, each consumed with their own thoughts, the only noise the clinking of utensils and the soft snippets of conversation from the tables around them.

Chapter Ten

It was nearly nine p.m. when Cole trudged up the back stairs of the castle mansion. The ancient hardwood stairs seemed steeper and more numerous than usual. A door opened as he made the first-floor landing, and Frau Newhouse held it wide. She wore a purple floral house dress, and a tired look of worry filled her caring face. She tottered out onto the landing and reached up, pulling Cole in for a hug. He bent down and laid his head against her soft, white hair. She stepped back after a long moment but held his hands in hers. "How is Michele doing? I have been so worried about her. She is such a wonderful girl." She shook her head. "It's been all over the news. What kind of madman would do such a thing?"

Cole looked deep into his friend and landlord's eyes, shrouded by the wrinkles that come from eighty-seven years of laughing and living. "She's stable now. She'll need to stay at the hospital a few more days, and then she can come back here, back home, to recuperate. It's not going to be easy; she has months of rehab in front of her. But I know she'll be okay."

Frau Newhouse nodded her head in agreement. "Ja. That girl is strong. She will make it just fine." She squinted, "Maybe it's you I should be worried about. You look like the horse that plowed one too many fields."

Cole laughed. "A couple days of little sleep and lots of stress will do that to a fella."

"Go on up and get some sleep, but let me know how Michele is doing and what I can do to help her." She went back into her home and pulled the door shut behind her.

When Cole reached the second-floor landing, he pushed open the door to the expansive second floor he now shared with Michele, wanting nothing more than to stagger to his bed and sleep until morning. He had tried to call Michele on his way back from the restaurant, but Debbie picked up and told him she was sleeping. "Just let her know that I'm thinking about her," he told Debbie, before saying goodnight.

Soft sconce lighting illuminated the long hallway, and Cole was halfway to his bedroom when Jim nearly collided with him coming out of the large kitchen with a glass of ice water. "Scuse me," he said.

"My bad," Cole said. "I wasn't paying attention. I don't know how you're doing, but I'm bushed."

"Yeah, my head feels like it's stuffed with cotton right now. I feel bad for leaving Michele and Deb, but I hate hospitals, and I had to get out of there for a bit." He gestured with his free arm. "This house is something else. When you said locals called it the 'castle mansion,' I didn't really know what to expect. It's beautiful, and it's big. Enormous even."

Cole laughed. "It is big. It took me a while to get used to it, but it's a magical kind of place. It was built in 1891 out of red brick and sandstone, and it's been on the National Historic Register for more than forty years. It's almost ten thousand square feet, and it cost Frau Newhouse's family patriarch, August Newhouse, nearly one hundred and twenty-eight thousand dollars to build. In today's dollars, that sum would be closer to seventeen million."

"You sound like a tour guide who knows his business," Jim said, his head on a swivel, noting the high ceilings and rich woodwork. "And, while seventeen million dollars is way out of my price range, it seems like it might be a bargain."

"I think you're right," Cole agreed. He noticed Jim's rumpled khakis and button-down shirt, the same outfit he'd had on at Michele's talk and in the hospital. Cole studied him further and noticed lines on the older man's face he hadn't seen the night before. "When's the last time you ate something, Jim?"

The question caught him off guard. "I don't know exactly." He thought back. "I guess it would've been the ham sandwich and tomato soup I had for lunch yesterday."

"Well, let me change out of this suit, and I'll get you something before we turn in."

Cole was at the stove ten minutes later, dressed in loose grey sweatpants and a faded orange V-neck T-shirt. He'd tossed some breakfast sausages into a frying pan, and their sizzling joined with the steady, low hum of the stove's fan to create a peaceful white noise in the room. "White toast or rye?" he asked Jim.

"I never turn down rye toast. And if you're gonna ask me how I want my eggs, I'll tell you right now that over-easy would be just fine."

Cole put a generous slice of butter in another pan and turned the heat to medium. As it began to melt, he turned to Jim and pointed with his spatula. "Coffee cups are in that cupboard just behind you."

Jim got up and retrieved one Cole had picked up long ago at George Webb, a famous local chain of classic diners. It was a standard white mug with a colorful blue, yellow, and red smiling character, and bore the line, *It's always breakfast time!*

Jim read the line out loud and poured a cup of coffee from the half-brewed pot. "Truer words were never writ," he laughed.

"I can't believe you asked for coffee this late," Cole said. "I remember my parents would drink it playing cards at night, and they never seemed to have a problem sleeping. I love my coffee during the day, but if I had a cup now, I don't think I'd sleep."

"Never been a problem for me, and I'm so tired tonight I could drink the whole pot and fall asleep. If it's not peaceful, well, that'll be no fault of the coffee."

Cole plated the eggs, sausage, and toast and slid them in front of Jim. Then he went to the fridge and popped the top on a cold IPA, pouring it into a glass so that he could enjoy the color and the frothy head before taking a sip.

"I haven't had much use for liquor since Deb sobered me up a long time ago," Jim said.

"I hope you don't mind me prying, but what inspired you to stop drinking alcohol?"

Jim stopped eating and picked up his coffee, staring into it. "I was one of the last groups to see combat in Vietnam. One minute I was playing baseball for my high school team, and the next I'm slogging through the jungle carrying an M16 and a rucksack of bad memories I couldn't drop in a thousand lifetimes. I lost friends there, wore their blood and gristle on my shirt for days sometimes. But the worst was the men I killed. I used to be a steady shot with a hunting rifle before leaving the States, and I hit what I aimed at with that M-16, too. You put that thing on full auto, and you became the Grim Reaper.

"I came home from the war without a scratch on my body but with welts and scars all the hell over my brain and maybe even my soul. I thought I was a badass when I came back, but when I drank, I was mostly just an ass, an ass who did bad things. When I met Debbie and started hanging out with her, she told me it was either the booze or her, and it was an easy decision. Not so easy to pull off, mind you, but an easy decision. Took me a couple tries before sobriety took, but she stayed with me. We're closing in on fifty years now."

"Thank you for your service," Cole said.

Jim raised his mug, "And for yours."

Cole took another sip of beer, his face clouding over. "I'm pissed at myself for letting someone hurt Michele. I try not to think about it, but she could've been killed." He paused and looked across the table at Jim. "And tonight, my team raised the possibility that she might have been attacked by someone trying to get back at me. That's tough to own."

"I'm her dad. Try being in my boots. I'm supposed to always protect my little girl from harm. Hell, at the auditorium when that guy attacked her, I was frozen in my seat. If you hadn't flown down the aisle and hurdled the stage to grab the guy, he might've finished the job."

"Thank you," was all Cole could say.

Both men were tired. Jim sopped up warm egg yolks with his toast while Cole sipped his beer, and a comfortable silence enveloped them like a soft blanket.

Cole cleared the dishes when Jim finished and stacked them in the dishwasher. He showed Jim to a spare bedroom and said goodnight. His cell phone rang just as his head hit his pillow.

"This better be good," he said, answering the call with his eyes still closed.

"It's Ty. I know you need the sleep, but I thought you'd want to hear this. The human trafficking hotline just passed along a call they received tonight. It's about a bunch of minors allegedly working illegally at a poultry processing plant."

"Poultry," Cole mumbled.

"You know, chickens and turkeys and such."

"Yeah. I get it. So where is this poultry processing plant...and try to say that three times in a row fast sometime."

"Just outside Ladysmith."

Cole tried to clear the fog in his head so that he could drop a pin for Ladysmith on his mental map. "I'm not placing it."

"Don't beat yourself up. I Google mapped it myself. It's in the northwest part of the state, about an hour or so north of Eau Claire. It's got three point five thousand residents and a Dairy Queen."

"We do love our Blizzards, especially with the chunks of Snickers blended in there."

"I'm more of a chocolate chip cookie dough Blizzard man myself," Ty said. "But anyway, the hotline tip came from someone who works at the plant, and the information seems both credible and actionable. I'm having it transcribed right now, and I'll text it to your phone in the next thirty minutes. I know you've got your hands full right now, and I'd like to help, but it's way outside my jurisdiction."

"Okay. I'm in my boxers right now, by the way."

"TMI!" Ty laughed.

Cole sat up in bed. "We'll come up with a plan of attack first thing tomorrow morning, and hopefully, we'll execute it tomorrow night. I'll let you know how things go. Thanks for calling."

"No problem. One other quick thing, though. The caller who left the tip said Rusk County has a 'report a crime' phone number that they publicize. It's supposedly monitored by the county sheriff's department. Our tipster called in the information to them a week ago, the same information she gave us tonight. She thinks the Rusk County Sheriff is in cahoots with the plant's owners."

"In cahoots, huh." Cole mulled that over. "I'll keep that in mind when we put together our plan. Thanks, man."

"Sweet dreams, buddy!"

"Not likely," Cole answered, ending the call. He wanted nothing more than to lay back down, but instead, he scrolled through his contacts and hit the number for Gary Schettle, a senior agent who worked out of their Eau Claire offices. They had served together the past seven years and Cole trusted the big agent completely. Schettle was a cerebral six-foot-four giant of a man who started on the offensive line for three years at the University of Wisconsin-La Crosse.

"Hey, boss! To what do I owe this honor?"

"Hey, big Gar! We just got a tip that there's a poultry plant in Ladysmith, about an hour north of you, that's using underage kids for labor and in some pretty dangerous positions at that." He looked at his phone and saw that it was ten p.m. "I need you up there and in place in less than sixty minutes, because I'm guessing that's when the second shift lets out. I don't know how you're going to do it, but I don't want it obvious that you're watching the plant or that we're on to them."

"I'll figure something out when I get there."

"Good. It's not like you're a little guy who can stay out of sight easily. I'll bet you sucked at 'hide and seek' when you were a kid."

Schettle laughed, "The plant's gonna be outside the city limits a ways, and I have an idea on how I can hide in plain sight. I've hunted deer around Ladysmith before, and I've got a nineteen sixty- nine Chevy pickup that I can hunker down in across from the plant entrance. Even if they see me sitting there this time of night, they'll just think I'm glassing the fields for big deer ahead of the gun hunting season.

"Works for me," Cole said. "I know it's gonna be dark, but if you can get some shots of kids coming out of the plant, it'll help us get a warrant. We're acting on a tip that should be enough; it's specific and indicates kids are being endangered. But photographic evidence is always nice."

Schettle pulled on a brown barn coat over a red and black checked flannel shirt while he talked. He also threw snacks, bottled water, and an empty gallon milk jug in a bag. Once he was in place, he'd be able to sit in his truck until the plant's first shift came on at seven the next morning. That would be enough time to let him observe two shifts of employees come and go. He was ready. "I'm heading out now."

"Godspeed and be safe," Cole said before ending the call and falling into a restless sleep.

Chapter Eleven

Michele's eyes fluttered open and she turned her head to the window, the parted drapes giving her a view of a glorious sunrise painted in brilliant orange and plum. It warmed her face and her soul, giving her the feeling that today would be a good day. Her mother was sleeping soundly in the recliner. Michele could hear her gentle snoring, and it made her smile. Her mom looked tired but at peace, and that was important to Michele; she didn't want her worrying herself sick. She was grateful for her parents and knew they would do anything for her. She picked up her phone from the nightstand and looked at the time; it was early, but she took a chance and hit Cole's number.

"Morning, sunshine!" Cole answered on the first ring. He had just pulled out of the garage and was on his way to work. "Are you seeing this amazing sunrise? I'm taking it as a good omen."

"Yes, I see it. It's breathtaking."

"Like you."

"Flattery from the early bird?" Michele whispered, careful not to disturb her mom's sleep. "It's not even seven yet, and I was afraid my call would wake you. I'm just checking in to see how my beau is doing."

"Your beau, huh? I kinda like that. And I'm doing pretty well, considering you scared me half to death. I'm just glad you're gonna be okay."

Michele had asked her mom the night before to place the roses Cole had brought her onto her bedside table, and she picked one up now and held it to her nose. She breathed in its sweet perfume. "Thanks for helping me."

Cole frowned as he moved slowly in the morning traffic, the sunrise distracting more than a few drivers on their commute. "I haven't done nearly enough. I'm sorry about that. Ty has been leading the investigation into your attack, and your parents are making sure someone's always at your side. And we got a tip last night on the human trafficking hotline that the team is following up on. It's likely we'll be conducting a raid tonight on the other side of the state. No rest for the wicked, as they say."

"You're anything but wicked," Michele said. "Watch yourself, and don't be afraid to share details with me. You know I like to help solve puzzles."

Cole turned east off the interstate right into the sun. He pulled down his visor. "This one seems pretty straightforward right now, but I'll definitely lean on you if we have questions."

A nurse walked into Michele's room after knocking lightly on the door, and Michele told Cole she had to go. "Love you!" she whispered.

"Love you, too."

The nurse wore deep blue scrubs and a warm smile. She pumped some gel onto her hands and rubbed them together to sanitize them before pulling on a pair of vinyl gloves. "Good morning! I'm here to take out your chest tube."

"Great!" Michele said.

The nurse had a syringe in her hand. "Your doctor prescribed a dose of morphine for you, so that you don't feel as much discomfort when we remove the tube. I'm going to inject it into your IV, and then we'll give it a few minutes to kick in before we get to work."

"Morphine?" Michele's brows hiked up. She knew 'discomfort' was a code word for pain, but she didn't think it would take that long to remove the tube from her chest. She'd written true horror stories in the past about hospital patients who became addicted to pain meds during their stay, and she didn't want to become another statistic. "That's pretty strong stuff. Do you think you could remove the tube without giving me the morphine?"

The nurse shrugged. "Sure, if that's what you prefer." She set the syringe down and went to Michele's bedside. She unsnapped the buttons on the shoulder of her gown and pulled it down to expose her upper torso. Then she put dressings around the tube before carefully snipping the sutures that held it in place just below her ribs. She had one hand on Michele's ribs, her arm braced, and she had a strong grip on the tube with her other hand. Michele thought she saw the muscles in the nurse's forearm flex. The RN paused and looked at Michele, "When you're ready, take a deep breath."

Michele nodded and breathed in. The nurse pulled on the tube hard. It felt to Michele like her intestines were being yanked from her, and she gasped before screaming, startling her mom awake. The nurse winced and quickly applied gauze to the small opening. "Sorry," she offered.

"Shoulda taken the morphine," Michele groaned to nobody in particular.

Chapter Twelve

Agent Schettle texted Cole more than a dozen photos of what looked like kids entering and leaving the Ladysmith poultry plant. Most were taken at night, but the high-output LED flood lights at the plant entrance had made the photos clear enough. Schettle also sent a couple photos taken just an hour before, but he indicated that far fewer people had entered the plant for the third shift. He thought maybe the plant's third shift was devoted to deep cleaning and maintenance, but he wasn't sure.

Cole had already shared the transcript of the hotline tip with his legal team, and he forwarded the photos now. One of their attorneys would work with the federal court based in Milwaukee to obtain a search warrant. He wanted it by early afternoon so they could serve it this evening when the second shift was in full swing. The tipster had indicated minors were employed more widely on the second shift when they were easier to hide from prying eyes. So that's when they would 'raid' the plant if at all possible.

By eight-thirty p.m., Cole assembled a group of seventeen law enforcement officers at a quiet crossroads two miles away from the Ladysmith poultry plant. Most Special Agents in Charge of FBI offices didn't lead operations like Cole was doing now. A SAC's job was primarily to direct personnel, not to get his hands dirty. But Cole had an understanding with Gene Olson, and he always led a couple of key investigations while also directing his team. He never wanted to be the guy who led from behind. He felt his agents, analysts, and other staff appreciated the fact that he had to file his own reports and follow every nitpicky, onerous new policy and procedure handed down from D.C. just like everyone else.

Besides the FBI's Milwaukee field office, Cole was in charge of six other resident Bureau offices dispersed throughout Wisconsin. The Milwaukee office was the furthest from Ladysmith, and Cole, Li, and two other agents had made the drive in four hours, a half-hour less than what it would've taken to drive the posted speed limits. Cole had pulled one agent from each of his other state offices, and they had driven three and a half hours from Madison, three from Green Bay, and two from Madison and Wausau. Agent Schettle hadn't shown up yet, but Cole was expecting him back from the Eau Claire office at any time. Cole had also called on the Wisconsin State Patrol, and they had given him four uniformed troopers to help secure the premises, preventing anyone from leaving or entering the grounds once the raid began. The other officers were from the Department of Homeland Security, specifically its Immigration and Customs Enforcement Division (ICE). A key role of ICE was targeting employers involved in criminal activity and labor exploitation, and Cole was confident its officers would earn their paychecks this evening. Nobody from the Rusk County Sheriff's Department was involved in the operation due to the potential that one or more of its officers was compromised.

They had been lined up on the side of the barren road for ten minutes, and nobody had driven past. Other than widely separated farms, these roads didn't pass much else but uncultivated forests and woodlots for miles. Cole was standing outside his team's black Suburban enjoying the cool evening air when a set of headlights appeared over the crest of a hill and grew larger as the vehicle got closer. The pickup stopped next to Cole and idled while a big guy got out from behind the wheel and approached him.

"Great work, Agent Schettle," Cole said, shaking his agent's hand. "Glad you'll be with us when we go inside the..." he stopped, a look of concern on his face. "What's with the shiner? I can't picture you getting into a bar fight after you left here this morning. What gives?"

The big agent looked down at his boots and shrugged before returning his attention to Cole. "A little while after I sent you those photos, I got a visit from a couple of sheriff's deputies. They didn't like where I was parked and told me as much. They pulled me out of the truck and asked me what I was doing. I told them I'd come up from Eau Claire to scout deer for the gun hunt coming up. I left my FBI credentials at home, and they didn't get anything when they ran my driver's license or my truck's plates. I don't think they had a clue I was in law enforcement. I thought they were done with me and were going to send me on my way when one of the deputies sucker-punched me. Pissed me off, but I just let it go. When this is all over, I might come back up here and remake his acquaintance, or better yet his face."

Cole's face went dark and his eyes hard. Any doubts he had about the local Sheriff's department being crooked were gone. To everyone assembled, he yelled out, "Mount up!" Then he walked around to the passenger side of Agent Schettle's truck and hopped in. He looked across the truck's cab to his agent, and, in a measured tone, said, "Lead us to the plant now, and I guarantee you we'll deal with the sheriff later. You have my word on that."

It was nine p.m. when the law enforcement convoy rolled through the open gates of the Ladysmith poultry plant. State troopers were the last in line and they pulled their blue and white Dodge pickup across both lanes at the entrance and set up sawhorse barricades on either side of it. The pickup was one of just a couple employed by the State Patrol as a cruiser. Bold red *Wisconsin STATE PATROL* lettering stood out on the side of the truck against an outline of the state in brilliant white. They hit their lights without the siren, and alternating bands of neon blues and reds strobed the sky.

The remaining vehicles parked in the plant's visitor entrance, and when everyone was out of their cars, Cole grabbed their attention with a firm voice that carried, "I said earlier that I don't expect to be met with violence tonight, but I want everyone ready and steady. Each of you has a job to do here tonight, and we all have each other's backs." He looked around the group and saw determined faces, and he gave them a confident nod. "Are my remaining troopers ready?"

Three uniformed troopers stepped forward. "We are."

"Then get to it. And be careful," Cole called over their shoulders as the troopers split up and moved to cover the other three sides of the large building. There was just the one main road in and out of the complex, but the plant itself covered one hundred and eighty thousand square feet and had multiple exit doors through which someone could try to escape and run into the neighboring woods and fields. The troopers had the job of shutting those options down.

Cole led the team into the plant's front entrance, where they were met by a uniformed security guard who was clearly rattled by the sudden appearance of more than a dozen officers in FBI and ICE windbreakers. "You, you...you can't go any further," he said. "This here's, uh, private property."

Li stepped up and showed him the warrant. "Here's a search warrant signed by a federal judge. Do you need me to read it to you?"

The guard didn't pick up on her sarcasm; he just squinted at the warrant's official-looking heading and small type and shook his head, sweat beads appearing on his forehead. "I need to call the boss."

Cole stepped forward, invading the guard's personal space, and read the man's laminated badge. "You do that, Officer Nowak, but not until *after* you take us inside the plant. And bring me whoever's in charge of the operations here tonight. We need to see that person immediately. I don't want to have to arrest you for obstruction. Understood?"

"Okay," he nodded in surrender before turning and leading them down a long, narrow hallway and through two heavy doors. They pushed through them into a whole different world. When their eyes adjusted to the bright lights, they stood stunned. Hundreds of fresh, plump chicken carcasses whirled jerkily around the giant room at eye level in a serpentine pattern, carried on automated conveyor hooks. A seemingly endless conga line of headless chickens. Workers in white aprons and hair coverings looked over their shoulders at the officers, too busy to step away from the line for even a moment, the eyes of many of the uncovered faces wide with obvious fear.

Cole stood at the head of his team transfixed, trying to take it all in, his senses overloaded. The bright lights, incessant whir and clang of the overhead conveyors, and the obnoxious smell of blood and chemicals hung in the moist air.

A short, heavyset woman with a tight smile on her otherwise pleasant face stepped forward, "Good evening. Or maybe not, I suppose. I'm Jeri Widen, second shift manager here at the plant. I'd say 'Welcome,' but I'm not sure the owners would feel that way. What can I do for you?"

Cole tore his gaze away from the assembly line and focused on the woman in front of him. He guessed she was in her late fifties. She wore a white apron, and orange-dyed strands poked out from under her hairnet. The look on her ruddy face told Cole that she would cooperate, and he stepped forward to introduce himself. "I'm Cole Huebsch, special agent in charge of the Milwaukee FBI field office. He gestured to his team. The rest of these officers are from the FBI and the Justice Department." He purposely didn't mention ICE, because the acronym had a way of setting off alarm bells for some. "We're executing a search warrant after receiving a confidential tip that you're utilizing underage workers."

Widen shook her head and wrung her hands. "I told the dipshits in suits this would happen one day. They wouldn't listen." She paused, considering her next words. Cole thought maybe her eyes were tearing up. "But I want you to know that everybody in this plant right now is just doin' the best they can to do their job, feed themselves and their families if they got em. They're good people, every last one of 'em."

Cole nodded, believing her.

"What do you need me to do?" she said.

"For now, keep the plant operating while you walk us through a quick tour, tell us how things work here, and reassure your people that everything is going to be okay."

Widen turned to Officer Nowak, who'd been standing there listening, wide-eyed. "Ray, I need you to go on the overhead PA system and tell folks that everything is gonna be okay. Say it in Spanish, too. *Todo estará bien.* Repeat that every fifteen minutes or so until the shift ends. Can you do that?"

"Total etcetera bean?"

"Lord, no! *Todo estará bien.* Write it the hell down like it sounds so you don't butcher it so bad. Got it?" When he still looked confused, she softened. "Just do the best you can, Ray. If you say it like you mean it, maybe at least one soul in this god-forsaken place will believe it." With that she turned on the heels of her clean white tennis shoes and started the tour, all the while hundreds and thousands of fresh chicken carcasses whirled around them.

"We process six hundred thousand chickens at this plant every week," Widen said proudly to the group like a tour guide. "They call ours a three 'D' job, meaning *dirty, demanding, and dangerous*...but, I think it's pretty dang clean for what we do here and how much of it we do. And it's sure as heck hard work, but we try to keep ourselves and each other safe. We employ five hundred here at the plant, maybe thirty or so being contract labor. We have close to one hundred fifty employees working tonight."

It felt surreal to Cole as he followed Widen through the tour of the working plant. Each section was a new, mostly sanitary hell, as they walked from the slaughter area, to chilling, cut-up, deboning, aging, packaging, storage, and distribution. The sights, sounds, and smells were pervasive and jarred the senses a little differently as they moved from area to area within the huge plant. Cole felt like he was starring in a bad remake of *Willy Wonka and the Chocolate Factory*. Maybe it would be titled *Scary Jeri and the Poultry Plant*. The absurdity of it all was made worse when Officer Nowak's faltering voice came over the PA precisely every quarter-hour to assure everyone that "Everything is going to be okay. *Total etcetera bean*."

It took an hour for the tour to wind its way back to where it started, and on cue, the guard attempted once more, with even less success, to convince everyone in the plant that things were peachy. When the last of the guard's butchered Spanish echoed around the big room, Cole muttered, "*Ay, caramba*!

"Jeri," Cole raised his voice to catch Widen's attention over the constant whir of the machinery. "I need you to shut the plant down now so that we can interview everyone here. You said that your team moves one hundred forty birds a minute down the line and through the plant. Stop the line the way you would at the end of the shift so that you don't lose any product. I don't want to waste any birds needlessly. We can wait until you've cleaned up. She got right to it, and within a half hour, the employees were organized into lines as officers checked for identification. Cole walked around, answering his agents' questions the best he could and letting the ICE agents do their job. Most of the agents selected for the raid spoke Spanish, some fluently. But as Cole moved about, he couldn't help see the fear etched into the faces of many of the workers, afraid they were being rounded up to be tossed out of the country.

Agent Schettle called Cole over and introduced him to Santos Garcia. Cole took the young boy's hand, noticing his blood-spattered apron. In a quiet, friendly voice, he said hello, *"Hola, Santos!"*

"Hello," Santos replied.

"He's twelve," Schettle said to Cole while looking at the small boy. "He goes to the public grade school during the day and reports here to work right after. Then he goes to a relative's home to sleep and does it all over again in the morning. He's from San Marcos, Guatemala, near the Mexican border. He said San Marcos was full of violence and lacking in jobs, so his parents snuck him into the U.S. They died months ago in Texas, murdered by the coyote who took them over the border. He didn't waste a bullet on Santos, just left him for dead. But the boy's a survivor and remembered his uncle in Wisconsin. He miraculously found him. The sad thing is he likes his life now, making money, going to school, making friends. He misses his parents desperately, but he sees how this is a better life than what he had back in Guatemala. He's worried about what will happen to him now."

Cole shook his head. He wasn't sure there were going to be happy endings when the dust settled here.

Chapter Thirteen

Without the constant noise of the machinery, the large room was library quiet, with pockets of subdued conversation creating nothing more than a murmur in the background. Cole was still considering Santos' predicament and uncertain future when the front doors to the room banged open, heralding the entrance of a loud-mouthed sheriff, a deputy, and two men in suits. Cole assumed the suits were either the owners or their lawyers. The relative calm was shattered.

The sheriff was at least six foot two and broad-shouldered. Cole watched him with a mixture of anger and amusement from sixty feet away. "Who the hell authorized this?" he bellowed. "This is Rusk County, and I'm Sheriff Ron Eager. This is my jurisdiction. Where's the dumbass who thought it would be a good idea to enter this plant without my involvement?"

Cole raised his hand but not his voice. "The dumbass is right here." He knew the sheriff was crooked, taking money from the plant's owners to look the other way when they hired undocumented or minor workers. Or he was blackmailing them. But that would take initiative, and Cole's first impressions told him that Sheriff Ron Eager lacked both initiative and brains.

The sheriff came at Cole, closing the distance quickly with long, menacing strides. Cole saw Agent Schettle get up from his seat and take a step toward Cole, no doubt to put himself between his SAC and the sheriff, but Cole shook his head and waved him off.

The sheriff stopped in front of Cole and looked down at him. His face was red, and his black-bearded jaw was tense. The sheriff's open brown coat strained to keep his muscles in check over his white dress shirt with his badge on one breast and a U.S. flag on the other. He had gold pins stuck in the collar of his shirt, and Cole wondered idly what they signified as he watched the ignoramus preen before him.

Eager was right in Cole's face, and Cole thought he smelled beer on the man's breath. "This is *my* county, and this should have been *my* bust, or you should have run it *through* me. What part of jurisdiction don't you understand?" He was so close that his spittle sprayed Cole's face. He was trying to intimidate the smaller FBI man but was getting even angrier as he realized it wasn't working. Cole leaned to the side and in, speaking low but clear right in the sheriff's ear. "I didn't bring you in on this because I have reason to believe your department is compromised." He nodded to the machinery that wound its way into the distance. "Crooked as that assembly line right there." Cole flashed the sheriff a sly grin before turning his back, effectively dismissing him. "You can go," he said.

The sheriff grabbed Cole from behind and shook him. "Who the hell do you think you are?" he yelled.

As soon as he felt the bigger man grab him from behind, Cole instinctively slid his right leg behind him and fell back against the man's chest hard. The sheriff tripped over Cole's leg and suddenly found himself falling backward. Now he was going to the ground holding Cole, and he needed to make a decision, let him go and try to break his fall, or hold on and land on his back, likely banging his head. He released Cole with his right hand and twisted as he fell, reaching out to take the brunt of his weight with his hand and arm. The sheriff didn't know that his elbow joint wasn't designed to take the weight of two grown men under momentum. But Cole did. The man's muscles might be bigger than normal, but the ligaments and tendons that held his joint together were nothing special. Cole didn't think the sheriff's elbow joint would hold if they were falling onto a thickly padded wrestling mat. He was sure it wouldn't when they landed on the concrete. That thought was still running through his mind when Cole heard the splat of the sheriff's palm hitting the hard floor and an "oof" from the man himself. Then he heard his high-pitched scream as his elbow shredded. Cole landed on top of the sheriff and rolled off.

To anyone watching, it would have looked like Cole had been attacked from behind by the sheriff, and the bigger man had been hurt accidentally when they tumbled to the ground. But Cole knew different. He had used an old wrestling move, and the sheriff had reacted instinctively, only to find out when he did that his elbow wasn't meant to take the weight of two grown men. Not falling at speed toward an unforgiving surface. Mass and momentum had done him in. That and a certain FBI agent from Milwaukee.

The state troopers had alerted the local volunteer rescue squad when they set up at the entrance in case there were any injuries during the raid. They were quickly inside and tended to the sheriff. When they slid off the man's coat and rolled up his shirt sleeve to get a look at the injury, Cole noticed that one of the man's bones was protruding through his skin. It was a bloody mess. The sheriff was crying. What with the blood and the grown man's tears, Cole felt a little guilty. But only a little. Agent Schettle was at his side, and he shook his head. "Now that was a freaky accident."

"It sure was," Cole agreed, brushing himself off.

In a much lower voice, Schettle said, "Remind me to never, ever piss you off, boss."

Chapter Fourteen

Li and the other Milwaukee agents took turns driving when they left the plant in the wee hours of the morning. Since ICE had packed up all the confiscated computers and personnel files, Cole had half the roomy backseat of the SUV to himself, and he slept the entire way back to the city. He had asked to be dropped off at the hospital, so Li woke him when they pulled under the building's canopy. It was eight a.m. Cole looked at his phone and noticed an unread text from Michele's mom. *Good news! Shelly has improved to the point where they moved her out of the ICU and onto the med/surg unit, Room 410.*

"Mind if I join you?" Li asked, putting the Suburban in park.

Cole shook his head. "No. Not at all. Michele would love to see you. Let's go." They said goodbye to the other agents, and got out of the vehicle, then walked through the wide rotating glass doors together. Li looked at Cole as they walked through the spacious lobby. She had a mischievous glint in her eyes. "You look a fright," she said.

He pushed the elevator button for the fourth floor and turned to Li as they waited. "Really?" He studied Li. She was wearing a white button-down shirt tucked loosely into tactical pants, which he likened to professional cargo pants. Her military boots, a cross between hiking boots and Cole's old wrestling shoes, were untied, and her open blue windbreaker with the bold yellow FBI lettering seemed to hang from her slender frame. "I would say you look rumpled," he said, turning as the bell chimed and the elevator doors opened. "But don't worry, I'm not planning on writing you up."

They got off the elevator on the fourth floor and were nearly to room

410 when a chorus of laughter came from the open door. They stepped into the room and were greeted by Michele, Jim, and Debbie, the hospital administrator Alan Anderson, and Wisconsin U.S. Senator Eric Rhodes and his wife, Karri. Li knew everyone, but Jim and Debbie, and Cole quickly made those introductions. "Full house, I see," he said to the room. "But I've got some bad news…" His voice trailed off, and the room grew quiet. "We got a call from the fire marshal, and you guys have exceeded the official occupancy limit for this room!" Everyone laughed again.

"You just missed my surgeon," Michele said, holding up her bandaged arm. "Apparently, I'm a model patient. Everything looks good. They just changed my arm dressing, and the wound looked nice and pink, which means there's good, healthy blood flow to the area. Not a hint of infection either!"

Cole bent over the bed, doing his best to avoid the bandaged arm and the IV tubing in her other arm, and he gave her a heartfelt but awkward hug while gently kissing her forehead. "Best news I've heard in a long time," he said.

"The doctor told us that the first twenty-four hours after the chest tube comes out are the most critical, and so far, all systems are a go," Michele said. "He told me I could likely go home as early as tomorrow."

"Even better news!" Cole said. And if you ever start writing fiction, you just gave me an idea for the title of your first novel. He wrote the title in the air with his finger as he said, *The Impatient Patient*. The room broke up in laughter again.

Senator Rhodes turned the conversation to the previous evening's raid. "We heard about your visit to the poultry plant up north last night. The intersection of human trafficking, immigration, and child labor is messy and seems to be becoming a bigger and bigger issue nationally. I'm hoping when you have a chance to digest what you learned in this case, that you'll share it with me so that I'll be better informed on the issues involved. It's obviously hitting our state now."

"It is. We found a number of undocumented workers at the plant, and at least twenty were kids, as young as twelve years old. And most of the jobs the kids were doing are dangerous; a couple of months ago, a teenager from

Guatemala was caught up in the conveyor belt he was cleaning in a poultry processing plant in Mississippi. Similar plant to the one we raided last night. That kid was dragged up to the high ceiling by the machine before they could stop the line and help him. He died of asphyxiation and blunt trauma. He didn't 'go gentle into that good night,' as Dylan Thomas might say."

"That's horrible," Karri Rhodes said.

"It is," Cole agreed. "But Eric's right; it's complex. These plants are typically located in rural communities tucked away in the middle of nowhere, and they're desperate for workers. And the immigrants are equally desperate for meaningful work and a living wage. Everybody knows what they're doing is illegal, but they're drawn to each other like the north pole and the south pole of two strong magnets." He looked at Eric. "You and your colleagues need to figure this immigration thing out."

Eric smiled in acknowledgment. "We're on the same page there. Do you know anything else about Michele's attack? We assumed it was a crazy fan or stalker."

"Funny thing about that," Cole said. "In law enforcement circles, it gets said a lot that the obvious answer is usually the right one, but that rarely seems the case with ours."

"Hey, wait a minute!" Michele said, the conversation meandering like a wild Wisconsin stream. "I forgot to tell everyone that my agent, my publicist, and my publisher all called me separately. They each wanted to see how I was doing, of course, but mostly, they wanted to let me know that *The Killer Sermon* is number one on every nonfiction list out there, from Amazon to Goodreads to the *New York Times*. Apparently, getting attacked is good for book sales." She wasn't much for self-promotion, and she was blushing. "The networks are, and I'm quoting here, 'pushing and shoving' to see who will be first in line to interview me when I'm out of the hospital."

Alan said, "If you'd like, our public relations staff can work with your publicist to set up a press conference in the hospital lobby right before you're released. That will give you the chance to not only talk about your book, but to brag on the great care you received while you were here. That could help you and wouldn't hurt my cause with potential donors either."

"I like it," Michele said. "Your team has been amazing!"

The conversation grew lighter then, and the senator and his wife gave Cole a lift home from the hospital a few minutes later. After a quick shower and a short drive of his own, he was seated in his office in his customary dark suit and tie. He squinted into the bright sun and enjoyed the view of Lake Michigan for a moment. It was already sixty-eight degrees this morning, and he would have enjoyed nothing more than to walk along the shoreline, breathe in the moist air, and listen to the gentle murmur of the waves caressing the sand.

He turned when he heard a rap on the doorframe and saw Li and Lane standing there. He nodded in the direction of the table and settled in with them. Lane slid a mug of steaming black coffee over, and Cole thanked him.

"The ICE team we worked with last night has already sent us a preliminary report on the raid," Li said. "They're saying at least twenty-two of the employees or contracted workers at the plant on that second shift alone were minors. The plant manager called the jobs at the plant '3D' jobs, because they're dirty, demanding, and dangerous, and it's illegal for them to hire minors into any of those roles. Poultry processing plants are considered meatpacking plants by the Occupational Safety and Health Administration, and minors aren't allowed to work in any meatpacking plant in the United States because of the inherent dangers involved."

"I read yesterday that one hundred poultry workers die every year on average," Lane said. "Hard to believe the owners would use kids in those jobs. And they're not alone. There's been a sixty-nine percent increase in child labor since 2018."

Cole sipped his coffee, wondering how much good they'd actually done the night before. "It's a mess, isn't it? I mean, the plant needs workers to be able to process all the chickens being raised in that area, and there aren't enough adults with U.S. birth certificates or visas who are willing and able to do the jobs required. So, what happens now...to the undocumented workers, adults, and minors we detained, to the people in Ladysmith and the surrounding area who depend on that plant for their economic survival? It's a damn mess."

"You're right about that," Li agreed. "The ICE report says that some of the children interviewed at the plant were working there voluntarily; it was safer than what they left behind, the pay was good, and they could go to school. But others were forced to work there by non-related adults who housed them and were taking some or all of their wages. The other thing ICE shared is that the plant was accepting fake or stolen IDs from the kids, IDs of people who were as much as twenty years older. They obviously weren't scrutinizing them."

"Now *that* pisses me off," Cole said. "Since ICE is taking the lead from here, there's not much else for us to do right now." He looked at Li, "Do me a favor and forward everything you got from ICE to Ty. He brought us the tip, so he should know what went down. Also, I wonder if anybody on the task force can help the kids involved."

Lane spoke, "Not to change the subject, but have you had a chance to put together the list of people who might have paid DeMario to go after Michele?"

Cole went to his desk and brought back two sheets of paper, placing one in front of Li and the other in front of Lane. It was the list of people he thought possibly held a big enough grudge against him to have Michele attacked. There could have been five pages of names, but Cole had included only five names total, the ones he determined might possess both the will and the means to plan and, more importantly, pay for the attack.

"Geez, you could've used a Post-it Note for..." When Lane started to protest about the shortlist, Cole cut him off. "Remember that someone paid DeMario a hundred thousand dollars to go after Michele. A lot of people might want to see me or those I care about hurt, but not many of them could pay someone that kind of money to make it happen, especially if I helped squash their operations, put them behind bars, or worse."

The list included two rival gang leaders that Cole and his team put away for life, a dirty police chief from a local suburb, the head of an organized crime ring they caught moving tens of millions of dollars of knockoff goods from China into the country through Milwaukee's harbor, and a Congressman from the Green Bay area that they'd put away after filming him taking bribes from Russia and North Korea.

Li looked up from the list. "I hope there's a special place in hell for traitors. And crooked cops, too! They smear all of us in law enforcement."

Lane looked at Cole and smiled. "From what I heard, you could add a certain sheriff from Rusk County to this list, maybe at the top, if you didn't just make his acquaintance last night, that is."

"Hmm. I wonder what exactly you heard," Cole said, looking at Li now. "And whom exactly you heard it from."

Li smirked, covering her face with her tea mug. "Yeah, Boss, I wouldn't expect a Christmas card from him this year."

"And if you do get a card," Lane added, "make sure you have the bomb squad open it for you."

"Ha. Ha." Cole said, shaking his head. "The crooked sheriff from Ladysmith hurt himself when he attacked me, cowardly from behind, I might add. And you're right about another reason he's not on the list. He had no beef with me until our feet accidentally got tangled last night. So, he's not on the naughty list, and we move on. 'Potential' naughty list, I should say."

"The American Pharmaceutical Advocacy Group isn't on the list either. They should be number one," Lane said.

"Their CEO is dead."

"Could be a board member, or another executive," Lane said.

"Okay. Duly noted. We'll add APAG to the list and follow it up."

"There's still a name missing," Li said.

Cole raised his eyebrows.

Li pointed to the framed hole in the wall behind Cole's desk, "You forgot your old buddy, FBI Special Agent Collin Jeffers. Accent on special."

Cole's face scrunched. "Nah. He's a dickhead for sure, but a mostly harmless dickhead. We may not be besties, but there's no way he's behind the attack on Michele."

"Hmm," Li said, unconvinced, as she and Lane gathered up their notes and left.

FBI Deputy Director Gene Olson called Cole that afternoon, and Cole turned down the speaker phone's volume to protect his eardrums and the structural integrity of his windows. "Cole!" Gene boomed.

"Hey, Gene! To what do I owe this honor?" Cole knew Olson was much too busy to check in on him this often unless something was up.

"I just wanted to let you know that you've made the news again. The CBS affiliate in Minneapolis just broke the story of your raid on the poultry processing plant in Ladysmith. Every other station up there is piling on, and the national networks will pounce, too. I saw the early reports, more than twenty minors were found working on the second shift alone, almost all undocumented workers. Kids as young as twelve and using the IDs of thirty-year-olds in some cases. Yikes! I wouldn't want to be the owner of that plant right now."

"It'll be a shit storm, that's for sure," Cole said.

"The television reporters reached out to our Minneapolis field office and got a big 'no comment.' ICE officials gave them the same. Now they're calling here trying to get a response."

Cole smiled to himself. He loved the fact that the Minneapolis field office was closer to Ladysmith than his office and was the one being deluged with media calls concerning the raid. Dealing with the press was one of the few aspects of his job as special agent in charge that he didn't relish. "Tell them that we acted on a hotline tip by a concerned citizen, and make sure they know how dangerous those meatpacking jobs are. Make them aware that it's illegal for any minor to be employed in the industry precisely because of how dangerous it is. Or you can just refer them to Homeland Security. Your call!"

"Good advice," Gene said. Then his voice went flat, "Care to tell me what happened between you and the sheriff up at the plant?"

Cole sighed. The new agent they'd taken along on the raid last night had transferred from D.C. Gene had told him that Cole would be the best mentor he could have, but Gene had also no doubt asked him to keep an eye open. Cole might've gotten mad at Gene or the new agent, but he couldn't. He had learned the hard way over the years that Olson cared deeply about him and only wanted the best for him. "Would you believe we got our legs tangled, and he hurt his arm when we fell to the ground?"

"That's the official version. I'm looking for the unvarnished one."

"Fair enough. But keep in mind that the Rusk County sheriff is dirtier than Pig-Pen and not a tenth as nice!"

"Well said and duly noted."

"Okay, you should also know that just before I met the sheriff, I was introduced to Santos Garcia. Santos is a twelve-year-old kid from Guatemala who had lost both his parents, but who was still grateful to have a job risking his life in a foul-smelling—pun-intended—factory. That was tough for me to see. Then the sheriff made a loud entrance and asked me why I hadn't included him in the raid. When I told him we had received a tip that his department may be 'compromised,' he grabbed me from behind. Without turning around, I leaned backward and tripped him. He tried to break our fall but broke his elbow instead. Compound fracture."

"Sounds painful."

"I'm sure it was. Even with provocation, I think I would have handled the sheriff differently, more gently if you will, if his deputies hadn't sucker punched one of my agents, one of *your* agents, earlier in the day."

Gene sighed. "In that case, I would've preferred you broke both of the arsehole's arms." He paused a beat. "You know, the only reason I lean on you like this is because you have a special set of skills. Thanks for using them with reason."

"Always," Cole replied, and both men laughed. "One other thing," Cole said, "and this won't make your life any easier. I'm going to have to pay a visit to the APAG offices again."

"I wondered about that. I don't need to remind you that the top folks at APAG have a direct line to the president and to our director. I'd tell you to tread lightly, but I'm not sure you know how to do that."

"I'll be the stealth agent," Cole chuckled.

"More like the stealth *bomber*!"

"Seriously," Cole said. "If APAG is behind the attack on Michele, nothing will keep me from taking them down."

"And I'll be right there with you," Gene said. "I've got one more thing too."

"Shoot."

"Special agent Collin Jeffers is back at the Hoover Building."

"What the hell? You called him back to D.C.?" Cole was dumbfounded. "You only banished him to Anchorage five or six months ago. He's going to miss out on the mind-numbing cold and the impossibly long nights. What kind of lesson do you think he'll have learned?"

"Hold on now. Bringing him back was not my doing. I just found out about it yesterday. Nobody but the director would have had the balls or the short-sightedness to do such a thing."

Chapter Fifteen

"If you want to find out what a man is to the bottom, give him power. Any man can stand adversity — only a great man can stand prosperity." — Robert Ingersoll

One hour ahead and eight hundred miles of winding asphalt and concrete away, three people convened in an intimate dining room of the Cosmopolitan Club, which the *New York Times* once referred to as "the oldest and most exclusive private club in Washington, D.C." The club was formed more than one hundred sixty years ago, and the current brick and limestone Renaissance revival building in which the privileged trio now gathered was completed in 1908. It was situated conveniently just two blocks from the White House. Presidents Grant, Harding, Hoover, Kennedy, Taft, and both Roosevelts had been members through the years, along with countless generals, admirals, and other people of influence and affluence. The three people sitting in the club's dining room fit the membership requirements just so, as they touched their glasses in the quiet, softly lit room, sipping the finest spirits money could buy. Flames licked at split lengths of birch and oak in an ornate stone fireplace, projecting a living dance of shadow and light across the room. The logs popped and hissed as they burned.

They were known to a select few as the Trinity, and they had been meeting in private now as needed for more than thirty years. The membership changed from time to time when one of the three died. Once a member had rotated off when he lost his power base. That was rare, however, as the power of the three was entrenched. The deck stacked overwhelmingly in their favor. The game rigged, so to speak. The two men in the room were outfitted in suits and ties as required by the club, and the woman wore a formal black evening dress with a simple string of pearls and earrings to match. None of their clothes were off the rack, and the cost of their combined attire sans the pearls could have easily covered the sixty thousand annual tuition for a deserving student at nearby Georgetown University. The senior man looked to be in his late eighties but could've been older. His face had a reptilian appearance, with beady eyes set in deep sockets shrouded by folds of saggy skin. He ran his thick, blackish tongue over his upper lip. The woman loathed him and everything he represented. She was in his age range, although she might pass for a decade or two younger due to the work of several gifted surgeons over the years. The plastic surgery had another benefit; it pulled her skin so taut that it hid her emotions to an extent. She shook her perfectly coiffed shoulder-length hair, colored a rich auburn, and looked at her perfectly manicured nails. She relished her seat at this particular table but hated her companions. The feeling was shared by all and rather thinly disguised. The other man who sat at the head of the table was roughly half their age. If you asked the wait staff who served them this night to describe the small group, they might mistake them for family, perhaps grandparents treating a favorite grandson to a special birthday dinner. But they weren't family. Rather than tied by blood, they were tied by greed. They had power, prestige, and privilege rivaled by perhaps just a few dozen people across the globe. But it wasn't enough to satisfy their appetite for more. Not nearly enough.

The man in his early to mid-forties took a sip of whiskey from his crystal tumbler and let the twenty-five-year-old liquor linger at the back of his mouth, tasting soft oak, vanilla, and caramel. He sighed wistfully. "If only our latest plan had finished as perfectly as this bourbon."

The octogenarian laughed at that and shook his head, "But it didn't. It went down as crappy as this Bordeaux." He swirled the blood-red liquid in his wide-mouthed glass and said, "All we can do is move on and do better next time." With that, he rang a bell to summon a waiter, and he had a new bottle of a high-end cabernet opened and poured for him within minutes. The conversation stalled until his wine was poured, and the waitress excused herself. The old man leered at the younger woman as she walked to the door and left the room.

The older woman rolled her eyes. "Jesus, Bob, wipe the drool off your face. If a young woman like that ever gave an old goat like you a go, you'd have a heart attack for sure. As much as that might please me on so many levels, I don't want to break in a new majority leader any time soon. So, keep your tongue in your mouth and your pecker in your pants."

"Well said," the younger man agreed. "Now, what do we do about Michele Fields? I've heard she's making a nice recovery and could go home from the hospital as early as tomorrow, maybe the following day."

"Do we really need to have her…to have her removed?" the woman asked.

The older man slugged half the glass of the expensive cab. "Yes, we do," he said, wiping his mouth with the back of his hand inelegantly. The woman winced. "What?" the man said. "Don't get weak-kneed now."

"I'll do whatever it takes. I've shown that over the years. I can be more ruthless than you," she sneered. "But I also don't want to do anything rash. Careless. Fields is wounded now. It sounds like it will take her some time to fully mend. She's got a book out now that she'll be promoting when she's back on her feet. I don't see her meddling in our business anytime soon."

"You said she has a book out now," the younger man said. "And thanks to us, it's the best-selling book on the fucking planet. Shades of Salman Rushdie. I guess we should have seen that coming. Her book was going to sell a lot of copies regardless, but the attack on her gave it free non-stop worldwide media coverage for days. I've read a few of her stories, and she's damn good. She could do a lot of damage to our interests if she advocates for change to her millions of followers. I don't think we can allow that to happen."

The other two nodded their assent, and the room went momentarily quiet, each lost in their own thoughts. The older gentleman broke the mood, "Do you have someone who's up to the task when the time comes?"

The younger man nodded and smiled, "I believe I do. In fact, I'd like to introduce him to you." He rang the waitstaff and they ushered in a good-looking man in a dark blue suit and a crimson-colored tie. Now, it was the woman who openly leered at the man half her age. "This is my old college roommate and current FBI Special Agent, Collin Jeffers."

Chapter Sixteen

Cole found an open space on the street a block from the hospital and pulled his Dodge to the curb. His dust-coated cream-colored Charger was provided for his use by the Bureau, but it was more than ten years old, and its odometer had rolled past the 200,000-mile mark a month ago. The Bureau had pushed him to get a new vehicle for more than five years before they gave up. *Would the Lone Ranger trade in Silver? Would Roy Rogers put Trigger out to pasture? Hell no!* Cole said to himself. He patted the dash reassuringly and stepped out into the early evening air. He took a deep breath and walked toward the hospital. He wasn't strolling the beach as he'd daydreamed about doing earlier, but after being cooped up in his office all day, this street wasn't half bad. The towering trees overhead had begun donning their fall wardrobe, and the last of the day's warm sunlight filtered through the canopy's collage of reds, yellows, and greens. He walked unhurriedly, like the cars slowly moving down the side street, and he took in the crisp, clean air that hung in the sky before the leaves died. The temperature was perfect, with no hint of the bitter, cold winds and snow that would punish the city and its residents in three or four months time.

Cole talked briefly to the special agent assigned to Michele's protection once he reached the hospital's fourth floor. When he pushed open the door to room 410, he half expected to see her entertaining a room full of friends. Instead, she was by herself, seated in a large recliner, and the brilliant smile she flashed was for him alone. If he didn't know better and she wasn't sitting in a hospital room, he would have thought she looked normal. *If someone as beautiful inside and out could ever look normal,* he thought. He went to her and hugged her clumsily, kissing her forehead.

"Not good enough," she smiled, pulling him in for a long, passionate kiss. When she finally let him up for air, Cole said, "Wow! I'd say you're making a strong recovery. Where are your parents?"

"I sent them to the cafeteria to get something to eat. I love them to pieces, but it's getting old having them hover over me day and night. I told Dad he needs to get back to the farm, and I think he might head back tonight. I'm trying to talk Mom into going with him. Neighbors have been milking our cows twice a day, and that gets old quick. They've got their own farms to worry about."

"Is your doctor still letting you come home tomorrow?"

"Yes," Michele sighed. "And I can't wait. They've had me up and walking the halls, and there's nothing they do for me here that can't be done at home."

Cole loved how Michele thought of Frau's home, his home, as hers as well. "How about your therapy?"

"Most of it I can already do on my own, but a physical therapist will be coming to the house three times a week for the first few weeks to make sure I'm making progress and meeting key recovery milestones. I would have been getting my therapy in an outpatient clinic, but Alan stepped in and said he didn't want me leaving the house. He's keeping an eye out for me."

Cole's stomach growled, "Have you eaten dinner yet?"

"I did have dinner, or at least what passes for dinner in a hospital. They try, but it's not easy making sure everything is served at the right time when you're having a dinner party for six. Try doing it for a hospital with a hundred patients! I have a craving for a Kopp's cheeseburger, fries, and a quart of their macadamia nut custard.

"I'll get you your custard fix tomorrow night," Cole laughed. "Promise. And I'd like to suggest we pair our burgers with a nice Sonoma cabernet."

"I like the way you think," Michele laughed.

Cole's phone buzzed in his suit coat, and he pulled it out. The caller ID read *Janet Wifey*, and he held it up for Michele to see before taking the call and putting it on speaker. "Hey, Janet," he said. "I'm with Michele at the hospital with the phone on speaker, so don't say anything too risqué!"

Michele punched him in the arm.

Janet Stone was Cole's ex-wife and current anchorwoman for Fox News nationally. Cole had never bothered to change her caller ID on his phone, and she and Michele had become friends after their initial disaster of a meeting on national television. "Hi Michele," Janet said. "How are you doing?"

"I'm okay. My parents are here, and between them and Cole, I can't get a moment to myself."

"Wow!" Cole laughed. "And here I've been beating myself up, feeling I haven't been with you enough!"

"Oh, and they're letting me go home tomorrow!"

"Was that tidbit off the record?" Janet teased.

"Hell yes, that was off the record," Cole said. "No kidding about this, Janet. Michele was attacked, and we're not sure who's behind it." He looked at Michele with an apology in his eyes. "There's no guarantee they won't try something again. I hope that's not the case, but if it is, we don't want to give them anything they can use." He turned his focus to his ex-wife again. "We especially won't want to give them much-advanced notice that Michele is being released."

"Got it," Janet said. "I hope you guys know that I wouldn't do anything to put Michele in danger." It was quiet for a moment, and Cole wondered if each of them was remembering the evening a few months ago when the two women had met for the first time. Janet was interviewing Michele on national television, and it ended up in a catfight. But the two connected after that and became friends. Michele was a regular commentator now on Janet's show, and she bumped up the show's already high ratings whenever she appeared.

"Are you sure this DeMario guy isn't just some crazed stalker who lost it? That's what everyone's assuming," Janet said.

"I know, but there's more to it than that." He took Michele's hand in his, thinking it odd that he was talking so openly with his ex-wife and the woman he loved at the same time.

"That has me thinking," Janet said. "Michele, do you remember a couple weeks ago? The last time you came on the show?"

Michele shook her head and then realized Janet wouldn't be able to see her reaction. "No. No. Sorry. I hit my head pretty hard when...when that guy attacked me, and my memory of the past couple of weeks is fuzzy. I don't really remember anything about the attack itself either."

"Well, when you were with me, I asked about your book, obviously, since it was going to be released the following week. Congrats on having a runaway bestseller, by the way."

Michele blushed, and she was grateful Janet couldn't see that via the phone. "Thanks!"

"You're welcome. Anyway, after we talked about your book, I asked you what other projects you were working on or that you might like to explore. And you got very passionate about two things: big pharma and term limits. You don't remember that?"

Michele shook her head again and then blurted, "No. Not at all."

"I'll send a copy of the show to you, Cole, but Michele laid out some things in just a couple of minutes that would have made big pharma execs or anti-term limit folks very uneasy." Janet thought a moment, "Regarding big pharma, you said that the United States paid three times as much for our medications as any other country, costing us billions and billions of dollars annually, and that the reason we didn't set drug prices like other countries was because big pharma spent more money lobbying both sides of Congress than any other industry...more than big oil and the defense contractors even. You painted a picture that big pharma had the House of Representatives and the U.S. Senate in their pocket. That means they own the Food and Drug Administration as well, so that big pharma heavily influences when new drugs are approved. Some get rushed through the approval process and endanger the public, while other drugs are needlessly delayed, protecting the uber-expensive drugs they would replace. And you pointed out something that every American has noticed but never really thought much about...that drug ads have flooded the media at every level. Television especially, but even online ads. The press, including stations like mine, is supposed to be the watchdog of people and companies with ill intent, but big pharma has been feeding us, not under the table but openly, with billions of advertising dollars. If any big pharma execs were listening to my show that night, they would not want your message to get out. You have a way of easily and clearly connecting the dots on what is a complex issue for others."

"The American Pharmaceutical Advocacy Group is on our shortlist," Cole said. "For the reasons you just outlined, they have substantial influence with the president and, because of that, his political appointee, the FBI Director. It makes investigating them almost impossible, but if they're behind Michele's attack, I won't let them get away with it."

"I'm sure you won't," Janet said. "As for the term limit conversation, Michele, you pointed out the situation that Washington, D.C., and the country are in right now. Our United States representatives and senators get into office and latch onto the power and money like ticks on a bloodhound. They become so beholden to the special interests that shower them with cash election cycle after election cycle that they become little more than proxies for special interests like big pharma, the health insurance and defense industries, and more. And once you're an incumbent, the election deck is stacked so heavily in your favor that you'll likely get re-elected no matter how bad an actor or inept you become. You ended that segment of our interview by pointing out that according to the last five national polls on this issue, eighty-two percent of Americans want term limits. That includes eighty-nine percent of Republicans, seventy-six percent of Democrats, and eighty-three percent of independents. It's about the only issue Americans agree on right now!

"Then you asked how these current entrenched politicians can claim they represent their constituents when they blatantly ignore the four out of five Americans who favor term limits. My show is watched by a lot of elected officials nationally, and virtually all of their aides tune in, so it's no secret in Washington now that you plan to dig into the issue of term limits a lot deeper at some point down the road. There might be people watching my show who would rather that not happen, especially when you've now attracted a huge following."

Michele leaned forward in the recliner, concentrating, trying to corner a fleeing thought in her head. "I don't remember my last visit to your show, but I do recall looking at different articles on term limits a while back. It's incredible to me that even though it's the clear will of the people, our U.S. senators haven't brought the issue of term limits up for a vote in thirty years."

Cole scratched his cheek absently. "That's a lot to take in, Janet. And I don't like admitting this, but the people who paid for Michele's attack could have been trying to hurt me by hurting her. If that was their intent, it worked. But I'll definitely take a look at the show if you send me a copy."

"Already sent to your work inbox."

"Thank you. Take care of yourself," Cole said.

"You also. And take care of Michele, too."

Chapter Seventeen

When Cole arrived at work the next morning, the first thing he did was step into the small office of his new executive assistant. The last EA had served the St. Francis office of the Bureau for more than forty years before retiring. Cole missed her. Annie knew more about the workings of the FBI and its local office than most of its agents and analysts ever could, and she had a matronly way about her that Cole found somehow comforting.

Annie hand-picked the new assistant from thirty-three qualified applicants, and to Cole's eye, they couldn't be more different. Jenny Contreras was twenty-five years old and looked even younger. She had long black hair and kept herself in great shape by running and doing yoga. Her smooth skin was a light caramel color, and her eyes were like large circles of dark chocolate. *Edible,* Cole thought, before picturing Michele in the hospital and hating himself. But if he was asked under oath whether Jenny was pretty, he would have to admit that she was. Stunning even. And that made him uncomfortable. It shouldn't maybe, but it was what it was. As Clint Eastwood once said, *A man's got to know his limitations.* Cole went so far during the interview process to have Li and Lane interview the top candidates for the position, and they independently sided with Annie in recommending Jenny. She had been the assistant for a high-ranking agent in the FBI's New York field office for three years before applying for a transfer to be closer to her parents in Chicago. When Lane asked if they needed to worry about her absconding to the home of the Cubs and the Bears if a similar job opened up ninety miles south, she laughed out loud. "I adore my parents, but I'm not sure I want to be *that* close to them. Milwaukee's perfect. When I was younger, we'd come up for Summerfest every year, and I got to know the city pretty well. I think it's severely underrated." Li and Lane loved the answer.

Cole reached out to Jack Gokey, the head of the FBI's New York field office, and he said he didn't know Jenny. That wasn't really a surprise, since the New York office was the largest in the Bureau, composed of more than two thousand agents and support staff. But Jack personally checked in with her boss and called Cole back with a glowing review.

Cole hated letting go of anything or anyone he liked, but he finally relented, deciding you probably couldn't discriminate against beauty any more than you could discriminate on other grounds. Jenny had started in her new role two weeks ago and after a few days' transition working with Annie, she was now on her own.

Jenny was busy typing on her computer when Cole rapped on the doorframe and said, "Good morning."

Jenny looked up, her brown eyes wide. She gave Cole a broad smile. "Oh. Sorry. Good morning, Cole! Annie told me the monthly internal newsletter should go out tomorrow, and I'm putting the finishing touches on it. I'll have it ready for your review by late morning."

"That's fine. One other thing I need you to do is to try to get Li and me an appointment with the Chief Executive Officer of APAG. Annie should have the contact information on her computer somewhere. I doubt they'll be excited about seeing us, but the sooner you can make the meeting happen, the better."

"I'll try right now."

"Thanks," Cole said, before leaving. He picked up a coffee in the cafeteria before heading to his office. He was still getting settled in when Jenny stopped by minutes later, surprising him with the news that the APAG meeting was set for five p.m. Central Standard Time that day. He wasn't surprised when she said that the CEO would also have counsel present, but it caught his attention when she added, "someone named Roger Beneker."

"Fuck," Cole said, the word slipping out.

Jenny raised her eyebrows in a question, but Cole waved it off. "Sorry. It's nothing, really. I've met the guy before, and, well, let's just say he's not the most helpful. Or the most pleasant, for that matter."

Cole called Li and Lane into his office and had Jenny get Ty Igou on a Zoom call. Ty's camera was showing a close-up, and his face took up most of the flat screen's surface. Cole started the impromptu meeting as soon as the hellos were out of the way. "You got a damn big head on your shoulders, Ty, but you look sharp in your captain's uniform. Thanks for joining us with little notice."

"You're welcome, I think. I need the larger-than-life head to house my big brain and even bigger thoughts. And thanks for noticing the duds. It's not a spiffy suit and tie combo like yours, but it holds up better in a street fight."

"You get into a lot of those, do you?" Cole asked.

"Not really. Certainly not nearly as many as you," Ty admitted. "These days, the biggest brawls I get into are with members of the Common Council and the mayor of our fair city."

Cole laughed. "We have our share of politics to deal with, too. As a matter of fact, I plan on rattling a cage later today, and I'm sure we'll get some blowback. That's the reason for this call. When Michele was first attacked, it seemed like a clear matter for MPD to investigate. Now that it looks like someone from out of state is behind the deed, it changes things. I don't mean this to be a power play, but I think we should lead the investigation."

"That's fine," Ty said. "What do you want me to do from my end?"

"I'm not sure what else MPD can do, Ty. The one thing I thought of was that people had to register to attend Michele's author event. Did you happen to run the list of attendees? I doubt that the person or people behind the attack would show up in person, but stranger things have happened."

"We did run the list, and we didn't see anyone who attended that raised eyebrows. Other than Michele's agent and publicist, everyone else in attendance at the library was from the metro area. We did come across something else that raises red flags."

Lane broke the silence, "You're making us wait here to build suspense, right?"

"I learned a lot from you guys during *The Killer Sermon* murders," Ty deadpanned. "Anyway, the library streamed the talk live, and people who attended online had to register as well. Seventy-five people were watching from a computer when Michele was attacked. We were successful in tracking down the IP addresses for all but four of those folks. The routing of those four addresses bounced all around the world and makes them untraceable. It's pretty advanced stuff. And the names those four registered under are bogus. Combine that with the one hundred grand that the people paid to have Michele attacked, and it seems like the people behind it are sophisticated and well-funded."

"And the assholes wanted to watch it take place, too. Voyeurs," Li said. "They could have paid for the hit and then waited to hear back, but they got off on seeing it happen live."

"We really need to get the bastards," Lane said.

"To that end," Cole said, trying to keep his own anger in check so that he could focus. "Let's talk about the next steps we need to take to find the people who paid for Michele's attack. I've been thinking about DeMario's daughter, Megan. Someone had to figure out that she had this rare type of cancer. Apparently, there are only a handful of places offering the experimental treatment that could help her. To be part of a clinical trial like that you would have to be enrolled. And you'd have to apply first. So, Megan would have been on a waiting list at one of those clinics. We should reach out to the clinic and find out if they were hacked. Did they have a data breach? If not, most of them have electronic medical records now, and they should be able to look into their system to see if anyone unauthorized accessed Megan's information."

"Good stuff," Lane said. "I'll dig into that today."

Cole sighed and took a sip of his coffee. It was tepid and he preferred it piping hot, but he drank it down anyway, hoping for a pick-me-up. The erratic scritching noise that Timer, his ancient wall clock, made as it struggled to drag its arms in a circle relaxed him with its familiarity. "I sent you guys a video last night of Janet's most recent interview with Michele. Did you have a chance to watch it yet?" When everyone nodded, Cole asked,

"What do you think of Janet's theory that someone might have gone after Michele because of issues she was thinking about pursuing after her book tour? During that interview with Janet, Michele put big pharma and anyone who's against term limits on notice that she'll be digging into those areas next. She's already got some explosive information, but I'm not sure what to make of it."

"It's one more sign pointing directly at APAG from where I sit," Li said, her voice rising. "This would be right out of their playbook. We couldn't prove it before, but we know they paid goons to kill journalists and other critics who had a big enough megaphone. They made them look like suicides or accidents, but we know better."

Cole caught Li's eyes and noted the fire in both. "But they're under new management, so to speak. I was really hoping that their CEO had gone rogue and that those kinds of practices would've died with her."

"I guess we'll find out," she said, returning his stare.

"Okay," Cole said. "Anyone got any other leads they'd like to follow up on?"

Lane answered, "Our agents interviewed the first five people on your list of those individuals who might want to get revenge on you, and at this point, we don't think any of them are behind Michele's attack. The two gang leaders are locked away in the Supermax prison in Boscobel. They mostly sit in their small cells twenty-three hours a day thinking bad thoughts. But if they could get to anyone outside their jail cells, it would likely be their successors. Seems the people who stepped up in their organizations are enjoying their newfound power and cash and have cut them off altogether."

Li added, "The head of the group that was bringing in knockoff goods from China is actually sharing a cell in a minimum-security federal prison down in Florida with our crooked Congressman from Green Bay. It's no Supermax prison, but it's not exactly cushy either; they've got eight more roomies in an eighteen by twenty-two-foot room. But both of them will be getting out within the year, and it doesn't seem likely they'd jeopardize that."

"The dirty police chief might hate you the most," Lane said. "He's in a medium-security prison in the middle of the state, and it's no secret he's a cop. He's got a bit of a paunch, not exactly in his prime anymore, and he's had a couple scuffles already. 'Punish the pig and all that'. So, he's definitely not enjoying his stay, and he still has another ten years to serve on his sentence. But when we took him down, we also recovered all of his ill-gotten gains, so he would have no way of paying for the attack on Michele."

"And then there were two," Li deadpanned. "The American Pharmaceutical Advocacy Group and Collin Jeffers."

"Li and I are leaving in a few minutes for a face-to-face with the APAG CEO," Cole said. "And Gene Olson told me that the FBI Director himself, good ol' Jim Trudell, personally made the call to bring Special Agent Collin Jeffers in from the cold, so to speak. He recalled him from Anchorage back to D.C."

"That sucks," Lane said.

"Yeah, it's a damn shame he never got to experience a fine winter in the land of the midnight sun," Ty agreed.

"He's always had motive," Lane said, and all eyes in the room but Ty's followed his to look at the framed hole in the wall. "And now that he's been pulled back into the lower forty-eight, it looks like he had the opportunity. We'll have to dig into that some more."

"But very carefully. You don't accuse a brother in law enforcement of being bent lightly," Cole said. Before he could thank everyone and end the meeting, Ty interrupted. "Hey, I heard that Michele is going home today. That's good news!"

"She is, but how'd you hear about it?"

"I was listening to the radio, and they just announced that Michele was holding a press conference at the hospital in a half hour. I assumed it was to thank people for their well wishes and to say she was being released from the hospital."

"You assumed correctly," Cole said. "Michele's parents and Frau Newhouse are going to help get her settled in while Li and I are in D.C., and then her parents are heading back to take care of the farm. It'll be nice to have her back," he said, before thanking everyone and ending the call.

Chapter Eighteen

The FBI offices in St. Francis sit just two miles away from Milwaukee's General Mitchell Airport as the crow flies, and Jenny got Li and Cole on a nonstop flight to Ronald Reagan Washington National Airport. Their one-thirty p.m. Central Time flight landed two hours later, which was four-thirty on the east coast. According to most reports, D.C. traffic is the third worst in the country, behind only L.A. and San Francisco. Jenny had picked Washington National Airport because it was less than five miles from APAG's offices in downtown D.C., some of the most prime and expensive real estate in the U.S. Li and Cole took an Uber to APAG's gleaming high-rise office building. Their firm's executive suite took up an entire floor of the building, and Cole and Li were checked in and seated in the expansive lobby fifteen minutes before their scheduled meeting time. The FBI pair had sat in the same chairs less than two months earlier when the former CEO had toyed with them like a cat with a cornered mouse before dismissing them. She seemed beyond the law, but she was murdered during an apparent robbery less than twenty-four hours after their meeting. Fate? Or perhaps the flipside of divine intervention. Those were the thoughts swirling through Cole's head when an assistant arrived and took them to the interim CEO's office.

Cole remembered the building's layout from their earlier fruitless visit, and he noted that they were being led down the opposite hall from the former CEO's office. When they stepped into the exec's office, it was impressive with its floor-to-ceiling glass, but it wasn't over the top like the former CEO's. The assistant introduced Cole and Li to APAG CEO Clint Washington and

Roger Beneker, the firm's retained legal counsel and lobbyist.

"Welcome," Washington said as they settled in around a dark wood table polished to a high gloss. The man's greeting seemed forced. Cole had read up on Washington on the flight from Milwaukee. He had served as the former CEO's second in command before rising to the interim CEO role upon her death. He was on the short side and appeared almost frail, with thinning white hair and small eyes behind thick glasses. Cole wondered if Nichole Sebastian had selected him because she felt she could control him, that he wouldn't be any threat to her ruthless leadership style.

"What do you want?" Beneker said, looking at his Patek Philippe timepiece. "We have an important dinner meeting to attend after this. Your assistant was vague, and you're frankly lucky Mr. Washington here made time for you. Spit it out, Agent Huebsch."

Cole gritted his teeth. This was only the second time he'd had the distinct displeasure of meeting Roger Beneker the fifth and the first time the highly paid hack had rushed his meeting with a top executive from a different company. Cole hated few things more than a bully, and Roger Beneker, esquire, was exactly that. He was Cole's age, but he'd left the oldest and wealthiest lobbying firm in the city a decade ago to found his own firm, Capitol Gains, and it was now the biggest lobbying firm in the nation. Beneker's bespoke suit whispered *I'm better than you* and his round, polished designer eyeglasses screamed *I'm the smartest guy in the room.* He wore his arrogance, his sense of entitlement, naturally, like the kerchief in the breast pocket of his obscenely expensive suit jacket. Cole wondered if it was inevitable when you were at least the fifth generation to be flush with power and money. Maybe now it was ingrained and immutable, like part of his DNA...passed down from Beneker man to Beneker man from generation to generation.

"I told you, the clock's running," Beneker said, interrupting Cole's thoughts. "If you've got nothing to say, you can be on your way." He started to rise.

"Leave, if you want," Cole said, "But I have a few questions for Mr. Washington."

Beneker sat back down. "Then make it damn quick."

Cole ignored Beneker and looked directly at Washington. "Did you know that Agent Li and I were in these offices less than two months ago? We were here investigating APAG concerning the deaths of journalists who had written stories critical of current practices within the pharmaceutical industry. We traced offshore payments made by APAG to the journalists' killers."

"Stop it!" Beneker said. "That's enough. Do you have a real question for Mr. Washington? Or are you just going to blather on? The only thing you could prove conclusively was that the two of you came here and hassled APAG's then-CEO, Nichole Sebastian, *without me present, by the way.*" He turned to Washington as he said the last, emphasizing the mistake he thought she'd made in meeting with the FBI agents alone.

Washington did a comb-over of his hair with his fingers, and Cole saw beads of sweat collecting on his forehead. It wasn't warm in the room. The stop-gap CEO was out of his element and already rattled. Cole said to him, "Did you know that someone paid a man one hundred thousand dollars to attack Michele Fields, another journalist who was quoted on national television saying that she was going to look into big pharma when her current book tour is done?"

"Jesus!" Beneker said. "Is this about your girlfriend? It seems obvious to sane people that she was attacked by an overzealous fan. And speaking of overzealous, your attack of Mr. Washington is over the top!"

Cole tried to ignore him, looking directly at Washington, who kept turning away. He knew that Beneker was trying to get in his head, but he couldn't help wondering how in the hell the asshole even knew that he and Michele were together. His voice grew louder as he questioned Washington. "Did you know that the journalist's attacker needed the money to try to pay for an exotic new drug in a last-ditch attempt to cure his daughter's rare cancer?"

"Interview over!" Beneker shouted.

But Cole's voice, though even keel, was even louder and more commanding. "Do you believe in coincidences, Mr. Washington? Because, even if you do, there are way too many here to ignore. I suspect you haven't been personally involved in any of your firm's illegal activities." He looked around the room. "Nichole Sebastian set you up here in an office that's about as far away from hers as possible without placing you on a different floor. I'd bet she didn't share a lot of the company's darker secrets with you. If you work with us now, then any wrongdoing can likely be laid at your predecessor's gravestone. All of it."

"Get out!" Beneker yelled. "Get security in here!"

"If you stonewall us, Mr. Washington, then I'll do everything in my power to bring you down with the firm. Think about that. It's up to you."

Beneker hit a button on the sidewall near his chair, and three large security officers burst into the office. Cole immediately stood and pulled out his FBI credentials. Without turning around, he held them out for the guards to see, saying over his shoulder, "You don't want anything to do with this."

The security officers stepped back but stayed in the room by the door. Cole continued to focus his attention on Washington, "Keep in mind that if things go sideways and we find out APAG is behind the attack on Michele Fields, that you won't be able to avoid going down with the ship. Not once we leave here." He nodded to Beneker, "Cool Rog here won't be able to help you then. And he's known as the Teflon Tool, nothing sticks to him. If you need help later, he will be conveniently unavailable."

"Fuck you, Huebsch. You're an insignificant nothing," Beneker said, fuming, his face a blotchy red. Nobody talked to him like this, not if they knew better, knew who he was and the power behind him. Huebsch should have understood this after their last encounter.

Cole looked at Washington again, and the deer in the headlights persona he radiated now stuck to him like a mask. Cole thought he might be going into shock. He decided it was no use talking to him anymore. He turned to face Beneker, and he would have loved nothing more than to knock the sneer off the dandy's face. Instead, he pointed at the lobbyist's cheeks, "You've got some red, blotchy thing going on with your face, Rog. I'm no medical expert, but it could be dermatitis or psoriasis. Maybe rosacea. You should get it checked out. It may be nothing, but then again, there might be some underlying auto-immune thing going on. I can't believe it would be something as stupid as you simply blushing like a thirteen-year-old because you're embarrassed. Not the great Roger Beneker the fifth! Next, you'll be sucking your thumb and calling for daddy." Then he looked at Li and nodded to the door, before pushing through the wall of security officers and into the hall. On his way, he yelled back over his shoulder. "Great seeing you again, Rog! No need to see us out. We know the way!"

Li turned to Cole when they were on the elevator and moving down to the main floor. "The Teflon Tool? That's one more Christmas card you won't be getting this year!"

They reached street level and walked outside in the waning sunlight to hail a cab. Cole's head was on a swivel as they stepped to the curb. He half expected a Bureau car to be idling nearby, waiting to take him to FBI headquarters for a dressing down from the director. That was exactly what happened the last time he locked horns with Roger Beneker in this city. But a cab pulled up instead of a telltale black SUV. Cole felt relieved. Li ducked into the taxi's backseat and Cole was in the process of joining her when he froze, catching sight of a man in a suit reading a newspaper at the street corner. But the light had turned green, and the man paused a beat too long before folding the newspaper and moving along. Cole hadn't made out the man's features, and his back was now turned to him as he walked away in a mass of people, including dozens, maybe hundreds of other men in suits who were still streaming out of the concrete high rises all around them.

"Is something wrong?" Li asked from inside the cab.

"Nothing more than usual," Cole answered, getting in and slamming the door shut behind him.

Chapter Nineteen

Roger Beneker leaned back on a plush sofa inside the Oval Office of the White House less than an hour later, the half-ton resolute desk not more than fifteen feet to his right. His legs were crossed, and he tried to relax in what amounted to his second office, but his earlier meeting with Cole Huebsch made that all but impossible.

President Charla E. Howard sat on the couch facing Beneker, waving her arms to emphasize some point she was making that was apparently of great import to her, but didn't interest him in the least. He tuned her out. Beneker smiled, and the president thought perhaps she was finally getting through to him. But Beneker was smiling to himself, thinking perhaps he should go sit on the other side of the resolute desk and show her who really ran things. Strip away the pretense.

The president was an outsider who had been the CEO of a big tech firm before throwing her hat in the last presidential race and improbably winning. It was another case of the public telling anyone who would listen that they wanted meaningful change in the way the country was run. *She has a lot to learn,* Beneker mused as she prattled on.

He remembered the first time he had come to the White House. His grandfather led him to this very office to show the nine-year-old Benker that he owned the man behind the resolute, that he owned the office. It made an impression on the young boy. Indelible.

A frown pulled at Beneker's mouth as thoughts of Huebsch's earlier insolence crept inside his head. The FBI agent had mocked him. Nobody did that. Ever! Beneker began to seethe. His face, usually a mask he controlled precisely, morphed into a portrait of pure hate. The president stopped talking, witnessing Beneker's transformation. "Roger, is everything alright?"

Beneker caught himself and forced another smile, "Yes, of course. Carry on. I'm following."

The president haltingly started talking again, then picked up steam. *She does love to hear herself talk,* Beneker thought. He kept his forced smile in place while he tried to turn his mind to something else, something to salve the slow, hot burn of his encounter with Agent Huebsch. He thought of his new girl, and a genuine smile appeared on his face. The President reciprocated the smile, thinking she was finally connecting with the odd kingmaker in front of her.

But Beneker was now focused solely on thoughts of his new girl. This was the time of discovery he relished in a fresh relationship. Learning the girl's smell, taste, the sound of her voice, and her different looks. He relished it indeed, and his smile twisted into something sinister. The president noticed and stopped talking again. But Beneker was lost in his thoughts of his new girl and all he would soon learn for the first time. Her look of terror. The smell of her fear. The taste of her hopelessness. And the sounds of her screams.

Chapter Twenty

Cole and Li had booked a late departure back to Milwaukee, and Cole slept fitfully the entire flight, Michele's attack playing on a loop in his brain. When the plane touched down, he was no better rested. He and Li said goodbye at the airport's surface lot and Cole drove above the posted speed limits, hoping Michele might still be up when he got home.

It was closing in on eleven p.m. when Cole trudged up the back steps of the castle mansion. He flinched when Frau Newhouse opened her door as he reached her landing. She eyed him up and down. "Cole, I'm glad you are home. But you look tired. You are working too much."

"It was a long day," he said, wanting to go up and see Michele, but not wanting to offend his friend. "How's our girl?"

"Good. Good. She likes being here with us, and I like having her here. No offense, but it's nice having another woman around. You and I shall nurse her back to good health together. *Ja?*"

"Sounds like a plan," Cole said. "I'm going to head up and see her now, if she's still awake."

"*Ja*. Of course. I thought I heard her footsteps up there not too long ago, but I thought also that I heard you come up the stairs before. These wooden floors are very old, like me, and they creak a lot...like me too," she added, laughing at her own unintended joke. Cole laughed along with her, said goodnight, and continued up the stairs. He'd only taken a few more steps when her words echoed through the fog in his brain. *I thought I heard you come up the stairs before.* He slowed his ascent. Had Lane, or Ty, or one of

Michele's friends come over to check up on her? Or had someone else come over with other ideas in mind? The old house did creak a lot, and Cole thought his fatigue might be aiding and abetting his paranoia, but his senses were on high alert as he made it to the top landing and put his key in the door.

Chapter Twenty-One

Cole kept his Glock nine-millimeter pistol in its compact hip holster as he opened the door and walked as quietly as possible down the hall. No lights were on, which wouldn't be unusual if Michele was sleeping; the dim light reaching the hallway from the outside through the windows cast things in murky shadows. Cole didn't want to scare Michele needlessly if she was still up by holding his pistol out in front of him, but he did want to protect her and himself if they were in danger. He touched the handle of his gun once, reassured that it was in its place. *Like you dropped it somewhere?* He shook his head. Now was not the time to have an argument with himself. He kept the handgun holstered. He didn't clear the rooms exactly as he walked down the long hall, but he did poke his head in every room he passed to see if anybody was lurking around. Michele had round-the-clock protection in the hospital, but she had forbidden it when she was home. Her parents were back up north tending to the farm, and she had insisted she was safe. Cole couldn't remember a time when an FBI agent's home had been targeted for invasion, and he had gone along with Michele. He was second- and third-guessing that decision now.

He was halfway down the hallway and starting to feel foolish when a man stepped out of the kitchen with a pistol held steadily out in front of him, pointing directly at Cole's center mass. *I guess this guy wasn't worried about scaring anyone,* Cole's inner voice snarked as the man got the drop on him. The gun had a suppressor, but it wouldn't be completely silent if fired. Cole thought Frau Newhouse would register the sound if the guy pulled the trigger; her hearing was acute for her age. But if that happened, it meant

Cole, Frau Newhouse, and likely Michele would be dead before the night was over, and he would sacrifice anything and everything to avoid that fate. The intruder wore black jeans, a black turtleneck, and a black balaclava. *Bad guy formal wear,* Cole thought absently before the man said, "Good evening, Agent Huebsch. Nice you could finally make it home."

"I'd return the sentiment," Cole said, "but I'm kinda hoping your evening isn't so good." His voice came out a low growl. "I don't like it much when a guy enters my house without an invitation, wearing a cliché villain costume and pointing a gun at my heart. I don't like it at all."

"I apologize for the inconvenience then," the man said. "Come along now, and we'll go see the lovely Miss Fields. She was waiting up for you, but when she met my partner, she just swooned and fell back on her bed, like he was Elvis or something."

The calm, polite words of the would-be assassin enraged Cole more than if he had barked orders at him, and he fought to keep his cool. He needed to think. The gunman knew their names, and anyone but a professional would be nervous as hell at this moment. This guy came across as a stone-cold killer. He had mentioned a partner, but could be alone, with Michele tied up and gagged in another room. That would be best case, but Cole didn't think the people behind Michele's attack would send a lone hitman. Better to send two or more to ensure the job was done right this time; money didn't seem to be a barrier to them.

The gunman took a small step back into the kitchen and waved his pistol to indicate Cole should lead the way down the hall. Cole anticipated the wave of the gun, appearing emotionless and aloof, but inside, his adrenaline surged, and he felt every muscle in his being coil like a rattlesnake preparing to strike. Just before the gunman flicked the pistol forward to indicate Cole should move, Cole launched himself at him. Before the man registered what was happening, his gun was already moving to point down the hall, and Cole was on him before he could stop its momentum and turn it back on Cole. Cole shoved the man's right arm, holding the pistol away from him, and it went off close to his ear. He could feel the heat and hear the deafening bang, and he thought in the moment that feeling and hearing at that point were good. It meant he was still alive. When the man turned and swung his left elbow at Cole, Cole grabbed that, too. Now he was behind the guy holding his right arm with his own right hand and the guy's left arm with his left. The guy tried to stomp on Cole's instep and pull away, but Cole anticipated it and tripped the man headfirst into the oak kitchen table. With both arms held behind him and Cole's weight coming down on top of him, the man hit the hardwood table mouth first and hard. Cole heard the shattering of teeth and bone and felt the man's neck snap back; when it passed the point God intended it to go, Cole heard the loud "crack" of the spinal column breaking. Cole fell to the floor on top of a dead man. Before he could even sigh, he heard the beat of shoes running down the hall toward him. They were too heavy to be Michele's.

"Did you get him, Declan?" a man said, staying just around the corner from the kitchen, hesitant. Cole moaned, hoping the dead man's pal would either assume it was Declan or that Cole was hurt and not a threat. Cole had his Glock up and pointed at the doorway. When the man didn't make a move, Cole thought, *Plaster be damned.* He aimed his gun just to the left of the door, pulling the trigger four times in rapid succession, moving the barrel an inch or two left with each shot. The man yelped and landed with a thud on the other side of the door. Cole stepped around into the hall with his gun out in front now and saw the man writhing on the ground, blood pooling on the floor. He had dropped his gun when he was hit, but Cole didn't want to give the guy the opportunity to leave or, worse yet, come up behind Cole when he went to check on Michele. He leveled the gun at the man's head and saw the pain in his face replaced with fear. Pure terror. Cole decided to keep the guy alive for questioning later, and he kicked the guy in the head hard twice. He wouldn't be getting up under his own steam for a while. Cole continued down the hall, unsure if there were more gunmen in the house.

What if she's dead, his inner voice whispered. "Then I'll go back and empty this gun in the skull of that guy lying in my hallway. And then I'll spend the rest of my miserable existence dedicated to finding and destroying whoever the hell is behind all this," he said aloud. He wanted to run down the hall, but he couldn't be foolhardy. He was Michele's only chance at making it through this. When he got to her room, he saw her sprawled across the covers on her bed. She was dressed for the day, and the bed was made. She lay perfectly still. Cole's gun didn't have a silencer, and he knew the shots and scuffling caused a racket. He wondered how she could've slept through it. He went to her and pulled her to him, "Michele? Michele? Wake up!" But she was unresponsive. Limp. A dead weight in his arms. He gently laid her back down and felt for a pulse; it was there, faint and erratic. And then he heard a noise in the hall. Close. He turned and raised his gun. All his fear and anger boiled up and over, and he started to pull the trigger, aiming inches left of the doorway as he'd done with the man he'd just shot. But he held up, considering Michele lying nearly lifeless next to him. *What if she died?* He was tired of losing people he loved. He heard the person in the hall step closer, and he lowered his gun a little. Suicide by cop was a thing where a bad guy ended his life by pointing his gun at police with no intent to shoot, knowing the cops would protect themselves and each other by ending the threat and the life. Well, what about suicide by crook? Maybe he should just keep his gun pointing vaguely at the doorway and take whatever came his way.

Cole's emotions fought for control as another creak sounded just around the door frame. His Glock wavered, but some part of his brain whispered that Michele still had a chance, but not if he gave up now. He snarled and began to pull the trigger when Frau Newhouse toddled into the doorframe, her nightgown flapping and a halo of white hair flying around her frightened face. Cole cried out and dropped his gun. Frau came to him quickly, holding him in her slight but surprisingly strong arms, hugging him close.

"I need to call 911. They hurt Michele," Cole cried. He hadn't checked her for wounds, and he didn't feel any blood when he'd held her. Her face had been angelic and peaceful when he looked at her. "They might have poisoned her," he said.

"Shh. Shhh. I called 911 as soon as I heard the first shot. Help is coming." Frau had barely uttered those words when they heard feet pounding down the hall and the loud shouts of MPD. Within a minute, the room was filled with uniformed police and paramedics.

Michele was examined briefly and whisked away to the hospital. Cole walked Frau Newhouse back to her landing and went inside with her. He doubted she'd ever seen a dead person whose life was ended by violent means, and he wanted to make sure that she was okay. His ever-mounting worries now included one that she would think of him forever more as cold and ruthless. A killer. But Frau read his thoughts. "You are a good man, Cole Huebsch. You are a special man. You killed two very bad men tonight because they wanted to hurt a very good woman and to hurt you. Maybe they would have hurt me too," she trembled as she said it. "You know I love you like a son. I worry so much about you."

He teared up again but forced a smile. "You would think by now that the bad guys would know that you and I are both tough as nails."

"Michele, too," Frau said. "We will be like a family again soon. Go upstairs and get to work. They need you. I will be fine here."

Cole nodded. He started to leave but turned back to his old friend. "You may have saved Michele's life by calling 911 when you did. And you showed incredible courage to come up and check on us, not knowing if the bad guys were still up there, alive, I mean. Thank you."

He said goodnight then and headed back to his floor. Ty had arrived, and he was directing the team of MPD officers and techs. The two bodies lay on the hardwood floor, mere feet apart. The guy Cole shot through the wall hadn't made it. Cole had hoped they'd be able to question him, but he was otherwise unfazed by the man's death at his hands. *Enjoy the ride to hell with your pal,* he thought.

"You really know how to throw a party," Ty said, looking at the dead men. "But the cleanup is gonna be a bitch."

Cole stepped around the body in the kitchen, filled a glass of water from the fridge, and sat down at the table. Ty joined him, careful to avoid contaminating the crime scene. "We should've figured whoever paid for the attack on Michele would send someone else. That's on me. I'm sorry, pal."

Cole looked at him and shook his head. "It's on me too. But I can't dwell on that right now because I already hate myself enough over all this shit.

The other thing is, these guys were different from DeMario; they weren't amateurs. When that guy by your feet held his gun on me and looked me in the face, he showed no fear or emotion. It was just a day's work, something I'd bet he'd done plenty of times before. I never saw the second guy's face until after I shot him through the wall. He was a careful bastard. And when they do the autopsy, they're gonna find out that I kicked him twice in the head after he was already down, because I didn't want him to come after me from behind when I went to find Michele. And I didn't have time to cuff him. I wanted to keep him alive, but, between you and I, not that badly. It's a cluster."

"We'll figure it out, buddy. Are you okay?"

"No. I'm not. I don't know what they did to Michele, but she was in a bad way when I found her. She barely had a pulse, and it was anything but steady. If she doesn't make it, I don't know what I'll do. And I almost shot Frau Newhouse tonight. Christ!"

Ty put a hand on Cole's arm. It was a little awkward, but he wanted him to know that he was there for him. "Michele will pull through. She's young, and she loves her life. She's got every reason to fight, and she's strong."

Hearing Ty's words, Cole couldn't help but wonder about the feelings regarding his own life and its worth that had battled for center stage in his head over the course of the last hour or so. But he was fried, tired from stress and the adrenaline dump that had helped him get through the worst of it. At least, he hoped it was the worst of it. If Michele didn't pull through, then the worst was yet to come. He wasn't proud about some of the thoughts he'd had, but at least he'd pushed through and done what had to be done.

Ty snapped his fingers. "You still there? I think I lost you for a minute."

Cole sighed heavily and clapped his friend on the shoulder, thanking him, before grabbing a jacket and moving to the door that led down to the garage. Ty followed him. "We'll lock up when we're done," he said as Cole hurried down the stairs.

Chapter Twenty-Two

Cole drove to St. Joseph Hospital. Its large red *EMERGENCY* sign, lit up brighter than neon, pulled him to its main doors like a moth to a flame. He checked in with the front desk when he entered the ED, showing his FBI credentials, not bashful about getting a little preferred treatment. All he wanted was the best care for Michele and to be kept informed.

He called Michele's mom on the drive over and got her out of bed. He'd forgotten how early mornings started on a dairy farm and how equally early farm families usually went to bed. "Hello?" Debbie sounded sleepy, but Cole's next words hit like a defibrillator, shocking her wide awake when he told her that her only daughter was back in the hospital. She listened quietly, but Cole could hear her panicked breathing and almost feel the hammering of her heart as he told her the unvarnished truth about the intruders in their house and the state that he had found Michele in. He left nothing out. He said that Michele was still breathing when he found her, but that her pulse was faint. He said he hadn't seen any blood on her or the bedding and that all he could think of was that maybe she'd been poisoned. "The more I think about it, though, that really doesn't make sense either, since the men who entered our house didn't seem to have any aversion to using their guns. Unless they thought they could poison her and make it look like a heart issue or something and that they got noisy only when I entered the picture." He realized he was thinking out loud and worried it would only send Debbie into even more of a panic.

"Okay, Cole. I'm going to throw some clothes together and head back down to Milwaukee. Jim will have to stay here for the time being. The cows won't milk themselves, as they say, and we've already leaned too hard on the goodwill of our neighbors."

"I'll be here in the same ED we sat in just a few days ago. I'll hold a chair for you," Cole said, shaking his head at his lame attempt at humor. "If I learn anything new before you get here, I'll call you right away. Please tell Jim that I'm sorry about all of this."

"Not your fault, Cole. See you as soon as I can get there." She hung up, and Cole sat and fidgeted.

He was still alone an hour later when Alan Anderson entered the waiting room with a petite, youngish-looking woman in a white lab coat. Cole guessed her to be in her mid-thirties, and he could tell by her grimace that she came bearing bad news. They were an unlikely-looking pair, the hospital administrator towering over the woman as they made their way across the waiting room toward him. Cole felt acutely alone and wished with all his soul that Debbie was here holding his hand so he could share the burden that was about to be handed to him. He didn't know if he would be strong enough to bear it on his own.

Cole rose from his seat, and Alan introduced the physician, "This is Doctor Broor. She is a board-certified neurosurgeon, one of the most skilled in the country. He looked around the waiting room, and it was thankfully quiet. He gestured for Cole and Dr. Broor to sit down and said to Cole, "Dr. Broor has some news to share about Michele's condition, and it will be hard to hear." He looked at the doctor. "I told her to be completely forthright. Painfully honest." He looked back at Cole, "I want you to understand the seriousness of the situation, but also to know that there's hope. There's always hope. Miracles happen within the walls of this building every day."

Cole blew out a lungful of air in a rush and shook his head. "Please, just let me know what's going on."

Dr. Broor nodded and began, "The paramedics called our emergency department on their way to the hospital. One of our ED physicians, Dr. Julie Shimp, then pulled up Michele's medical records and ordered a CT scan based on the injuries she sustained during her original attack at the library. She suspected based on the patient's recent head trauma and current symptoms that she could be experiencing a brain bleed." She paused, "That proactive measure by Dr. Shimp may well have saved Michele's life. When she arrived at the hospital, the team immediately addressed her airway by intubating her, then they gave her fluids and drew blood for lab work. Within minutes, she was wheeled back to radiology, where the CT scan confirmed an intracranial hemorrhage. A brain bleed."

Broor read the confusion on Cole's face. "I know you suspected poisoning, and we are running lab tests to rule that out, but we are now confident that Michele's current condition was caused by the head trauma she sustained when she was attacked during her presentation at the library. The hospital performed a CT scan on Michele when she was initially brought in after her attack and again before she was released from the hospital. Both of them were negative for any sign of a brain bleed. Unfortunately, in about one percent of the cases of severe head trauma, the intracranial bleeding starts days, weeks, even months after the initial incident. That's what's happened here. Michele won the lottery that nobody wants to win."

"Okay," Cole said numbly. "So, what happens next?"

"Michele is in a coma, which is a common occurrence with severe brain bleeds. She's also recovering from surgery. I was paged as soon as the bleed was found, and as fate would have it, I was already in-house rounding on patients. A surgical team was here finishing another case, and we took her back for emergency surgery to reduce the pressure on her brain. Typically, we would need the informed consent of the patient to do surgery, but the law allows us to move forward independently without consent if it's deemed necessary to save the life of the patient. That was obviously warranted in this case.

Cole summoned his remaining courage and asked the question whose answer he feared the most, "Is she going to be okay?"

Broor pressed her lips together, stalling for time or steeling herself, maybe both. She looked at Alan and then quickly back at Cole. "The truth is Michele's prognosis is not very good. At one year, mortality ranges for people who've experienced an intracranial hemorrhage are fifty-one to sixty-five percent, depending on the location of the bleed. At six months, only twenty percent of patients are expected to be independent."

Broor let the statistics sink into Cole's brain, filtered by fatigue, fear, and grief. "You mean she's going to die or be on some kind of life support?"

"No. Not necessarily. Alan told you not to give up hope. We caught Michele's bleed and reduced the swelling as quickly as possible. Alan told me what happened at your house tonight, and I believe if those men hadn't attacked you there that Michele would likely be dead already. The paramedics said she swooned or fainted not long before you got there. If those uninvited guests hadn't stopped by, you would have found her in bed and likely thought she was exhausted. You might have covered her with a blanket, kissed her forehead, said a quiet goodnight, and left her to sleep until morning. But that would have been a sleep she would never have woken from. She has a chance now, thanks to whoever called 911, the quick work of the paramedics, and our ED and surgical teams." She paused again, knowing patients and their families needed time to process hard information when they were in states of shock, confusion, or denial.

Cole looked at Alan, his friend now for many years, and he saw both weariness and warmth in his big brown eyes. He turned to Dr. Broor and saw the heaviness and compassion in her eyes. He felt a lump in his throat; he wasn't alone in this. "Is there anything else?"

"Half of the deaths from intracranial bleeds happen within the first two days of their occurrence. Also, in situations like Michele's, if a patient is going to wake up from a coma, more than half do so within the first two days. If she doesn't wake up in the next week, then there's just a ten percent chance that she will, no matter how long we wait. But every patient is different; Michele is young and was in perfect health from what we can tell before her attack. That's in her favor, and that should tilt the odds her way a little. But Alan and I wanted you to know the facts. These next forty-eight hours are crucial."

She had just finished explaining things to Cole when Debbie burst through the ED doors. She looked frantic, and Cole yelled to her across the waiting room as she raced to the reception desk. She changed course and came straight to Cole and hugged him fiercely. When she let go, Cole introduced her to Dr. Broor and asked her to explain everything for Michele's mom's benefit. He hoped by listening a second time, he might retain more of the information. He watched the young physician walk through Michele's condition and prognosis again. He saw her gesture with her hands, tilt her head to listen thoughtfully and nod for emphasis. But her words and meaning weren't getting through to him, as the only thought he could keep in his head was the mantra: *please don't let her die!*

Chapter Twenty-Three

Debbie and Cole joined Michele in the ICU soon after she was moved from the recovery room. It hurt him to see her lying there. A tube ran from a bedside ventilator into her mouth and down her throat, and the machine that did her breathing for her sounded like Darth Vader. Michele's head was bandaged, and she had more tubes and lines running from her arms and chest. But her face looked surprisingly peaceful in the pale light. Cole pulled chairs up on either side of the bed, and he and Debbie sat on opposite sides, each holding one of Michele's hands, keeping vigil. They sat mostly in silence throughout the night, each saying their own prayers to the soft beat of the machine that tracked Michele's vital signs. Cole's eyes grew as heavy as his heart.

In his dreams, he saw DeMario climbing the stage and rushing Michele. He saw her knocked backward and heard the loud thud of her head slamming into the unyielding podium. It reminded him of a similar sound he'd heard once while vacationing in the Florida Keys. He had found a ripe coconut, but didn't have a decent knife, so he bashed the coconut against a rock to get at the sweet milk and meat inside. That sound now played over and over in his dreams and hammered home Cole's own pain in not reaching DeMario in time to stop him.

He woke up hours later, his head slumped awkwardly on the bed, still holding Michele's hand. He sat up, a ripple of cracks ringing out as his back straightened. He rolled his shoulders, the left one still a bit stiff from where he'd taken a bullet less than a year ago. He had a crick in his neck, and he tilted his head left, right, forward, and then back in an effort to loosen it up.

He noticed Debbie watching him with a smile on her lips. "She's still with us," she said, nodding to the monitor.

Cole's return smile was weak, but he said, "That's a blessing, for sure."

"She has a lot to live for, including and maybe especially you, Cole." Debbie saw the doubt, the complete and utter absence of hope behind Cole's stoic mask. She made sure he was looking at her. "She *will* pull through. She loves her life, you know. She calls us at least two or three times a week, usually on FaceTime, so we can see her, and she talks non-stop about her writing, her book, and about you. She is a strong, independent woman, but we all need someone to lean on. We need someone to keep us grounded when we get a little too full of ourselves and to lift us up when we're down. She found that in you. She will fight for that; she's fighting for that right now. Inside."

"Thank you," Cole said, forcing a bigger smile that made him feel like a fraud. Fear clung to him like a foul odor he couldn't scrub away. It covered him, swallowed him whole. He feared Michele never waking up and, maybe worse, feared her waking up a different person altogether. It was paralyzing. But through his own pain, he knew Debbie needed support, too. "When she's with me, she talks about you and Jim a lot," he finally said. "I haven't known you long, but I see both your qualities and Jim's in her, and she's proud of that. She's also grateful for everything you've done for her and credits you for encouraging her to follow her dreams. It's not fair that this has happened now, right when she's begun to realize those dreams."

"Not fair, maybe, but our struggles always seem to make us stronger in the end. I know that sounds cliché, but I believe it. There's a quote I heard once that I'll never forget. It goes like this, 'Without the darkness, we can't really appreciate the light.' That rings true to me."

"Thank you, Debbie. I'm seen as calm and cool at work, the guy who keeps his head when things are at their worst. I might look that way in my personal life, too, but inside, I can be a mess, giving in to doubt and worrying about all the most horrible 'what ifs.' But I think you're right." He looked at Michele. "It could take a while for her to come around and even longer before she is back to being herself. But together, we'll get her there. In the meantime, I should run into the office. I'm going to have to answer some questions after everything that went down last night. But I'll be back as soon as I can." He squeezed Michele's hand one more time, went around the bed, hugged her mom, and then left to face the day.

The morning had dawned gray and rainy. The wind flapped his wrinkled suit and drove the cold into his bones as he made the short walk from the hospital to his car. Wet leaves fell on him and his Dodge like sodden pieces of brown paper bags. The weight of the rain and the gusts of wind tore the leaves from the trees in bunches and bled the color from the canopies. Like skin sloughing off and whirling down the drain. Cole reflected on the change of weather and seasons as he gratefully pulled open his car door and shut it behind him, cocooning him from the icy breeze. As more wet decaying leaves splattered down on his hood and windshield, he thought, *it doesn't represent death, but more the state of dying.*

Gene Olson was sitting behind Cole's desk when Cole walked into his office twenty minutes later. The deputy director looked comfortable, reading a print copy of the *Journal Sentinel* while drinking coffee. Cole sat down heavily in one of the chairs facing Gene. "Morning, boss."

Gene looked up at Cole. "You made the funny papers again by taking down two more bad guys. Front page, above the fold! A lesser leader might be jealous of all the media attention you get." He removed the black cheaters he used to read and studied his protégé. "You look rough. Everyone in the Bureau thinks of you as Superman, but you must have sat on a lump of Kryptonite recently."

Cole had driven directly to his office from the hospital. He looked down at his rumpled shirt and suit and then back at Olson. "Your boy's been busy, Gene. It seems like a week ago, but it was only yesterday that I was in your neck of the woods pushing the interim CEO of the big pharma advocacy group on whether they were behind Michele's attack. I might have stepped on Roger Beneker's toes a bit while I was at it."

Gene smiled. "That's putting it mildly. Cool Rog, as you like to refer to him, was on the horn to the president, who was on the horn to the director, who was on the horn to yours truly, all within an hour of your meeting. I'm pretty sure my right ear is still bleeding. You seem to have a particular gift for pissing Beneker off."

"Good to know," Cole said. "Then I catch a plane back here and open up the door to my house, and get attacked by two guys with guns. You'll be glad to know that I actually used my own gun this time and shot one of the bad men."

Gene took a big sip of coffee. "I have given you a ration of shit about that in the past. Seems like when you're confronted you typically forget about your gun and just pile-drive the bad guys into the ground. Nice to see you showing off a different side of yourself. You are a talented lad indeed." Gene looked a little closer at his SAC, "You have good instincts; what's your gut telling you about APAG's possible involvement in Michele's attacks?"

Cole blew out his breath and beat a short staccato rhythm on the armrests of his chair. He hadn't had time to really consider it. "Well, DeMario attacked Michele out of desperation in order to get the pharmaceuticals his daughter needed to hopefully keep her alive. That's like a crazy big cartoon arrow pointing right at APAG. It screams, '*We're behind this*,' which either shows their arrogance or possibly their innocence. Would they be that stupid? And then this second attack featured the same kind of stone-cold mercenaries that APAG used to come after me before. Maybe it's connected, or maybe all the evil powers-that-be in our nation's capital rent their would-be assassins from the same wholesaler. *Mercs R Us* or some such."

He got up and went to the windows that looked out over Lake Michigan, stalling to gather his thoughts. The winds whipped the great lake into a frenzy, the waves large and erratic, scouring sediment from the bottom and tossing it high into the dark, heavy air. He could see legions of huge, frothy whitecaps and spray through the misting rain. His mind mirrored the churning of the big water.

"There are powerful people in this country who are up to no good. And yes, I know that's not a news flash. But when the CEO of APAG died suspiciously a couple months ago..." He paused, still looking out the window, feeling Gene's eyes boring into his back now. Cole and his team had believed the CEO, Nichole Sebastian, and her security chief were behind the attempted murder of Senator Rhodes and that they had successfully murdered a number of journalists critical of big pharma. When they couldn't conclusively prove it, they had backed off. At least officially. Cole had been on a flight to San Francisco when Sebastian had been killed, so the Bureau didn't investigate him. Nobody, including Cole, had confronted Li. Cole continued, "When Sebastian was killed, I think a lot of us just assumed that the head of the snake was cut off and that the body would die. I guess now that I've had a chance to ruminate on it, I think that still feels right. With Sebastian, her security chief, and their best mercenaries off the board, I just don't believe APAG has the will or the muscle to do this. I've met the interim CEO now, and he's a milquetoast kind of guy, not some genius mastermind."

Gene took that in while he drained the last of his coffee. "So, you think someone else attacked Michele and left the obvious trail of crumbs back to APAG's headquarters."

Cole turned back to him, "Yeah. At least, that's my best guess right now. But I've been a little distracted lately with everything going on."

"Of course, and that reminds me…now that you actually shot someone, I need to take said gun of yours for the time being and place you on paid leave."

"Seriously?"

"Yeah. SOP. Standard operating procedure. There'll be an internal investigation, our lawyers will get involved, and then there will be an official ruling on whether or not the discharge of your weapon was justified by the circumstances. Given the situation, it seems obvious that you were justified in your actions last night."

"You think? Those guys were armed intruders in my home. They had a woman held hostage. Has the Bureau ever heard of the Castle Doctrine? In Wisconsin, like most sane states, homeowners have the right to protect themselves and others under their roof with deadly force, if necessary. I'd say it was necessary in this case."

"I don't disagree. And the investigation shouldn't take more than a few days at most. You just need to trust the process…and hand over your gun for the time being."

Cole pulled the Glock from his holster and laid it on the desk in front of his mentor. He reached into his suit pocket, but Gene waved him off. "I don't need your badge. I brought an agent along with me from D.C., and right now, she's looking at the police report and interviewing the MPD detectives working on last night's incident. I wanted to get on this right away so that we can put it behind us. I will try to call you first to let you know the outcome of the investigation, and the attorneys will also send you something in writing. Until then, you're on leave. No work. No contact with your agents or analysts."

"You did say this was a paid leave, right?"

"Absolutely," Gene answered. He could almost see the gears in Cole's head spinning. "This leave comes at an opportune time for you. Go back to Michele's bedside, tell her Gene says 'hi,' and nurse her back to health."

Cole pushed himself slowly to his feet and smiled. "That's an order I'll be glad to follow."

"One more thing," Gene said, causing Cole to turn back as he was almost out the door.

"Yes?"

"For God's sake, go home and take a shower first!" His booming laughter echoed down the hall after Cole. Gene's eyes followed his favorite SAC until he turned a corner out of sight. He leaned back in the chair and closed his eyes. He had never been hurt on the job; most agents went their whole careers without being shot, stabbed, or even punched or kicked. He had pulled his gun twice, but never had to shoot another human being. Cole had been shot in the past year and been in other fights where his life had been on the line. He killed two men just twelve hours ago, one with his bare hands. Gene had seen the blood and gore from crime scene photos and knew it had been ugly. The woman Cole loved was also fighting against overwhelming odds for her life. Gene knew Cole better than anyone and had witnessed countless times the depth of strength in him. The grit, that unique blend of passion and perseverance that Cole possessed, had helped him to a collegiate wrestling championship and one of the most decorated careers in the Bureau's history. But Gene knew that every man and woman has their breaking point. And as he opened his eyes and looked out over the churning lake at the endless grey skies, he worried more than ever about his friend.

Chapter Twenty-Four

After a quick shower, Cole went back to the hospital in jeans and a soft flannel shirt and resumed his vigil with Debbie. They sat at Michele's side nonstop, aside from the occasional bathroom break. They each held one of her hands and discussed everything and anything. Michele's eyes remained closed, no matter the changes in noise and light levels as the myriad of caregivers came and went throughout the day and into the evening. She showed no response as they poked and prodded, drew blood, changed her bandages, or hung new meds.

Dr. Broor stopped in and updated them. She'd reviewed the nurses' and hospitalists' charting from the past few hours and did her own cursory exam of Michele. There wasn't much new to report, except that all of Michele's lab tests had come back, and they were negative for any type of poison. She told them that 'untraceable' poisons were mostly a myth found in mystery novels, especially when they were able to draw blood from a suspected victim as soon as they were from Michele. They also did a thorough inspection of obvious and not-so-obvious injection sites on Michele and found no evidence that she'd received one. They were focusing all their efforts on helping her wake up from her coma and continue rehabbing her arm as soon as possible.

Around nine o'clock, Cole's stomach began growling, softly at first, but then louder, more insistent. He couldn't remember when he'd eaten last. It turned out that Debbie and Cole shared a love of the Seinfeld television sitcom, and it cracked Cole up to hear Debbie tease him that his stomach was saying 'hellooooo' to Michele. The banter kept their minds off the unthinkable. Cole knew the cafeteria was long closed, and he was contemplating whether to hit the vending machine on the main floor when Debbie came around the bed and put a hand on his shoulder.

"You need to get something to eat and then go home and rest. I don't think anything will happen in the middle of the night, but if it does, you'll be the first person I call."

Cole looked at her and started to shake his head, "I don't want you waiting alone."

"I won't be alone," she said, nodding toward Michele's still form, "I've got my little girl here to keep me company."

He wasn't sure why, but he listened to her, and after hugging her again, he said goodbye to Michele and went home. As soon as he was in the door, he poured himself an IPA and fried a pound of bacon in a heavy black skillet. The hiss and pop and the hickory and maple smell had him salivating. If bacon and beer wasn't the breakfast of champions, it damn well ought to be. He added two fried eggs to the mix and sat at the kitchen table, savoring each sweet and smoky bacon strip as he thought back over the past couple of weeks. He tried to read for an hour, but couldn't concentrate on the words. He thought about going to bed but knew he wouldn't be able to fall asleep. He needed a change of attitude; instead of rest, he'd do the opposite.

Cole put on a pair of running shorts and pulled an old Marquette sweatshirt over his head with the hoodie up. The rain had stopped, but it was still windy and damp when he left home, the cold embracing him as soon as he stepped outside. He started slowly, burping bacon and beer, but soon settled into his typical six-minute per mile pace. He hadn't worked out for a few days, and it took a while to get into a comfortable rhythm. He didn't think about where he was running, setting his mind free to wander as his feet slapped the wet pavement like a metronome.

Before he realized it, he had turned up Wisconsin Avenue and onto the Marquette University campus. As he ran down the sidewalk, he couldn't help but notice all the new buildings that had replaced the old since he'd been a student. He slowed as he approached Johnston Hall; the tall Gothic building was more than one hundred years old and used to house the entire university. It had been home to the College of Communications for decades and had recently undergone a multi-million-dollar renovation. On the outside, it looked much like it did when it was first built, except even in the gloom, it looked brighter and updated. It was almost midnight now, and he liked seeing the old building in the dark, the day's rain still dripping slowly down the tendrils of ivy that clung to its gray walls. The sleek new buildings he passed were beautiful and impressive in their own way and spoke to the advances made by the University over the years. But somehow, he'd just always preferred the old over the new. And then he realized where he was headed, to the humble chapel that most students over the last sixty years saw as the beating heart of the school. St. Joan of Arc was tiny, originally built of stone and wood in 1420, in a small town in France, and it was now the oldest building in Milwaukee by more than three centuries. It had been rebuilt in Milwaukee in the mid-sixties, stone by loving stone.

Cole stood in front of the stout wooden doors of the chapel, the sweat from his run swept away by the cold breeze. He wasn't sure what brought him here or what to do next. He raised his fist hesitantly, meaning to knock on the door. For some reason, he thought of Martin Luther, standing at the door of another church in England, one hundred years after this chapel was constructed. But he didn't want to challenge the church or start a reformation, perhaps only find a little comfort or direction. Instead of knocking, he pulled at the heavy door and was surprised when it swung open. Without thinking, he stepped inside and pulled the door shut behind him. The chapel was dimly lit, and Cole squinted to see. It was warmer inside than one would have expected, given the stone floor and tall ceiling with dark timbers. Small wooden chairs were lined up before the altar, and Cole walked to the front of them, genuflected, and sat down.

He pulled the hoodie back and ran a hand through his hair. He looked straight ahead and listened as his breathing slowed. His eyes became accustomed to the gloom, and a soft, diffused light bled into the chapel from the stained-glass windows that flanked the spot where Cole sat. Two tall candles stood sentry on either side of the solid stone altar. Lit, their flames danced to a zephyr Cole couldn't feel, and he knew that he was not alone in the small chapel. Somehow, it was more comforting than unnerving. He waited, calming himself even more.

After a time, a young woman stepped out of the shadows behind the altar and came around to stand in front of him. From years of being on the job, Cole sized the woman up. She was about five foot two in height, dressed in unadorned jeans, a heavy red long-sleeve chamois shirt, and an open navy peacoat. Her eyes were large and set far apart, and her mid-length black hair was pulled back. She was reasonably good-looking but would never be described as beautiful. When she spoke, her voice was surprisingly low and sweet. "May I sit with you?"

Cole smiled at her. He thought she was probably a first- or second-year undergrad. "Sure. I'd like that."

They sat close, in comfortable silence, both facing ahead. They looked at the flickering candles and the small crucifix they seemed to watch over, and the woman said, "You must be quite devout to be here on a Saturday at midnight."

Cole shook his head, *"Au Contraire."* He looked around and added, "It seems like a lifetime ago that I was a student here. I used to wrestle, and there were many Saturdays during the offseason when I would attend midnight Mass in this chapel before hitting the bars afterward. The faith and sense of community that bound us together in this small place was palpable; you felt it the minute you walked through the door. But I lost my faith somewhere along the way, right around the time I graduated. And that was a long time ago."

When she had nothing to say to that, Cole continued. "I'm a cradle Catholic, grew up in the Church. I went to Mass every Sunday with my parents when I was little. They sent me to a Catholic grade school, and at that point, I attended Mass six times a week, even more after I became an altar boy. Back then, I took my faith for granted. I had the faith of an innocent and never considered it could be any different. And when I prayed, I believed. I prayed to a God I not only knew existed, but I knew in my heart that He loved me.

"But then life happened. I lost both of my parents before I graduated from

MU. Then I got married in the Church, telling God, my wife, and everyone else that my commitment was forever…until it wasn't. I guess that sacred vow I made didn't mean all that much to me in the end." His head had fallen down, but she put a hand under his chin and gently lifted it up, and he felt compelled to continue. "The other thing is, I believe things that are contrary to the Church's teachings."

When he hesitated, she said, "Please, go on…" And he did; it felt freeing to share these hidden thoughts with someone else, especially someone who didn't know him and wasn't judging him.

"For instance, I have met holy women who I believe have been called to be priests. But because of the Church's man-made rules, these women can't answer their call; we turn them away." The young woman only nodded, but Cole thought he saw a slight smile on her lips. "And I've known priests who have fallen in love and had to leave the priesthood. Some of the finest priests I've ever known, lost to us. God led them to find love; why can't they marry and still remain priests? It makes no sense! Can you imagine all the good our Church could accomplish if we allowed these inspired men and women to lead?" His voice rose as he became more impassioned. "I think we are not only holding these holy people back, but we are damaging our faith community at the same time. And I don't think it's God's will at all. Don't you see?" His voice bounced off the stone walls, and he blushed in the darkness. "Sorry," he whispered.

They sat in silence again, eyes drawn back to the altar. "I do see. In fact, I question the same things about our Church," the woman confessed.

"But?"

"But I love the Church too much to leave it. I'd rather work for change from within the Church than abandon it."

Cole stared at the young woman and saw the courage and conviction in her. The simple words she'd said so softly reverberated deep inside him. He had never stopped feeling like a spiritual creature, but he had most certainly lost his faith. He began to think that maybe he could find it again. He wanted more than anything to believe in something larger than himself. "I watched the brown and blackened leaves falling to the ground this morning and wondered if that is how life ends for us, as compost. I held the hand of the woman I love as she fought for her life, and I feared that might be her fate. You've given me strength and hope."

"Glad I could be of service," she said. She reached into her coat pocket and pulled out something wrapped in a napkin. "Should we celebrate with Communion?"

"What? Just the two of us?"

"For where two or three are gathered in my name, I am there among them. Matthew 18:20," she said. She opened the napkin, revealing a bread roll, and she broke it and offered half to Cole. "The body of Christ."

"It looks like a dinner roll," Cole said.

"It is indeed."

"Shouldn't it be unleavened?"

"I don't think the Lord will mind."

And that felt right to him, too. "Amen," he said. Then he ate the bit of bread and felt a deep warmth spread through him. He remembered another definition of communion, the sharing of intimate thoughts and feelings on a spiritual level. And he knew he had never felt communion so fully as he did just then.

The young woman took his hands in hers, nodded, and said goodbye. She turned and began to walk, but Cole called to her, "Wait!"

She turned back to him, and he said, "You never told me what brought you here on this cold and windy night."

She looked around the chapel and smiled, a smile as sweet as it was sad. "I've been coming to this chapel to pray for strength and guidance for some time." With that, she turned again and resumed walking, disappearing behind the altar, presumably going out a back door. When he stepped outside the chapel and pulled the great door behind him, the wind had picked up and it was raining again, not hard but steadily. But as Cole ran toward home, the warmth he felt in the chapel never left him. He was soaked by the time he reached the castle mansion. But as he made his way up the steps and into his home, a trail of small puddles in his wake, he saw the rain as a second baptism of sorts, and his spirit was renewed. He took a hot shower before falling into bed, where he slept soundly for the first time in years.

Chapter Twenty-Five

Cole carried two large black coffees when he entered Michele's room early the next morning. He felt better and more purposeful than he'd felt when he left less than ten hours before. He noticed the sunlight streaming in the window through the blind and thanked God for the gift of today. Debbie was awake next to Michele when he walked in, and she gratefully accepted the coffee. Cole had skipped breakfast, and he had barely settled in on his side of the bed and taken Michele's hand in his when his stomach growled. It was loud in the quiet room. Debbie said, "hellooooo" in a deep voice, and Cole couldn't help but laugh. He stopped short when he thought he felt a tiny squeeze from Michele's hand. His breath caught. He wasn't sure. He didn't want to say anything to get Debbie's hopes up. He supposed it could have been a muscle twitch. Then he felt it again, slightly more pressure, and he looked across the bed to Michele's mom. Her eyes were wide and caught his.

"Did you feel it?" she said. "Did she just squeeze your hand a little? Twice?"

Cole nodded, a huge smile spreading across his face. "That has to be a good sign, right?" He looked at Michele and noticed her head was turned toward him somewhat. He was sure of it. That was a change. And then her eyes blinked open.

"Hellooooo!" Cole said, and though the rest of her face was impassive, he could swear he saw laughter in her eyes. Debbie pressed the call button for the nurse, and she looked at Cole through a veil of joyful tears. Cole's face was wet, too, and they both squeezed Michele's hands tighter, letting her know as words never could that they would never let go of her. The nurse pushed through the door and flicked on a bright light directly over the bed, and Cole saw Michele's eye shut tight in a wince. She was responsive again!

Dr. Broor rounded on Michele a couple hours later. When she was done examining her, she asked Debbie and Cole if she could have a word with them. They got up from their chairs, intending to walk out into the hall, but Dr. Broor indicated it would be better to talk in front of Michele. She wanted her to process what could be expected in the days ahead.

"It's obviously a great sign that Michele has opened her eyes and is responding to stimuli again. She can hear, and she feels pain. When I ask her to blink, she does. When I ask her to raise one finger or two, she complies accordingly. This is a great start. Only in the movies does a person wake from a coma and say, 'What happened?' Every person is different, but Michele is showing the first signs of recovery, however fully she will ultimately recover.

"The swelling has started to go down, and there's less pressure on her brain now. This allows better circulation or blood flow in her brain. That's partially why she has begun to awaken from her coma. The swelling should continue to recede over the next few days, and she should show further signs of improvement. But…" She paused to look at Cole and Debbie to make sure they heard the next part.

"But?" Cole asked.

"Recovery from a coma is a gradual process. The dead and severely damaged cells in Michele's brain caused by her trauma will likely never heal or regenerate. There's some difference of opinion on this, but for the most part, we believe that brain cells don't grow back after they die. The brain can, however, recruit surviving parts of the brain to take over the functions of the damaged areas. It's kind of like rerouting the wires in the brain around the dead cells. Today is a good day, but there will be both good and bad days ahead for all of you. The path to recovery will not be straight, and it will not be without its bumps. Michele could have trouble focusing, speaking, walking; we'll learn a lot over the next few days and weeks. When we understand more about her deficits, we will come up with a treatment plan revolving around physical and occupational therapy."

There was a loud rap at the door, and Alan Anderson poked his head into the room. The hospital administrator's large frame filled the doorway. "Sorry to interrupt, but I heard our patient is making headway, pun intended."

Dr. Broor put her hand on Michele's shoulder and said, "I just finished telling Debbie, Cole, and Michele that our patient's recovery has just begun." Cole noticed Michele's eyes following the conversation. He was a lot more hopeful today, but he was still pragmatic. "Anything else we should know," Dr. Broor?"

"Nothing more from me." She looked at Debbie, "Questions?"

"No," Debbie said. "I'm just very grateful right now to you and Michele's team of caregivers. Everybody has been amazing."

Dr. Broor thanked her and said her goodbyes, and Alan looked like he was going to duck out with her, but Cole called to him. "Alan, do you have a minute?"

His friend turned and came over to the bed. "What do you need?"

"The list is long," Cole said. "But what I need from *you* is help in keeping Michele's recovery quiet. She's now been attacked twice, and I'm thinking maybe we won't be so lucky if there's a third attempt. I'd like you to limit the number of different nurses and doctors involved in Michele's care going forward, with everyone sworn to secrecy about her condition. I want her electronic medical record updated daily to show that she is still in a coma until we figure out and nail whoever is behind these attacks."

"You know I want to help, and I can limit the staff and swear them to secrecy. But it's against a number of federal laws to falsify medical records. I'm not sure I can expect any physician or nurse to go along with that. They could be putting their licenses to practice at risk."

"I work for the *Federal* Bureau of Investigation, enforcing *federal* laws. You tell the staff involved the reason behind the fake documentation that we're safeguarding the patient's life. I'll write each of them a 'get out of jail free' card on FBI letterhead. What do you say?"

Alan gave Cole a big smile, "I think they'll be proud to do it. But if anybody tries to go after one of my staff later, I expect you to shoot them."

"That's a given," Cole said, cementing the deal with a handshake. "And not to be greedy, but there's one more thing you can do for me to help a patient who's not even in your hospital."

Alan cocked his head. "I can't wait to hear this."

Cole put his arm around his friend and spoke quietly in his ear, explaining what he wanted done. A huge smile broke over the administrator's face. "That could actually be kind of fun. And there's nobody I like working with more than the distinguished U.S. Senator from Wisconsin. In fact, Eric gets into town later tonight and we're meeting up for coffee first thing tomorrow. I'll let you know how it goes."

They shook hands again, and when Alan left, Cole turned back to Debbie and said loud enough for Michele to hear, "Now let's see what we can do to get this girl back on her feet!"

Chapter Twenty-Six

The elder two members of the Trinity were gathered in the Lyndon Baines Johnson Room in the northeast corner of the U.S. Capitol. The room was ornately decorated and had a distinct nineteenth-century vibe. It featured an elaborate fresco ceiling designed by Italian Constantino Brumidi, Minton floor tiles, and a large, elaborate crystal chandelier that had been the object of a tug-of-war between the executive and legislative branches of government through the decades, ping-ponging between the two seats of power.

The two members' security teams had independently swept the room for listening devices and cameras while they waited impatiently for the youngest member to arrive. They had each entered the room fashionably late and were unaccustomed to being kept waiting by others; the third and youngest member of the Trinity was the one exception for them both. The woman looked at her reflection in the large, elegant mirror that dominated the space above the fireplace. She ran her index finger absently under her eye, wondering if a minor tuck or tweak could erase the new set of fine lines etched there. The hooded eyes of the older gentleman wandered absently over the three large portraits that hung prominently in the room. The John Adams and Thomas Jefferson portraits looked beautifully rendered but outdated and stuffy to the old man's untrained eye. He identified more closely with Lyndon B. Johnson, the third presidential portrait in the room. Hell, they were almost contemporaries. He had been elected to the U.S. House of Representatives in 1974, missing the tail end of Johnson's presidency by just six years. He was elected to the Senate in 1980 and hadn't looked back since. The Johnson portrait had been painted in an uber-realistic style by Norman Rockwell, and it appeared to the man that the brash Texan might step out of the gilded frame and sit down with them at any moment. The man and woman looked everywhere about the room, except across the table at the other. They saw themselves as having nothing in common, except their shared love of power and money. The room was quiet as a crypt, and the only sound the woman heard was the heavy breathing of the man. "Mouth breather," she hissed under her breath. Together, they turned in a huff upon hearing the quiet click of the door opening. The youngest member of the group entered the room, offered a dismissive wave of his hand, and sat at the head of the table. Collins Jeffers entered at the same time and sat in a side chair, observing.

"Sorry for my delay," the younger man said, straightening the cuffs of his suit. "It was unavoidable."

"You're an important man," the senator said sarcastically, but looked away when the younger man fixed his eyes on him. When he found his nerve again, he said, "I should be out on the campaign trail."

"Whatever in the reason for?" the younger man said. "You're a lock. You haven't had a close election since your very first one, and that's more than forty years ago. There's nobody even running against you this time. You've got a machine, for Christ's sake!"

"True," the older man said, "But I need to take that machine on the road to help other members of my party who aren't as fortunate. I've got coattails, as they say."

"Coattails? More like goat trails," the woman said under her breath. Louder, she said to the younger man, "Why did you call this meeting? Was it to discuss yet another failure in silencing the reporter and killing the pesky FBI agent?"

"On the contrary, Madame Speaker," the man said, favoring the woman with a withering look. "If it weren't so soon after lunch, I might be popping the cork on a Chateau Petrus Bordeaux at this moment. Although, I prefer to share a good red with people whose company I actually enjoy." He let his comment linger. Their positions gave them the illusion of ultimate power, and at times, he felt the need to disabuse them of the notion. "The reporter you mentioned is in a coma; she won't be talking to anyone for some time. We have remote access to her electronic medical record, and we'll know in real time if she so much as blinks. If you understand anything about intracranial bleeds and comas, not too many people wake up from them and return to their regular routine. I don't see her writing an exposé or sitting down for an explosive interview in the near term, if ever. As for the Special Agent in Charge of the Milwaukee field office, he is on leave right now. When he's reinstated, which is likely, by the way, I imagine he'll be distracted by his girlfriend's life-and-death struggle. It would have been cleaner if he was dead, but a side benefit to this outcome is that they both suffer more. Given they've been an irritant to us, I find that to be a delightful bonus. A gift. Either way, I think we can agree the threat posed by these two has been removed." He looked back and forth between the two of them. "Are we agreed on this?"

They nodded their assent.

"Did you bring your binders?" The two nodded again, like obedient schoolchildren now. Nothing the Trinity discussed and decided over the years had ever been electronically recorded or stored. When it came to documenting their business, old school ruled. The woman hefted her embellished leather Bottega Veneta briefcase off the floor and set it on the chair next to her. She unzipped it, pulled out a large leather binder, and placed it in front of her. Across the table, the older man pulled an identical binder from a large lockable attaché case that looked like it came from the props department of a bad 1970s spy movie. The woman rolled her eyes and let out a chuff of air. The man's lack of any sense of style disgusted her.

The younger man had his binder open in front of him, and he looked his two elders in the eye again. "Now, on to the next order of business. Who do we compromise next?"

Chapter Twenty-Seven

Alan Anderson stepped into the Sherman Perk coffee shop carrying his laptop and felt like he had just entered his second home. Bob Olin and his wife Pat had transformed the Perk from an abandoned filling station more than twenty years earlier. The building was nearing its ninetieth birthday, a rare standing example of Streamlined Moderne architecture, and Bob and Pat had transformed it into a thriving coffee shop. Bob greeted Alan warmly. "Welcome to our humble place of business!"

"Good morning! I thought you were mostly retired now, Bob. Kind of an absentee landlord."

"Don't believe everything you hear. I still get in regularly, especially when we have dignitaries such as yourself." He gave a mock bow. "The senator beat you in this morning. I think he's set up on the couch." Bob pushed a large Americano and a cruller across the counter, earning a nod of appreciation from the hospital administrator.

"I like a man who anticipates his customers' needs," Alan said as he paid, before stepping through a small entryway and down into the coffee shop's main room. It was colorful, warm, comfortable, and intimate, with eclectic seating for maybe thirty people. The Sherman Perk was one of the gems of Sherman Park, the most integrated neighborhood in an otherwise distinctly segregated city. The owners were purveyors of far more than coffee, hosting listening sessions, town halls, neighborhood meetings and musical events.

Eric stood and gave Alan a hug. Then, they sat down together on the couch. "You said on the phone last night that this wasn't going to be just a social visit," Eric said. "What do you have up your sleeve?"

Alan set the computer down on the coffee table in front of them and fired it up. He Googled Sacre Pharmaceuticals, and when he clicked on the *Contact* tab, he was sent to a phone directory. The company had offices in seventy different countries, and Alan dialed the 1-800 number for its U.S. offices. They listened through the speaker as it rang. Alan ignored the automated phone tree and repeatedly hit zero until a human being answered their call. "Sacre Pharmaceuticals! How may I help you?"

"This is Alan Anderson, president of St. Joseph Hospital in Milwaukee, Wisconsin. I am a customer of Sacre and would like to speak to your CEO, Jules LaRiviere."

"What? He's, he's the CEO. And he's in Paris..."

"Right. I know," Alan said. "So, you can just transfer me to his office and go on with your day. I should mention that U.S. Senator Eric Rhodes is with me this morning."

"I don't know. Um, I'm not sure what to say."

"You don't need to *say* anything," Eric jumped in. "You need to *do* something. You can talk to your boss, who will talk to his or her boss, etc., until we speak to your CEO."

It took almost an hour as the Milwaukee duo was passed to a supervisor, a director, over to the public relations department, up to the CEO of Sacre North America and, finally, to the head of Sacre in France. At eight in the morning in Milwaukee and three in the afternoon in Paris, the Sacre CEO said, "*Hallo*. This is Jules LaRiviere."

Alan noted the time difference. "Good afternoon, Mr. LaRiviere. Thank you for taking our call. My name is Alan Anderson, president of St. Joseph Hospital in Milwaukee, Wisconsin. I am a customer of yours. With me today is U.S. Senator Eric Rhodes. We have you on speaker."

"Wonderful," LaRiviere said. "I am sitting with my lead counsel and the head of our communications team. I don't often get calls directly from hospital presidents or senators, so this is a distinct honor."

He might have been sarcastic, but Alan couldn't be sure. LaRiviere had a heavy French accent that made Alan think of the old Pepe Le Pew cartoons he'd watched as a kid. "Thanks," he replied. "I'm calling to ask a favor.

There's a young girl in Pittsburgh who needs to be included in your trial at the Carnegie Clinic there. Your trials for the drug being studied are fully subscribed, so the father has been told that they need to come up with two hundred thousand dollars in order to get her enrolled in the study. They can't afford it. Senator Rhodes and I are calling you personally to ask that you include the girl, Megan DeMario, in your Pittsburgh study."

There was a delay, and Alan wondered if it could be caused by the distance separating them. But he thought he heard hushed conversations in the background. LaRiviere came back on. "A U.S. senator from Wisconsin advocating for a resident of Pennsylvania..." He struggled through 'Pennsylvania' like it was the first time he'd ever spoken it, which it likely was. "And a hospital president from Milwaukee who is doing the same for a young girl from Pittsburgh. How very interesting."

Eric whispered to him, "He sounds like Sacha Cohen's French character in Talladega Nights, Ballad of Ricky Bobby." Alan hit the mute button before laughing loudly. "Don't do that. We gotta make this happen." He put the phone on speaker again.

"Just think of me as a customer whose hospital does tens of thousands of dollars in business with your company every year. And I'm part of a health system that does tens of millions a year in business with Sacre Pharmaceuticals. Senator Rhodes is an up-and-coming member of the U.S. legislature."

"Yes, I see. What concern is the young woman to you both?"

Eric looked at Alan and answered for them firmly, "That's no concern of yours. Let's just say we're reaching out for a friend."

"These clinical trials are not, how you say, cheap. It would..."

"It would be bad form if you refused," Eric interrupted. "Sacre is one of the top ten, maybe even the top five, pharmaceutical companies on the planet. You had over fifty billion in sales worldwide last year. This is nothing to you and means something to us."

Alan and Eric waited while they heard more muffled discussions on the other end of the line. LaRiviere came back on, "*Oui.* It is done. We will make it happen."

"Merci," Alan said, "We appreciate it very much. Thank you for taking our call, and enjoy your evening." He fist-bumped his partner in crime. "We should celebrate before I text Cole the news. Maybe one more cruller?"

"Karri will kill me if she finds out," Eric said. "But we're living dangerously anyway, so what the hell?"

Chapter Twenty-Eight

Cole walked at Michele's side as she made her way hesitantly down the faux wood floor of the long hospital hallway. It was more shuffle than walk, measured in inches and not feet. Cole and Michele's caregivers were delighted by the progress she'd made in the week since first opening her eyes. The patient was anything but delighted, however. She wanted to be back to where she was before her injuries. Cole had called her the *impatient patient* during her first hospital stay, and that was an even more apt description now. Her mouth was set in a grim line, out of concentration and not pain. Such a normal thing as walking, putting one foot in front of the other, now required every ounce of her focus and effort. She stumbled, but Cole caught her by her right arm and steadied her. He saw a flash of anger in her eyes and squeezed her shoulder gently. She frowned and said, "Take me back to my room."

They had been moved out of intensive care and onto an inpatient rehab unit, and Cole helped Michele settle into a recliner, covering her with one of her favorite thick blankets he'd brought from home. She was a little down, but mood swings and bouts of irritability were common side effects during recovery from a brain bleed. Debbie had retreated back to the farm to help out, so Cole was practically living at the hospital. He didn't mind having Michele to himself for a while.

Michele fidgeted. Besides having to relearn walking, she was having difficulty remembering events in her recent past. More troubling, countless words had gone missing from her vocabulary. She would often stop mid-sentence while talking, searching her brain frantically for a phrase. It wasn't lost completely; it was there, tantalizingly close but just out of reach somehow. And that made it even more frustrating. For a person who made their living with words, it was her worst nightmare come true. From the time she was a small child, she had never had trouble expressing herself. It was a strength. Until now…

"It's okay," Cole said, reading the thoughts Michele couldn't articulate. "You've come so far in a week; it's amazing." When he saw her brows furrow and the sparks reigniting in her eyes, he put up his hands in mock surrender. "I know you don't feel the progress, or it's not fast enough for you, but every day you are moving forward. None of this is fair, but you're handling it better than anyone else ever could."

He saw her eyes cloud as she picked up the John Grisham novel her mom had left behind. "Can't even… Can't even read." Her eyes welled up, and tears leaked down onto her hospital gown. Cole stepped to her and took her hands in his. She shook her head. "Not being able to…to write…anymore. That is bad. Not being able…to…to…even…read…I can't…can't…imagine that life."

Cole knelt in front of her. "You don't have to. Your focus is coming back a little stronger every day, and more words are finding their way into your vocabulary by the hour. You've got this." He smiled and wiped away her tears. "*We've* got this."

His phone's ringtone went off, and Michele nodded at him to take it. Cole looked down at the screen and saw GENE OLSON in bright white. He put it on speaker. "Hey, boss, I'm with Michele, and I've got you on speaker. Choose your words carefully."

"Hello, Michele. I hear good things!" Gene said, and Cole thumbed down the volume quickly. He knew Gene well, but the blast of the man's voice always caught him slightly off guard.

"I'm…good," Michele said in return, shaking her head.

"We're both good," Cole quickly added. "Any news?"

"You are reinstated as of this morning. An FBI special agent in good standing."

Cole thought about that. "And still the SAC of the Milwaukee field office?"

Gene laughed. "That too, of course. This won't hurt your career at all. If anything, it just reinforces and embellishes your legend."

"That and five bucks will get me a cup of coffee these days," Cole said.

"Only if you take it black." He waited a beat. "You know you'll have a million emails and voicemails to get through when you get back in the office. Life happened while you've been at the spa with your girl."

"Spa?" Both Michele and Cole asked together, and she smiled at him.

"Whatever," Gene said. "Michele, you keep getting better. From everything I'm hearing, you're doing great. Try not to get down. And Cole, your new assistant, has your gun. Do your best not to shoot her when you pick it up. Everyone loved Annie, including me, but the new assistant seems like a great hire. Talk to you soon!"

They said goodbye to Gene, and Michele said to Cole, "Go into…the office. You need to…to get…away…not from…from me…but from…from here. Bring me…bring me back some…some…news."

Cole was torn. He didn't want to leave Michele alone, but it had been hard being completely out of contact with his team for a week. When Debbie called a few minutes later to say that she was on the road, headed back to the hospital, it was freeing. He felt a little guilty saying goodbye to Michele, but he would have felt equally bad staying away from the office any longer.

Cole drove through the city in bright sunlight, maneuvering his visor down and over as he turned in different directions. When he arrived at work, he went straight to Jenny's office. Lane was in the doorway, and Cole could tell by the way he was waving his arms that he was telling her a funny story. Cole walked up behind the analyst quietly and looked past him into his assistant's office. Jenny flashed a smile at him, and Cole tried not to notice how well she filled out her dark cashmere sweater or how much lower her neckline dipped than Annie's ever did. It was obvious what had drawn Lane to this spot. Lane finished his story with, "And that's how we solved that case," when Cole put his hand on his shoulder.

"Jesus!" Lane jumped. He turned and saw Cole. "Hey! Great to have you back, man! That was some stealthy shit you just pulled. I had no idea you were behind me."

"Thanks, pal," Cole laughed. "But I'm pretty sure a rhinoceros could have charged down the hall just now, and you wouldn't have noticed."

Jenny and Lane joined in the laughter, and Lane couldn't stop a blush from creeping into his face. "Well, ah, again, it's good to have you back. Is Michele doing okay?"

Cole hesitated, "I'll fill you in later. We have a lot to catch up on."

Lane wasn't sure what to make of that. "Okay, hopefully I'll see you later today."

"Count on it."

Lane said goodbye to Jenny, and Cole stepped into the doorway. "Do you have something for me?"

She raised her eyebrows at him and smiled, "That's a loaded question!"

Now Cole blushed like a schoolboy and felt like an idiot for it. "Sorry," Jenny said, laughing. "I should have added, 'pun intended' like you guys do." She reached into a filing cabinet and brought out his Glock, handing it to him with the barrel facing down. "I'm starting to catch on."

"That was a good one," Cole said, checking his gun quickly before sliding it into his hip holster. His face color slowly returned to normal.

"Seriously, how is Michele? Everyone around here is worried about her. I can't wait to meet her. I finished *The Killer Sermon* in two nights, stayed up until three in the morning on the second night. That was some adventure for you two!"

"It was," Cole said, "But that's one adventure I don't ever want to go on again." He almost told her that Michele had woken up from her coma and was making progress, but he changed the subject instead. "Could you see if Li and Lane could join me in my office after lunch? I'm going to try to catch up on emails and any voicemails before they fill me in on where we're at with different investigations."

"Sure thing," Jenny said. "I hope you don't mind, but I took the liberty of skimming your emails and voicemails and flagging those I think are a priority." She reached into another desk drawer, "And then there are these..." She handed him a stack of pink *While you were out* phone messages. "Oh, and Ty Igou called. He'd like to meet with you as soon as possible."

Cole fanned the messages like a deck of cards. "That's really helpful. I should get through all this in just a couple, ah, years maybe."

Jenny laughed, and her eyes studied Cole. He had come straight from the hospital, not knowing he'd be reinstated so soon. He was dressed in jeans and a classic, light gray ragg wool cardigan over a soft white button-down shirt. "You look good in casual clothes," she said.

"Thanks," he said awkwardly. "Tell anyone who asks that I'm working undercover." She laughed again, and he retreated to his office thinking *Undercover? Really?*

He closed the blinds facing the lake. The view was spectacular, but the sun was blasting through the window so brightly that it was distracting. He sat down at his desk and turned on his computer, taking comfort in the erratic noise coming from his wall clock and resolve from his wrestling memorabilia. He looked up at the framed hole in the wall and thought, *I'll get around to you soon, Agent Jeffers.*

Cole looked at the stack of *While You Were Out* memos and pulled one from the pile, dialing Ty Igou's cell phone. Ty answered after two rings, "Igou here!"

"Thank you, Captain Obvious. Didn't I show up on your caller ID? Maybe something like 'Coolest dude on the planet' or something? If you don't have that feature, maybe switch the ringtone for me to a song; Bette Midler's 'Wind Beneath My Wings' comes to mind."

"Yeah, I'm taking that under advisement," he said, and Cole could hear other voices in the background. "Gimme a moment here. I'm going to step out of a meeting." Cole heard a door close before it grew quiet, and Ty continued. "Good to hear your voice. How's Michele?"

"No change," Cole said, hating lying to his friend. He'd give him an update as soon as he saw him in person, but he wouldn't jeopardize Michele's safety by saying something over the phone. And he would keep the circle of people who knew her real condition a small one.

"Sorry, buddy. I'm sure she'll come around, though. She's one strong person."

"That she is," Cole agreed. "Now, what can I help you with?"

"The local Native American leaders would like to meet with you about some of the tribe's young women who've gone missing. We've been looking into the case but haven't made much progress. The tribal council president knows about our human trafficking task force and remembers seeing the press conference at FBI headquarters. You're a bit of a celebrity, especially when it comes to law enforcement, and they want the best."

"Buttering me up, are you?"

Ty laughed. "You know I'd never do that. I'm just repeating what they said to me. I would have disabused them of their lofty notions of you if they weren't so well connected to the powers that be, both in state government and on the national level."

"That they are. Can you get them here today at four or five p.m.?"

"I'll check. If they can make it, I'll call Jenny directly and get it on your calendar."

"You'll call her directly?"

"Sure," Ty said. "It's the least I can do with you just getting back and all. I'm sure you're swamped."

"That is soooo thoughtful of you, Captain Igou." He relished teasing the straitlaced MPD officer and faithful family man. "Okay, then. If there's nothing else, I'll see you later this afternoon."

Cole plowed through his emails and returned phone calls the rest of the morning. He had a couple of packets of tuna in his desk, and he wolfed them down with a coffee chaser for lunch. He had a lot more catching up to do, but it felt good to get back in the flow of things.

Li and Lane knocked at his door, and Cole joined them at the table after Li gave him a welcome back hug. "How's our girl doing?" she asked.

Cole held up a finger and went to close the door. When he sat back down, he said, "Officially, she's still in a coma, and that condition won't change until we're confident she's no longer being hunted. Unofficially, she woke up about twenty-four hours into her coma, and she's getting a little better every day. She has some cognitive and physical deficits she's working through right now, but she's doing great. I'm telling you two knuckleheads this and likely Ty when I see him face to face. The people who are after Michele are both connected and have a lot of resources available to them. I don't want this shared with anyone in any manner." He trusted the two literally with his life, but he looked at them a beat to make sure they understood how serious he was.

"Got it, boss," Li said.

"Our little—no, make that big—secret," Lane said. "And we appreciate you letting us know. We're pulling for Michele."

"I know you are," Cole said, sitting back in his seat and relaxing a little. "Now, any updates you've been dying to get off your chests?"

"Well," Lane said. "We checked out the cancer clinics that are doing trials on DeMario's daughter's type of cancer."

"Megan," Cole interrupted.

"Hmmm?" Lane said.

"DeMario's daughter's name is Megan."

"Right," Lane said, scanning his notes. "Sorry. Anyway, the three cancer centers that are doing clinical trials with the new drug targeting Megan's form of cancer are the Mayo Clinic in Rochester, Minnesota, Johns Hopkins in Baltimore, and the Carnegie Cancer Institute in Pittsburgh. I personally asked the executive director of the Pittsburgh clinic if their computers had been hacked within the past five or six weeks or if anyone had obtained unauthorized access to Megan DeMario's records. He said 'no.' I then asked him politely to have his IT experts run diagnostics on their systems to make sure, and they found out that someone inside the clinic had accessed Megan's files four weeks ago, someone they believe had no legitimate reason for doing so. It's a physician, as yet unnamed.

"They've opened up an internal investigation. If it turns out they're right that the individual had no business reviewing Megan's records, then it's a violation of the Health Insurance Portability and Accountability Act. That's a big 'no-no' for healthcare workers. One instance of a HIPPA violation is often grounds for dismissal and can end a career prematurely. They'll turn the doctor over to us if they determine a violation occurred."

"They know speed is of the essence here, right?"

"Absolutely."

"That's progress," Cole said. "Good job, Laney."

"Thanks. But the people behind Michele's attack wouldn't have had to access the Carnegie Clinic's servers to understand that Megan and her dad were desperate to get her into that clinical trial. I looked at her Facebook page, and I was directed to a GoFundMe campaign. They're trying to raise two hundred thousand dollars for the trial, but less than ten thousand has been raised to date. They had already tapped out most of their friends and relatives during Megan's earlier two bouts with her cancer. I guess you can only go to that well so many times."

"I thought patients don't usually pay for clinical trials," Li said.

"That's typically true," Lane said. "The only thing that's certain when a drug is still in the experimental stage is that a person's health insurance company won't pay for the treatment. Instead, the drug companies themselves usually foot the cost. It makes sense, because if the drug gets approved, it could mean hundreds of millions or more in new revenue. But, in this case, the trial was full before Megan finished her last unsuccessful course of treatment. Mayo and Hopkins couldn't fit her into their trials, and Carnegie said they would, but only if the family could come up with two hundred thousand dollars."

"Which is what ended up pushing old man DeMario over the edge."

"Old man? Isn't he roughly your age?" Lane asked.

"I don't think so." Cole thought about the situation and next steps. "Hound that Pittsburgh clinic, Lane. If they can figure out who accessed Michele's records and why, then we can sweat that person to see who put them up to it. Maybe follow that lead all the way back to the source." He leaned back in his chair, cradling his cup of coffee, feeling the first twinge of guilt for being away from the hospital.

"There's one other thing," Lane said. "Remember when Ty told us that there were four people who viewed Michele's attack remotely who couldn't be identified? Well, Ty was right when he said that they were using pretty sophisticated software to scramble their addresses, but our geeks back in the Hoover building got further in tracking them down than Ty's people. They were able to get a geo fix close enough to determine that all four of those unnamed viewers were watching live from somewhere in the D.C.

metro area."

"Huh," Cole said, scratching his head. "Not sure what to make of that right now. But it's something. Do they think they'll be able to make further progress, maybe dig down to the source locations with home and work addresses so we can go visit them with our guns drawn?"

"Sadly, no," Lane said. "The trail ended in an impenetrable brick wall. They told me they tried getting through, around, over, and under, before they gave up. They know how much that information would have meant to us." They were silent for a moment before Lane asked, "Do you think APAG is behind all this?"

Cole took his time before answering, but then slowly shook his head. "No. I don't. I've had plenty of time to run this over and over in my head these past few days, and I just don't see it. Now, if you ask me if I believe big pharma would do whatever it takes to protect their billions in income, I'll say, 'Hell yes!' Unequivocally. But I don't think for a minute that they would send someone to attack Michele in a way that screamed, 'We did it!'"

"I agree," Li said. "When we went to visit APAG's new CEO, well, let's just say that he doesn't strike me as an evildoer. He's not mean enough, and he's surely not devious enough."

"Wait a minute! Hold up there!" Cole said, cocking his head. "Did you really just say 'evil-doer?' Who are you anyway, Batman?"

"No, of course not. I would have to be Batwoman or Batperson," Li deadpanned.

"Which would make me Robin," Lane added. "I can accept that. It's a supporting role, of course. And I'm more of a leading man type. But that young man did a lot of good."

"And he also wore tights and a cape," Cole said. "Which could be the real reason you like it so much."

"There's nothing in the dress code that says an analyst can't wear a cape," Lane said, and they all laughed.

When the laughter died down, Li nodded toward the framed hole in the wall by Cole's desk. "What about Special Agent Collin Jeffers? We don't have much else to look into at this point. It's a little too coincidental that he got recalled to D.C. just before bad things started happening here."

Cole rubbed his stubble thoughtfully, and a picture entered his mind of when he was standing behind the podium outside these same offices what seemed a lifetime ago. Ty was talking about the work of the joint human trafficking task force and Cole had noticed a glint, a spark of light from a car parked in the distance. He was sure now that it wasn't the scope of a rifle, and it could still have been the car's mirror or windshield that had caught and reflected the sunlight just so. But it could also have been the lens of a high-powered camera. And then he thought about the man in the suit he'd seen outside the APAG headquarters a week ago. It could have been nothing, but Cole's gut told him it was something. He'd always trusted his gut, and that had served him as well as anything else during his FBI career.

"You still with us, boss?" Li asked.

"I am," Cole answered, standing up and walking around his desk. He sat down and hit the speaker function on the desk phone. "If you guys have nothing else, I've got to make a call to a man in a suit."

Chapter Twenty-Nine

Special Agent Collin Jeffers sat in his new office on the seventh floor of the J. Edgar Hoover Building in downtown D.C., just four doors down from the director's office. He looked around at his plush carpeting, modern furniture, and view of the U.S. Capitol. It was a far cry from the tiny office he was banished to in Alaska. And while nobody with any taste or sense of style would make the mistake of referring to the Hoover building as beautiful, it was at least massive, stark, and even menacing. The Anchorage offices had been housed in a squat, brick, two-story building with less bulk and character. He scanned his office again. *Nice bounce back,* he thought to himself.

The song *Enemy* by Imagine Dragons began to play on Jeffers' cell phone, and he didn't have to glance at his caller ID to know who it was. He gritted his teeth and waited until the sixth ring before answering in an even voice, "Agent Huebsch! It's been a while. If you're calling to gloat, you're more than two months late."

"Hey, Collin, I'm not calling to gloat," Cole said, fighting his every instinct and trying to sound friendly. "I'm calling to welcome you back to warmer climes. I read somewhere that the average temperature in Anchorage in January is eight below zero Fahrenheit, and it's even colder when you get further away from the Gulf. Makes Wisconsin seem downright balmy."

"I'm not a pussy like you, Cole," Jeffers spat. "But when the director picks up the phone and tells you he needs your help, then you do what you need to do. Not that the director's ever called you directly before."

"Well, no. He hasn't, actually. But he did personally pin a couple medals on my chest. Maybe you remember because it was for cracking that case we were working on together." Cole couldn't stop himself from one-upping Jeffers, but he sure could kick himself. He wanted the other agent calm, and this wasn't going to help.

"Fuck you. You went rogue."

"And I'm calling to apologize, to offer an olive branch," Cole quickly said. "We'll likely have to work together in the months ahead, and I don't want our past coming between us."

Jeffers looked out the window at the blue skies and billowing white clouds. He knew Huebsch was a straight shooter, but he still didn't like the agent. He blamed Huebsch for every trouble he'd ever gotten into in the Bureau. They had clashed since they first entered the FBI in the same class years ago. But he didn't want Huebsch to be suspicious. "I appreciate that," he said, finally. "I'd like nothing more than to start fresh too."

"Perfect. Say, as long as I have you on the phone, I wonder if I can ask you a couple of things. I know you're connected."

"Shoot!"

Not yet, Cole said to himself. *But maybe someday.* "Have you ever heard of a guy by the name of Albert DeMario? He's the big fellow who attacked Michele at the Milwaukee Public Library while she was giving a speech."

"I heard about Michele being stabbed, but I don't know much more. Never heard of any DeMario before."

"You wouldn't know anything about his daughter's cancer then, or that he attacked Michele in order to pay for her experimental cancer treatment. Her last hope."

"Sounds a little like someone put a twist on Denzel Washington's movie, *John Q*. But 'no,' I've never heard of either DeMario or his daughter, and I know nothing about anybody paying for her clinical trial, treatment, whatever."

Jeffers' use of the term "clinical trial" jumped out at Cole since he hadn't used it himself. But, it was plausible that an educated person would make the leap from experimental treatment to clinical trial. He was trained to detect lies and other tells, but so was Jeffers, so he would know how to hide them.

"Anything else?" Jeffers asked. "It's nice catching up and all, but I've got a lot on my plate."

"Understood. Thanks for taking my call."

They both clicked off, and Cole hit the button on his cellphone to end the recording, noting the time as he did. His day was nearing a close, and it felt like it had been a long one. With only one meeting left on his docket, he called Ty, "Change of venue..."

Chapter Thirty

Cole found an open spot in the sprawling Good Earth Casino parking structure and made his way across a skywalk into the main building. Ty was waiting for him with two public safety officers. After quick introductions, they helped him bypass the state-of-the-art security system, allowing both Cole and Ty to keep their weapons. "This system has fifty sensors and six cameras and uses artificial intelligence to detect threats," one of the officers said with obvious pride. "We've got one on each of our three public entrances and even on the staff entrance."

"Very nice," Cole said as they walked by endless rows of slots that strobed a dizzying array of light and noise. It overwhelmed his senses and made him glad he wasn't prone to seizures. Ty leaned in close to him and said, "A lot of the security officers here are full-time MPD. This is a side hustle. It's good for the casino and good for us. Our guys like the gig. It pays well, and it's nice work. They're proud of this place and their role, so humor them for me if you have to."

"You ever been here before?" the officer asked Cole as they walked.

"Not for years. I checked it out when it first opened. Before the hotel and before it went smoke-free." Cole wasn't much of a gambler, but he'd been to Las Vegas on golf trips twice and played a little craps, fed the slots, and mostly soaked up the atmosphere when he was there. This casino was much the same, offering people dozens of different ways to throw their money away. But he had nothing against the gaming industry per se. Most people only gambled what they could afford, and he saw it as just another form of entertainment. He had spent five hundred dollars for a seat near the court to see Marquette take on U-Conn in basketball, so who was he to judge how people spent their leisure dollars. He still remembered his only visit to the Good Earth Casino, and the faint sickly-sweet smell that hung in the air, regardless of the number or size of the commercial smoke eaters they'd installed. His nose and lungs appreciated the move to smoke-free.

"We've got over one point one million square feet to watch over here," the officer continued his walking tour. He pointed to another long row of slot machines. "And over three thousand slots, not to mention crap tables, roulette, and all kinds of card games. We even have sports betting now. And it's not just gaming; we've got restaurants, music venues, and every other amenity. No need to go to Vegas anymore."

"You had me at hello," Cole said, avoiding Ty's sly grin as they were ushered down a hall and into a conference room in the casino's administration suite. The security officer left them alone, and Cole noticed an array of beverage options on a side countertop. He surveyed his choices before filling a mug with hot water and steeping a bag of decaf green tea in it; he didn't want a caffeine jolt this late in the day. He sat in one of the cushioned leather seats at the high-gloss rectangular wood table and took a sip, the taste a strong reminder of why the hell he didn't like tea in the first place. He grimaced. *Idiot! You should've just had the decaf coffee!*

Ty read Cole's face. He shook his head at him and smirked just as a man and woman entered the room. The man was tall and slender and radiated strength. The woman was shorter and stout and held herself in a way that told Cole she was a person of substance. The man wore a navy blue suit with the jacket open, revealing a white dress shirt that had a brilliantly colorful floral design on one side. The woman wore a navy suit jacket and a white blouse over a long, colorful skirt. Both of them had dark hair and eyes that radiated intelligence and warmth. Cole liked them immediately. He walked around the table and introduced himself, suddenly feeling severely underdressed in jeans, a sweater, and casual leather slip-ons. *Not even socks, for Christ's sake,* Cole thought, before apologizing for his attire to his hosts. "I'm sorry. I hadn't expected to go in to work today."

"Not a problem," John Mishicot said, gesturing for the group to sit down.

"And I actually think the moccasins are a nice touch." He nodded to Cole's shoes as he said it, and the group enjoyed a laugh.

Mishicot sat at the head of the table, with Eve Keeshik to his left. Cole and Ty joined them. "Thank you for coming and meeting us here," Mishicot began. "I am the council president for the Good Earth Tribe in Wisconsin, and Eve is our vice president." He looked at her with fondness, "I'm hoping someday she will succeed me as tribal leader.

"Most of our lands, more than twelve thousand acres, lie three and a half hours north of here. If twelve thousand acres sounds like a lot, know that ours was once a much larger nation; we lost millions of acres when our people were physically removed from their lands." He looked at both Cole and Ty separately for a moment, trying to read them.

"I have nothing but respect for the Good Earth people," Cole said, sincerely. He knew that the people of the Good Earth Nation had been treated poorly, savagely even, especially during the early years of the country's 'settlement' by whites. Things had improved greatly for the tribe since the advent of Indian gaming some thirty-plus years ago. The tribe had built an initial casino with limited gaming options in northern Wisconsin and had followed with a much larger casino in Milwaukee. He knew that the casino revenue had lifted many members of the Good Earth community out of poverty and that gaming had helped provide good jobs, homes, and health care, not just to tribe members, but other Wisconsin residents.

Mishicot nodded, believing Cole. "We have fourteen hundred tribe members in the state, but less than half live on tribal lands. We couldn't watch over all of them if we wanted to and, unlike some tribes, we don't have our own law enforcement. We depend on local, state, and federal officers to help investigate any major crimes against our people."

"How can we help?" Cole asked.

Keeshik cleared her throat, and the chairman nodded to her to take over. "The lives of our people have improved immeasurably with the influx of gaming revenues, but we still have our problems like any other community. The importance of family is at the center of our tribal values, and we all feel the pain when members struggle with alcoholism and addiction, or when they turn on the family that raised them. It's not unusual in any culture for teenagers and young adults to run away from home for any number of reasons, but it has been happening more often in our community lately. Especially with our young women."

Keeshik paused, and Ty said, "May I offer additional information?" When their hosts both indicated their assent, he said, "In the past two years, four young women from the Good Earth Tribe have gone missing soon after graduating from high school. And none of these girls fit the typical runaway composite. They weren't from abusive homes, either physical or sexual. They weren't abusing alcohol or drugs, and neither were their family members. They weren't being bullied or running away to be with someone. And they weren't failing in school, just the opposite, they were thriving."

Keeshik broke in, "All of them graduated high school and one of them was a star, excelling in both the classroom and on the lacrosse field. Her name is Ashlyn Keeshik. She's my daughter, and she had been offered many academic and athletic scholarships, including the full ride she accepted from Yale University."

Cole was shocked. Keeshik's eyes were filled with tears, but she retained her composure and continued, "Ashlyn came to Milwaukee with a group of friends a few weeks ago, five young women celebrating the end of summer, the fruits of their hard work and moving on to a new chapter in their lives. Only four of those girls came back home. They told my husband and me that Ashlyn was trying on clothes at the downtown mall when they left her. She was supposed to meet them at the food court. They waited over an hour, and when she didn't show they split up and looked everywhere in the mall. When they couldn't find her, they alerted security. The security officers weren't that helpful at first; I guess kids leave their groups all the time for different reasons and show up later. But Ashlyn's friends wouldn't leave them alone. They pestered the mall cops until they eventually called the police. That was less than a week before my husband and I were supposed to take her to Connecticut to start her college career."

Ty took over again, "When MPD got involved, the first thing we did was look at footage from the mall's security cameras. It showed Ashlyn leaving the store accompanied by two people wearing baseball caps and sunglasses. They were close on either side of Ashlyn as they walked, and both their faces were down and away from the cameras, as if they knew where they were. Ashlyn didn't just make two new friends and walk out of the mall with them; the two people were likely either threatening her or her friends if she didn't go with them. She hasn't been seen since."

"And we've tried calling repeatedly," Keeshik said. "She doesn't answer, which isn't like her. Her voicemail has been full for days, and we can't even leave messages anymore."

"We tried to trace her phone," Ty said. "But it's either turned off, or it's been disabled."

It seemed obvious that the young woman had been abducted, but Cole had one line of questioning he felt he needed to follow, "Was Ashlyn excited about going to school? Or was she nervous or maybe a little scared about being far away from home? Could she have been worried about failing or letting her family down if she couldn't make it?"

Keeshik's face grew red, and Cole said, "Please know that I'm only asking the question to better understand the circumstances."

Eve took a deep breath and shook her head. "Ashlyn isn't perfect and there have been times when she's been humbled. But that girl has a grit to her that you would have to see in person to understand. She feels the weight of the pride that our nation has for her, and she doesn't shrink from it; instead, she wears it like a mantle. We've talked about it, and she knows it's a greater honor to strive at the highest level and fail than to never try." Tears began to trickle down her face, and she wiped them away. "Something bad has happened to her. I keep imagining the worst."

"I'm so sorry," Cole said. "Ty and I will work together to do everything we can to find Ashlyn and the other girls. You can help us by giving us photos and any other information you have on their families, friends, and last known whereabouts."

"I've got all that," Ty said.

"Okay, then," Cole said, standing up. "We'll get to work on it."

He parted ways with Ty in the casino parking structure and left a text for

Li and Lane before heading to the hospital. *Lunch at Luna's tomorrow with Ty and me. He's emailing you regarding a new case(s) involving missing women from the Good Earth Tribe. See what you can dig up before the meeting.*

Chapter Thirty-One

Cole was the first of his team to arrive at Luna's Mexican Restaurant in St. Francis, less than a mile from the FBI offices. The inside was simple, with honey-colored hardwood floors, a drop ceiling, and wood-paneled walls painted bright orange and yellow. Drink specials were scrawled in white on a large chalkboard. The restaurant had been in the same family for seventy years, and with its plastic tablecloths and paper placemats, they had never intended the restaurant to be fancy. The descendants of Felipe Luna wanted it instead to be *busy*, with plenty of satisfied customers coming back over and over for the quality of its food and service. Repeat customers like Cole and his crew.

Luna's was known for its hot tortilla chips, and Cole sat in a booth eating the salty fried corn triangles, dipping them contentedly in guacamole and the restaurant's red and green salsas. He was dressed in a dark gray suit and white button-down shirt and had spent most of the night and all morning at the hospital. Michele's motor skills and her mind were returning at a rapid rate, astounding her physician and nurses and comforting Cole and Michele's parents. She still got frustrated at times, but she saw the progress, also. It bothered her that she couldn't remember the night of the attack or most of the two weeks leading up to it, but Dr. Broor said that was normal and cautioned that those memories might never return. *No loss*, Cole thought to himself before noticing Li, Ty, and Lane had all sat down in the booth while his eyes had been closed.

"Who's Mr. Stealthy now?" Lane laughed when Cole finally realized he wasn't alone.

They talked about nothing and everything after they ordered their food and drinks. When Cole finished providing an update on Michele, he said, "Who'd like to start?"

After a brief pause, Lane said, "Violence against Indigenous people isn't new, of course, not across the country and not in Wisconsin. The Good Earth Nation is right to be concerned. Homicide is the third-leading cause of death for Indigenous girls and teens, according to the CDC; Indigenous females are three times as likely to be murdered as white women. Three times! We don't have formal data on those statistics in Wisconsin, but it was bad enough that the Wisconsin Department of Justice launched a Murdered Indigenous Women Task Force a couple of years ago. And things seem to have only escalated since."

Cole waited while their food was served, dipping a bite of his cheese enchilada in sour cream and plopping it in his mouth. He savored it, before saying, "Why are the women being taken, and why is it escalating? Best guess?"

"Sex," Ty said, disgusted. "No way these girls are being abducted for forced labor. They're being sex trafficked. I don't think there's any other explanation."

"I've read the statistics, including from your own task force, though, and these most recent women missing from the Good Earth Tribe don't fit the patterns in many respects," Li said. "The average age of entry into the sex trade is fifteen, with one in six starting at age twelve or younger. The last four girls who've gone missing from the tribe all graduated from high school, every one of them is at least eighteen years old. And none of these women exhibited the kinds of vulnerability that typically attracts sex trafficking predators. They were well-adjusted, strong women."

"I agree," Ty said. "And taking a young woman from a busy downtown mall was risky, too. This wasn't some runaway nobody would miss who was grabbed in a dark alley at midnight. Ashlyn is a strong, smart, athletic young woman who could put up a fight and whose connected family would raise the alarm at the highest levels if something happened to her. And they took her in broad daylight!"

They ate in silence for a minute. Lane followed a bite of his chile verde steak burrito with a forkful of rice and beans. "The greater the risk, the greater the reward," he finally said.

"This is why the FBI hires analysts," Cole said, "to analyze."

Li and Ty chuckled, and Lane waved them off with his fork. "Think about it. If they are taking a greater risk, they must be doing so because there is potentially a greater reward to be had." He took another bite of the burrito, keeping the table waiting. "And I think I know what it is..."

Cole sat back in his chair and wiped the corner of his mouth with his napkin. "This better be good."

"Oh, it's good," Lane answered, forgetting his food. "Everybody knows that the Good Earth Tribe makes a fair amount of money on its Milwaukee casino, but nobody talks about how much exactly. Their finances are not publicly reportable, but we can back into it. Every year, they pay twenty million dollars to the State of Wisconsin as part of the gaming compact. That's a fixed dollar amount. But, the payments the tribe makes to the city and to Milwaukee County are a percentage of the casino's net winnings in any given year. One point five percent precisely. Last year, the city and county were each paid just over six million dollars, which means the Good Earth Nation netted roughly four hundred fifteen million dollars from its Milwaukee casino operations." He looked around the table to make sure everyone was following the numbers.

"That's a lot of money," Cole said. "But I'm not sure what bearing that has on what we've been talking about."

Lane grew more animated. "You guys have all read *Killers of the Flower Moon*, right?"

Cole and Li nodded. "By David Grann," Cole said, "Subtitled, '*The Osage Murders and the Birth of the FBI*.' Good read."

Ty had shaken his head. "I don't read a lot of books, what with my long hours and little kids in the house. I did see the movie. DiCaprio. De Niro. It was amazing. Hopefully, I've got the gist of the story."

"It might've been quicker to just read the book," Lane said with a chuckle. "Anyway, the story's about the plight of the Osage Indian Nation, whose people were pushed off their native lands in Missouri and Kansas and onto a reservation in northeastern Oklahoma on rocky land that the government figured was worthless. Then oil was discovered under the land, some of the largest oil deposits in the U.S. And the government, in one of the few instances when they didn't completely screw over the Indigenous people of North America, allowed the people to retain the mineral rights. Overnight, the Osage became the richest people per capita on the planet at the time."

"Which brought them to the attention of unscrupulous white men who, in the nineteen twenties, quietly went about killing the Osage and taking their oil money," Cole said. He pointed a tortilla chip at Ty, "And when local law enforcement turned out to be either or both crooked and inept, the feds were brought in to solve the murders, leading to the birth of the FBI."

"Of course, local law enforcement would be the bad guy of an FBI story. And I'm still not seeing what it has to do with these missing girls," Ty said.

"Maybe everything," Lane said. "Across the U.S. today, most tribe members aren't wealthy, or even close to it. Some of them get an annual payment from the tribe, but it might only amount to a couple hundred or maybe a couple thousand dollars. A select few of the tribes give their members more, a lot more, and the Good Earth Nation is one of those. Their tribe members who reach the age of eighteen and get their GED or high school diploma receive an annual payment from the tribe. If they aren't a high school graduate, then they have to wait until age twenty-five to qualify for the money. The payment is a calculated percentage of what the tribe makes from its two casinos. Of course, the amount paid comes after those big payments to the state and local governments and after considering wages and other operational expenses. But it's still substantial."

"How much?" Ty said. "The suspense is killing me. You take as much time to tell a story as Scorsese."

"Ha!" Lane said. "I've found two separate estimates so far, and the annual payments to the tribe members look to range from between ninety and one hundred thousand dollars per member."

"Jesus," Cole said. "I think you could be on to something, Lane. We've all seen the photos of the most recent four girls to be taken, and I know it's subjective, but I think it's safe to say that they are all attractive to some degree. If they are being used in the sex trade, their handlers will have a variable stream of money coming in, depending on how often they are used. These girls are more valuable to the traders, because they could also generate a fixed income of roughly one hundred thousand a year per woman."

"That would make sense then," Li said, "why these young women are older than the typical sex trafficking victim. And they were likely targeted not for their vulnerability, but because they were well adjusted enough to have earned their high school diplomas. Otherwise, they wouldn't qualify for the payments until they were twenty-five. And that would be considered an advanced age for entering the sex trade."

"Greater risk for a greater reward," Lane said a little smugly.

"I knew there was a reason we kept you around," Cole said. Just then, four members of the waitstaff came to the table and placed an oversized red sombrero with gold trim on Lane's head, and Li, Ty, and Cole joined them in singing a rousing off-key rendition of "Happy Birthday."

"Happy thirty-first, Laney!" Cole said, raising his ice water in a toast. "Nice work indeed!"

Chapter Thirty-Two

Later that afternoon, Cole and Ty were seated in the same small conference room in the Milwaukee County Jail where they'd last interviewed Albert DeMario. When the inmate was led into the room and seated across from them, Cole told the guards they could leave them alone. As soon as the door locked shut, DeMario said, "You got Megan into the clinical trial. I don't know how you managed it, but thank you."

"I managed it without attacking any innocent people," Cole said, regretting it immediately.

DeMario turned ashen. "I'm sorry for what I did to Ms. Fields. I didn't know her at all. I didn't want to, because I was afraid if I knew something about her, I couldn't go through with what I had to do. But I've read the papers in here, and she sounds like an amazing woman. Now I've put her in a coma she likely won't come out of."

Cole could see his pain was genuine, and part of him wanted to tell the man that Michele was bouncing back. But he would never jeopardize her health and safety to assuage the guilt of the man who'd tried to kill her. "You have Alan Anderson and Eric Rhodes to thank for getting your daughter into the clinical trial. Alan is the administrator of St. Joseph Hospital here in Milwaukee, and Eric is a U.S. senator who represents the people of Wisconsin. They strong-armed the CEO of the pharmaceutical company that manufactures the drug that will hopefully save your daughter's life. As you can imagine, that's not an easy feat to pull off."

"Thank you and them then," DeMario said, tears of gratitude in his eyes. "There's something else too. That guy that you stopped from beating me up the first time we met, he's been protecting me in here. When I asked him why, he said it's because you told him to in so many words. Why would you do these things for someone who tried to kill the woman you care about?"

Cole thought about it. "I guess I believe your story, that you were desperate to save your daughter and would do anything to give her another chance at life. I'm not absolving you of your sins, but I can only imagine the desperation you must have felt."

"Well, if there's anything I can ever do to help you, please just tell me, and I'll try."

A pained smile tugged at the corners of Cole's mouth as he pulled out his phone, "Funny you should say that." He then proceeded to play the recording he had made of his recent phone conversation with Collin Jeffers. He also played four other recordings of other males reciting the same dialogue. Cole had asked Jenny to transcribe the Jeffers' recording, and then he had recorded himself reading that 'script' with Lane and three separate Milwaukee agents.

DeMario listened to all five versions, and Cole asked if any of the men he'd heard speak with Cole on the recordings sounded like the man who had instructed him to attack Michele. When Cole called Jeffers, he'd purposely gotten him to use words like *cancer* and *treatment* that he would've likely used if he'd been the one trying to convince Megan's dad to commit a crime. DeMario asked to listen to all five recordings a second time before he said. "I'm sure it was the first guy. He was cold. Arrogant. Cocky. I pictured him sneering at me the whole time he told me what he wanted me to do."

Cole was quiet. He nodded slightly to Ty, letting him know that Collin Jeffers had been the first recording that DeMario had listened to. It was hard for Cole to believe that Jeffers had fallen that far. He'd known from their first meeting that the man was self-centered, but he didn't think he was evil. And that's the only word that described someone who would entice a man to attack a woman to save the life of his only daughter. Pure evil.

"Does that help at all?" DeMario asked.

"Yes. It does," Cole said, studying the man across from him. DeMario looked tired, resigned to his fate. "How are you holding up?"

"Okay, thanks to you. My little girl has a chance now, and that's all I wanted when this whole thing was set in motion. But I've had a lot of time to think since I've been in here waiting for my trial to start. Too much time. I'm guilty and don't see any way I won't spend a lot of years behind bars somewhere. It's scary." He looked around the locked room. "I don't know how I'll hold up. Plus, I finally got through to Megan on the phone. This has been a media circus, and she's now a public figure, the dying daughter of a psycho. She says she hates me and never wants to see me again. That hurts worse than anything that could happen to me in prison." He sighed heavily. "But I deserve whatever's coming my way."

Cole went straight to the hospital after leaving the jail, and Michele's face lit up when he walked into her room. Debbie embraced Cole and then left to get a bite to eat in the hospital cafeteria. Cole stood to the side as Michele slid out of bed. She was no longer connected to any machines, and they walked side by side down the long hallway. Cole would've liked to hold Michele's hand, but she was at the point where it was important for her to learn to trust her balance and walk on her own. If she wasn't in her gown and didn't have the bandaged arm and head, a passerby wouldn't know that she was a patient. She had to concentrate, but her gait appeared normal. Cole looked at her and smiled. "I'm out for a stroll with my best gal," he said.

Michele looked at him, her eyebrows lowering slightly, "Your *only* gal, you mean!"

"Of course. That goes without saying."

"But I like hearing you say it!"

"My only gal!" Cole said, kissing her cheek and loving the fact that Michele's humor was coming back as fast as her motor skills. He filled her in on the case of the missing women from the Good Earth Tribe and then told her about his visit with DeMario. Normally, she peppered him with questions, but instead, she was quiet for a long stretch. He started to wonder if she was having trouble putting her thoughts into words when she blurted, "I want to meet him, the man who did this to me."

Cole stopped. "What? No." He shook his head. "That's a bad idea. Horrible even."

Michele took his hand and looked into his eyes. "I need to see him. I have nightmares of the attack, and I want to look my demon in the face."

"He's not a demon. He's a desperate man who did something terrible for a good reason."

"To give his daughter a chance to live. I know," Michele said. "But I need some kind of closure so that I can continue to move forward. I want my life back."

"We'll see," Cole said, hoping she'd forget the request.

She saw through him and shook her head, "If you don't get me in to see DeMario, I'll ask Ty to try to help me set it up. You know how persuasive I can be."

Chapter Thirty-Three

Cole and Debbie left the hospital together when visiting hours ended at eight that evening. They'd been allowed to stay past that time when Michele's life hung in the balance, but now that the patient was clearly on the mend, they were expected to follow the rules like everyone else. Frau Newhouse was waiting for them at the castle mansion, and she surprised them with a full meal of wiener schnitzel, red cabbage, and spaetzle. Debbie thanked her and politely said, "You shouldn't have."

Cole said, "No. You definitely should have," between forkfuls of the breaded veal, tangy cabbage, and warm buttered egg noodles. "This is delicious!"

Debbie stayed with Frau to help clean up after the late supper, and they shooed Cole away. Before leaving, he watched them chatting and laughing side by side at the sink, and he thought they both looked younger somehow, their fears forgotten for the moment. He went upstairs and slipped into a pair of old gray sweatpants and his favorite blue waffle sweater before pouring himself a cold beer and grabbing a ratty paperback copy of *The Old Man and the Sea*. He made himself comfortable in the two-story library, setting up near the fireplace in a leather chair and ottoman that felt like they were tailored to his frame. He'd been intimidated by the room's sheer size and number of volumes when he'd first moved in, unsettled seeing hundreds of signed, hardcover first editions of his favorite American authors and others from around the world going back more than one hundred years. But it had become his refuge within his refuge over time. He looked at the cover of the short Hemingway novel he'd selected, running his hand over the image of an old man adrift alone on a vast ocean, silhouetted by a rising or setting sun. *The sun also rises,* Cole thought to himself, but I think in this one it's setting. If he could only read one book for the rest of his days, it might be the one he held now. He was certain that life, the timeless story of struggle, suffering, perseverance, and love, had never been told as surely or as beautifully.

He started reading, wondering almost immediately if he, like the old man, was *salao,* which Papa Hemingway described as "the worst form of unlucky." He suffered and struggled to be sure, but he also had love and a job worth doing. He thought about Albert DeMario and his daughter. He thought about Santos Garcia, the young orphan he had met during the raid on the Ladysmith poultry plant. He and the boy had lost both of their parents, but Santos was only eleven at the time. Now twelve, he was fending for himself. Cole was surrounded by people who cared about him, who were there when he needed them. He decided he wouldn't trade places with anyone.

His phone began to vibrate on the side table, and Cole smiled broadly when he looked at the screen. *Janet Wifey.* He and his ex rarely saw each other, but they got along well these days. She didn't call him often, yet this wasn't the first time she had caught him when he was holed up in the library with a good book.

"Hola," Cole said.

"Hello. It's nine-thirty at night, and you answered your phone in Spanish, so I'm guessing you're reading that dog-eared copy of *The Old Man and the Sea* again."

Cole laughed. "Busted! Am I that transparent?"

"Only when you want to be. I always thought you had good taste in books, but especially in women."

Cole laughed again.

"How's Michele doing?"

Cole's laughter died in his throat. Janet heard it and felt bad, thinking Cole was hurting, seeing his partner in a coma day after day. "I'm sorry for asking the question, Cole, I was just hoping for better news than has been made public so far."

He had never lied to Janet when they'd been married or since their divorce, and it pained him to do so now. He trusted her as much as anyone in his life and wanted to let her know that Michele was getting better every day, but he wouldn't say anything over his cell phone. "There's been no change, but maybe you could come see her. I think she'd like that."

"Oh, okay," Janet thought it over. "I'm off this weekend. I could be there Saturday, mid-day."

"That would be great." There was a pause, and Cole added, "But that wasn't the reason for your call."

"No. I wanted to see if you were any closer to figuring out who was behind Michele's attack and the ambush at your house."

"Now I feel bad for even asking this, but I need to... This is off the record, right?"

"Of course."

Cole wouldn't share Michele's condition over an unsecured line, but he was pretty sure Jeffers already knew he was onto him. If his phone was being tapped, he didn't really care if anyone heard what he said next, "DeMario identified our old friend, Collin Jeffers, as the voice who called to convince him to attack Michele."

"He's always been a conceited prick."

"Incompetent at times, too, but I never saw him as a criminal. He must hate me even worse than I thought."

"Do you think he's working for big pharma, doing their bidding on this? Or is it just part of some personal vendetta against you?"

"We haven't completely ruled out the good folks at APAG, but we don't think it's very likely they're behind it. Probably just Collin losing his shit and going off the deep end."

"Have you considered the people who are protecting term limits? Last time we talked, I told you that Michele was clear during our most recent interview that she was interested in reporting on that down the road."

"With everything going on, we haven't pursued that angle yet."

"Well, I've been thinking about the attack coming so close after our interview. The only two things Michele talked about on my show beyond her book coming out were big pharma and Congressional term limits. And she would be asked about those things at every stop on her national book tour. Because that's what we do; we ask about an author's current project and about what they have in the works. Think about it: CNN, CBS, ABC, NBC, Fox, and all the others would have done stories on it. The *New York* and *LA Times*, the *Post*, and everyone else. They might have wanted to stop the message from getting out by literally killing the messenger."

Cole thought about it, nodding to the phone. "And if that's what they were trying to do, it worked spectacularly, with only maiming instead of killing the messenger. There have been zero conversations about term limits since the attack, with all the news focused instead on the attack itself."

"Maybe when you see Collin next, you can ask him about it. Politely, of course."

"Of course!" Cole laughed before they said their goodbyes.

Cole thought about Jeffers and the hatred he must hold for him in his heart. He started to set the book down with the intention of going to bed early. Instead, he settled back into his chair, took a sip of his beer, and rejoined Santiago in his small wooden skiff. He felt the warmth of the sun reflected off the gentle seas of the gulf and the cool spray of salt water in his face. He heard the creaking of the boat, the lapping of the waves, and the caws of birds attracted by the baitfish. He closed his eyes, breathed deeply, and for a few hours at least, he found peace.

Chapter Thirty-Four

Cole was in the heavens by noon the next day, somewhere high over Pennsylvania, he guessed, looking down at the cotton-candy white clouds below him. He would be in D.C. in less than an hour. He had swung by the hospital early before heading into the office. He had a lot more on his plate than Michele's attack and the case of the missing women from the Good Earth Tribe. Even though those two cases fought for his attention, he couldn't let them dominate it, because he had more than two hundred agents, analysts, and other staff in the Bureau's Milwaukee offices alone that needed his direction too.

He had no luggage beyond a simple backpack with a change of clothes and sundry essentials, and when his plane touched down, he made his way directly outside and joined the taxi queue. He got a text from Lane just as he got settled into the back of the cab and took off. *Call me asap! News from the cancer clinic about the doc who accessed Megan's records. You're going to want to hear this!* He hit the button to dial Lane immediately.

He was still thinking about the call twenty-five minutes later, when he was let out near the U.S. Capitol's visitor entrance at the back of the building. He cleared the airport-style security and made his way to the Senate wing. Cole was still a small-town boy at heart, and he was awed by the building's spectacle and majesty. Grand ceilings and marble everywhere, even on the floors, echoed and amplified voices and footfalls in a way that let visitors know that the work here was nonstop and vitally important. The kid in him was thrilled by it all, but the adult version of himself wondered if it wasn't just false advertising.

"Cole!"

Cole heard his name called and saw Eric Rhodes step out from the group of people who swarmed him. The senator's smile was big and genuine as he closed the ground between them and shook the hand of the Milwaukee SAC. "Good to see you!"

Eric led Cole down the straight, wide, and long hallway, accosted by greetings from all sides as they walked. Senator Rhodes was seen as a rising star on the national political scene. He stood out as one of only four Black U.S. senators, and he'd stolen the spotlight a few months ago when he delivered a widely acclaimed speech at his party's national convention. He'd hammered big pharma and the health insurance industry in that speech. Those watching in Fiserv Forum and across America loved the message and its presenter. But both political parties were still peeved at him for drawing attention to how little they were doing to police their two largest donor classes. Cole grinned at his friend. "You seem like kind of a big wheel, even here."

"I'm just keeping my head down and getting the work done," Eric said, pushing through a tall hardwood door and into his suite of offices. They walked across dark, uninspired carpeting past several desks staffed with aides working frantically on their laptops. Cole took in the big, polished stone fireplace in the middle of the room and the Wisconsin and United States flags that flanked it while Eric announced, "Everybody, this gentleman with me is Cole Huebsch, special agent in charge of the FBI's Milwaukee field office and all of its Wisconsin operations. He's both a resident of our great state and a personal friend, so treat him accordingly whether he's with me or on his own. Thanks!"

Cole followed him into his private office, and Eric shut the heavy door behind them. He walked over to another impressive fireplace and let out a long sigh as he settled into one of the plush wingback chairs set on either side of it. Cole stood for a moment, taking in the walnut-colored deep pile carpet and the matching wood of the built-in bookshelves and the large desk. He was struck by the frenzied chaos of the outer office and the calm order of the senator's private office. He took a chair facing Eric, "Nice digs!"

Eric nodded, "About as good as a first termer is going to get. I'm not complaining." He leaned in toward Cole, "I'm really sorry about Michele. Karri and I are heartbroken."

Cole nodded. "About that. One of the reasons I came here today was to tell you that she woke from her coma more than a week ago, and she's making great progress. 'Remarkable' is the term her neurosurgeon has used. I'm keeping that news close to the vest because she seems to have a target on her back. You're the fourth person I've told, and it's all been done in person."

"Understood," Eric said. "And that's awesome news."

"It is. The other reason I wanted to see you is to get your take on something. Not long before Michele's attack, Janet, my ex-wife, interviewed her on national television. Besides talking about the release of her book, she also talked about upcoming issues she might want to write about. She specifically mentioned big pharma and term limits for U.S. senators and representatives. Right now, we don't think big pharma was behind Michele's attack. They've gone through a leadership change recently and don't seem to have the stomach or the requisite resources at this time to do something like that. So, we're wondering about the people who like the status quo when it comes to term limits. Are there people in positions of power, influence, and/or affluence who would have a popular reporter attacked to keep the issue of term limits from getting more public attention?"

Eric leaned back in his chair and stretched his arms above his head, getting comfortable and taking his time in answering. "What you are asking me is if there are people in power here in Washington who would do whatever it takes to keep hold of their power. I think you know the answer to that. Yes! Unequivocally, yes!"

"Just to be clear, you think it's plausible that certain people in D.C. would have Michele attacked in order to keep her from writing a series of articles calling for congressional term limits?"

"Hell, yes, it's plausible. Likely even. You remember how I told you that I was told to shut up when I started raising a ruckus about big pharma and the health insurance industry's complicity in driving up health care costs? The leaders of my own party told me to back off, or they would do whatever it took to ensure I lost the next election. Would they go even further to protect their own power and money? Absofuckinglutely!"

"Who then?"

"That's easy," Eric said. "At a minimum, the House Speaker and the Senate Majority Leader would need to be in on the conspiracy."

"But the Senate Majority Leader is a Republican, and the Speaker of the House is a Democrat. I didn't think they spoke to each other, let alone banded together."

"Think about it. The last poll I saw on congressional term limits showed that eighty-six percent of republican voters favor them, and so do eighty percent of Democrats. So many of our elections go down to the wire and result in razor-thin margins of less than a percentage point. If any one party is seen as fighting term limits, they'll likely get hammered in the next election cycle. I don't know if you remember, but back in the 1994 national elections, the Republicans touted their 'Contract with America,' and the enactment of congressional term limits was one of the cornerstone pieces of that proposed legislation. It helped them pick up fifty-four House seats and eight Senate seats on that one election day, flipping both chambers. Not surprisingly, Newt and his republican colleagues rammed through every single one of the changes they promised except..."

"Term limits," Cole answered. "So, you're saying that the leaders of the Senate and the House are working together to keep term limits off the country's collective radar, because if either party is seen fighting it alone, it makes them vulnerable."

"Extremely vulnerable."

"Off the record, where are you personally on the issue of term limits?"

"I said when I ran for this office that if you can't make a difference in twelve years, then get the hell out of the way and let someone else do it. I still feel that way. Will I feel the same when my second term is coming to an end? I sure hope so. I've seen how power and money are addictive, and I want to think I'm above it, but I suppose you never know. Karri and the kids won't mind my coming home to a nine-to-five job, though."

Cole got to his feet and thanked Eric, offering him his hand. Eric shook it, "You on your way home right away? Otherwise, we could grab a bite to eat and a cold beer. I know of a small place within walking distance that has some great craft beers on tap. You can stay in the guest bedroom in the apartment. It just sits there empty when Karri and the brood are back home."

"I'll have to take a rain check," Cole said, heading for the door. "I've got a little work left on my agenda tonight."

Five hours later, Cole sat in the dark on a large white L-shaped sectional in a penthouse apartment with his back to floor-to-ceiling walls of glass that looked out over the city lights. A cold mug filled with pale ale was sweating coaster-less on the glass coffee table in front of him. The beer was brewed by DC Brau Brewing, who'd christened it, *On the Wings of Armageddon*. The beer was excellent, but Cole was hoping the name wasn't prophetic when he heard the front door snick open.

Collin Jeffers loosened his tie as he stepped into his apartment and flipped three switches just inside the door, bathing the large, modern, great room in light. He dropped his tie on the end of the sectional furthest from Cole and then shed his suit jacket and dropped it on top of the tie, revealing the shoulder holster that held his Glock under his left armpit. He ignored Cole and walked to the fridge. He pulled out a light beer, cracked it open, and drank from the can. He leaned on the large granite island countertop and finally addressed Cole, "To what do I owe the displeasure?"

"I'd like to say I came for the beer, which is excellent, by the way. I didn't know your taste was this good," Cole picked up his mug and took a big sip before setting it back down. "But the truth is I thought it was time you and I had a heart-to-heart, a tete-to-tete, if you will. It's long overdue, actually. I think you'd agree."

"You'd think wrong then, because I have no interest in having any conversation with you, especially after you broke into my apartment. And some shmuck left that beer here," he said, nodding toward Cole's glass. "It's way too fruity for me. More your style, to be sure."

Cole looked around the apartment. "Some place you've got here. The guy who let me in when I showed him my creds said it rents for nine thousand dollars a month. Can't be easy to swing that on what we get paid. You got a side hustle of some kind?"

"Not your concern. And you know as well as I do that the Bureau watches us. They know that, unlike you, I come from old money. I don't do the job for the small wages we make; I do it to serve my country."

Cole laughed, "Jesus, you almost made me lose some good beer with that whopper. Cue the national anthem!"

"Fuck you," Jeffers said, taking a few steps toward Cole. "And you can leave now. I told you that I'm not going to chat with you, so get out."

Cole stood. "I'll go, but not before you tell me who told you to set up the attack on Michele."

"God, you're dense," Jeffers said, shaking his head. "I told you I had nothing to do with that."

"And you were lying," Cole said, stepping around the table and toward Jeffers. He stopped when he was three feet from the other agent, close enough where he could reach him before he could draw his gun and fire if he decided to. "I played five recordings of men's voices in conversation with me for Al DeMario. I asked him if any of them sounded like the guy who called him and convinced him to attack Michele. It shouldn't come as a surprise that he fingered you. We also caught up with the doctor who accessed Megan DeMario's medical records. He said he was told to do so by a federal agent who flashed his badge and said he was working to catch a sadist who was preying on young women with cancer. A real sicko. We showed him photos of several agents, and guess what? He fingered you. He said you had a mustache, but he was sure it was you. Two different people fingered you as the guy who set up the attack on Michele, and now I'm giving you the finger, proverbially. You're either sloppy or stupid, and I'm guessing both."

Jeffers' face was a mottled red.

"Who put you up to it, Collin?"

"Nobody's going to believe you. Not based on the word of two criminals."

"That's funny, because neither DeMario nor the physician had ever committed a crime until *after* they met up with you. Not so much as a misdemeanor. You put them both up to it. And your reputation isn't exactly sterling right now. You just got back from your assignment in Alaska where you were sent to get your head on straight. Looks like that didn't work."

Jeffers stepped forward and snapped a jab at Cole's chin which Cole blocked with his left forearm. Before he could launch his own attack, Jeffers kicked him in the chest, sending him backward, where he landed hard on the coffee table. The glass top spiderwebbed with cracks, but held for the moment, keeping Cole from being slashed to ribbons. His beer was knocked onto the floor, and that pissed Cole off more than a little. He rolled off the table and ripped off his own suit jacket as he rose to his feet, just in time to block a front kick from Jeffers.

Cole stole a deep breath. "We've sparred at least a dozen times over the years, Collin. I kicked your ass every single time. Why in the hell do you think it'll turn out differently this time?"

Jeffers kept coming. "Because I worked out for hours every day while I was in Alaska. Not much else to do up there besides get in the best shape of my life while dreaming of ending *your* life."

Cole smiled. "So, you're dreaming of me now..."

Jeffers snapped another kick, and Cole blocked it with his left forearm, the arm going numb temporarily. Cole shook his arm out and backed up more, buying himself time and space. He was adept at boxing and kicking, but they weren't his strengths. And while Jeffers had spent the past few months training for this fight, Cole had spent weeks of it sedentary by the side of a hospital bed, the lack of exercise and sleep dulling his edge.

Neither man had drawn his weapon, and Cole wondered if it was a pride thing for both, wanting to beat the other with just his bare hands. He shifted around, moving in a circle in an attempt to continuously change angles on Jeffers until his back was to the coffee table again. Jeffers threw a straight right hand at Cole's face, and Cole brushed it aside and stepped close to his adversary, holding his left arm while grabbing Jeffer's head and throwing him over his right hip. Jeffers hit the coffee table with his hands first, and the table shattered. He was momentarily stunned, but then he noticed the blood flowing from his hands and arms. He looked at his white dress shirt, now shredded and stained crimson, and he cried out. Cole bent down and grabbed Jeffers' belt and the back of his shirt. He lifted him off the glittering remains of the table and dumped him face-down a few feet away.

Jeffers was bleeding from several places, including his hands, arms, and chest. A gash on his left wrist was flowing heavily, and Cole noticed Jeffers putting pressure on the wound to try to staunch it. "Ouch! That looks bad. I'm no medic, but if that's your radial artery, you could lose consciousness in thirty seconds, maybe bleed out in two minutes or so. That can't be good."

Jeffers stopped worrying about his blood loss long enough to reach under his armpit and pull his weapon with his good hand. He was rolling to his back and raising the Glock when Cole kicked the hand hard, and the pistol flew all the way into the kitchen area, bouncing once on the marble tile before banging loudly off the stainless-steel refrigerator. Jeffers covered his left wrist again and looked up at Cole with hate-filled eyes. "So now you kill me while I lay here unarmed?"

Cole looked down at him and shook his head. "No. I probably should, and I will likely regret this, but now you tell me who asked you to set up a hit on Michele. If you won't, then I kill you."

Jeffers laughed. "Ha! Mr. Goody Two Shoes himself, the baby boy scout, is going to break the law? I don't think so. You don't color outside the lines. Not your style!"

Cole kicked Jeffers' hand hard again, knocking it off his damaged left wrist, allowing the blood to flow freely onto the white carpet again. "You really think that?"

He kicked Jeffers' hand again, and Jeffers screamed in pain, looking at Cole uncertainly.

"When you were in Alaska, tell me you didn't hear about me taking on big pharma and the APAG CEO. The director personally told me to back off, and a few days later, that CEO was murdered in a 'robbery gone bad,'" Cole used air quotes.

Jeffers hesitated, confused, before his face hardened again. "Bullshit! Everyone knows you were on a plane headed to San Francisco when that bitch was killed."

Cole smiled down at him and sold the lie harder. "That's the official story. The fact is they built me up so high in the media, pinning every medal they had on me, that the Bureau couldn't afford to have it become public knowledge that I'd gone rogue. I'm like a fucking Wall Street bank that's become too big to fail. The FBI protects its image as much as it protects its country. What do you think would happen to the FBI's brand if the general public and the media found out that its most decorated agent had taken the law into his own hands and killed a CEO?

"Now, you're going to tell me everything I need to know about who put you up to having Michele attacked. If you don't, I'll stay here and watch you bleed out instead of getting you the medical attention you need. And if you still think that I won't do whatever it takes to protect the people I love and to see justice served, well, then you're every bit as dumb as you are corrupt."

Chapter Thirty-Five

Cole took the earliest direct flight out of D.C. that he could find the next morning, and he touched down in Milwaukee just before ten. He hadn't slept after Jeffers finally told him his story and named the people behind the attacks on both him and Michele. He had taken Jeffers to the nearest emergency department to get the medical attention he needed and then brought him and his newly acquired seventy-six stitches back to his apartment. It turned out that Collin's radial artery was intact. Cole suspected as much but had used Collin's fear of bleeding out to get the information from him that he needed. He didn't trust Jeffers, but he wasn't cold-blooded enough to kill him. And he couldn't turn him in, at least not now, not without tipping the people off who were behind all this. He didn't want them covering their tracks. Jeffers went to bed while Cole lay awake on his sectional. He used Jeffers' guest shower in the morning and felt somewhat relieved that the man didn't try to kill him while he was cleaning up. His suit was trashed from the fight, so Cole tossed it in the garbage and put on the pair of jeans and the blue and gray flannel shirt he'd carried in his backpack. He called the office after he landed in Milwaukee, but he drove directly to the hospital to pick up Michele.

She was still officially an inpatient when Cole led Michele out of the hospital via the loading dock with the help of Alan Anderson. She said a tearful goodbye to her mom before Cole drove her to the jail. "I'm still not sure about this," Cole said as he and Michele sat waiting in the sparse interview room. "Your mom made it clear that she and your dad aren't keen on the idea either."

Michele looked at him. He could tell that she was trying to hide her nervousness. "I respect all of your opinions and understand you have my best interests at heart, but I need to do this. I don't know if it's closure I'm looking for or what, but I feel in my bones that I won't be able to ever put this behind me if I don't meet the person who did this to me." She held up her bandaged left arm for emphasis.

Cole looked at her and nodded. He didn't really know what she was going through, but what he did know was that she was strong and smart, and he trusted her instincts even more than his own. The dressing on her head had been removed, and she was wearing a loose Brewers baseball cap to cover the part of her head that had been shaved for surgery. He saw steel in the beautiful big brown eyes that peered out at him beneath the lid. He nodded to her and said, "You know what you're doing," when there was a rap on the door, and Albert DeMario was led in and seated across from them.

DeMario's bulk was wedged into the seat, and his large, meaty fingers thrummed nervously on the armrest. Michele leaned forward and stared into her attacker's eyes. DeMario tugged on the loose collar of his orange top uncomfortably. It was cool in the room, but small beads of sweat collected near his hairline. He was a large physical presence, and Michele was even more slight than usual because of her health issues. But if anyone was watching through the one-way mirrored glass, they would see that the woman was in charge of the situation.

"Albert DeMario, meet Michele Fields," Cole said, breaking the silence. Michele nodded across the table. "Thank you for agreeing to meet me this morning. Please, tell me about your daughter."

With that, a dam broke inside DeMario, and the big man began sobbing hysterically. He looked down and away from Michele, but she reached over the table and took one of his hands in hers. Tears streamed down her face. "Please, it's okay. I just need to understand."

Cole wiped the tears from his own eyes as he watched the interaction. Michele mostly listened at first as DeMario answered all her questions. He held nothing back. He told her why and how he did what he did and said he was sorry at least two dozen times. At some point, he noticed a turn in the conversation and saw that Michele was comforting DeMario, assuring him that things would be okay. He felt like she was trying to reassure herself that things would work out as well. It took almost two hours before the pair were talked out, and when DeMario reached out to shake Michele's hand before he was led back to his cell, Michele pulled him in for a hug instead, which caused the big man's sobbing to begin anew.

Michele sat quietly, thinking, after DeMario was led out of the room. The little space didn't seem as cold and sterile as it had when they'd first sat down. She turned to Cole, "He needs to be with his daughter. Nothing will be served by him sitting in a jail cell for the next dozen years or more. Can you help me get him out of here?"

Cole steepled his fingers and thought about it. Slowly, he began to nod. "I believe we can. If you don't want to press charges, then technically, there is no victim, and there is no crime. The District Attorney has filed charges of first-degree attempted homicide against DeMario. He had an open and shut case with lots of reliable witnesses and video. The man bought airline tickets, flew halfway across the country, had a special knife, etc., so the D.A. would have easily been able to show the attack was premeditated. It would have been a slam dunk with lots of positive media attention, but if you say you want the charges dropped, he won't have much choice."

"Then that's what I'll do. She may not appreciate it right now, but Megan needs her dad, and he needs to be with her."

Cole drove Michele home from the jail, and one of his agents was waiting at the castle mansion with Frau Newhouse when they arrived. He wasn't overly comfortable leaving Michele at the house. The hospital electronic records still showed her as admitted with little change in her condition, but someone could have seen her leave the hospital. *Or seen her arrive here,* he thought, scanning the area quickly. But she couldn't stay at the hospital, and she would have been even more exposed if they had moved her into a rehab facility with all new staff assisting her. So, they'd privately contracted for off-duty hospital staff to come to the house to help with rehab. All he could do now was provide her protection and hope. He told the agent he was going into the office and instructed him to stay with Michele until he returned. Before leaving, he pulled the agent aside and reminded him that she'd been attacked twice already. The agent knew that Cole and Michele were in a relationship, and the message was clear: be hypervigilant.

The sun was playing hide and seek with the white, fluffy, early October clouds as Cole pulled into the FBI parking lot in St. Francis. The cool air blowing off the lake reminded him of fall after-school hunts with his dad for grouse, rabbits, squirrels, and other small game. He realized he was still in his jeans and flannel shirt and laughed out loud. He was dressed for hunting! He got a few strange looks as he walked through the building. Everyone was used to seeing him dressed in conservative suits, and within just a few days, they'd seen him in jeans twice. "No, we won't be adopting casual Fridays," he told more than one person.

He said a quick hello to Jenny as he passed her office and went into his own, and she followed him in. He had just sat down behind his desk when she came through the doorway. She had on a gray wool skirt that stopped mid-thigh and a V-neck crème-colored cashmere sweater that drew the eye to her cleavage. He didn't think her dress was inappropriate or crossed any lines, but it was far different from what Annie wore, and it made him a little uncomfortable. He wondered if he'd get used to it. She came to the side of his desk and leaned in, setting down a stack of phone messages and fanning them. "I have these arranged front to back in order of importance. The most important seems to be from Deputy Director Gene Olson, and there's one from John Mishicot, Chair of the Good Earth Tribe. There's one below that from Captain Igou."

"I'll be sure to let him know you had him pretty far down on the list of importance," Cole said, smiling.

Jenny laughed and straightened up, but she didn't move away from the desk. Cole could smell her perfume. The fragrance held notes of vanilla, roses, and sandalwood, and it was intoxicating. He shook his head. "Is there anything else you need?" Jenny asked.

"Nope. No. Nothing I can think of," Cole said, shaking his head. "I'm good."

"Well, I'll be in my office if anything comes up."

"Okay, thanks," he said as Jenny walked out the door. Her scent seemed to hang in the air when she was gone, and Cole caught himself breathing it in deeply. *What the hell is wrong with me?*

He picked up the top pink note on his pile, the one with Gene Olson's number. He considered for a moment, before texting Li and Lane instead. They were in his office ten minutes later, and Cole joined them at the table. They had barely said their hellos when Cole's stomach growled. "Sorry about that," he said, realizing the only thing he'd eaten all day was the tiny bag of pretzels he'd been handed by the flight attendant on his morning flight from D.C. His stomach complained again, and they all laughed. They were still chuckling a minute later when Jenny came in carrying a cafeteria tray. "I thought you might be hungry," she said, laying out a tuna sandwich with two bags of chips and a steaming mug of coffee.

"It's perfect," Cole said, grabbing the sandwich and taking a big bite.

"I know where you keep your tuna packets, and I had some twelve-grain bread that I brought in. I hope you like it."

"Thank you," Cole said. As she retreated again, both Cole and Li noticed that Lane's eyes never left the new assistant.'

"Laney's got himself a crush," Li said. "The word that comes to mind is smitten."

Lane blushed. "Jesus! Stop it. She's pretty and all, but she barely knows I exist."

Cole was grateful the attention was on Lane. He didn't need any directed his way when it came to Jenny. He felt awkward enough already.

Li turned to Cole, "How did your meetings in D.C. go yesterday?"

"I learned a lot," he said. He walked them through his conversation with Senator Rhodes first and then his confrontation with Collin Jeffers. He talked about the fight he'd had with Jeffers and how he'd forced him to open up. He told them he'd gotten him medical attention and finished by explaining his final conversation with Jeffers before he left this morning.

"Wait a minute. Did you really warn him about Michele by saying, 'Anything goes wrong, anything at all... your fault, my fault, nobody's fault...it won't matter—I'm gonna kill you. No matter what else happens, no matter who gets killed, I'm gonna kill you?'" Li asked.

"I did," Cole said.

"Whoa! Hold on there, pardner! I see where Li is coming from," Lane said. "You stole that hokum! John Wayne says that to Richard Boone in the movie *Big Jake*!"

"I didn't steal anything. Paraphrased it, maybe," Cole said, shrugging and finishing his sandwich. "And if it's hokum, then it's damn good hokum."

"You really think Jeffers is going to heed your warning?" Li said. "You've never described him as the trustworthy type to us before."

"I know," Cole sighed. "But the three people he named as being behind Michele's attack and the attack at my house are the Speaker of the House, the Senate Majority Leader, and Roger Beneker the fifth. That fit right in with what Eric told me. We're going to need somebody on the inside in order to have a prayer of bringing those three down. Even with that, I don't know that we have much of a chance."

"Have you told Gene Olson any of this yet?" Lane asked.

"No," Cole admitted. "Director Trudell has caved to Beneker alone before, and I imagine he'll swoon entirely if the Speaker and Majority Leader lean on him. If I reach out to Gene, I'll likely be putting his job in jeopardy again."

"Our prayer will have more of a chance of being answered if we've got Gene on our side, even as a silent partner," Li said.

Cole leaned back and took a long drink of the coffee, willing the caffeine to do its best work. "You're right. I know you're right."

Six hours later, Cole swung by Classic Pizza and picked up a twenty-inch hand-tossed sausage, pepperoni, and mushroom pie on his way home. He had called Michele earlier and told her he was going to bring food home, but he figured she would give him a hard time when she saw how big a pizza he got. He opened the door and turned the corner into his kitchen, stopping short when he saw Michele and his ex-wife drinking red wine at the table. "Surprise!" Janet said. She noticed the mammoth pizza, "Are you clairvoyant? How did you know you had company?"

"I didn't," Cole said, setting the pizza on the counter and grabbing his own wine glass. "I'm just a glutton who loves leftovers." He poured the rest of the Cabernet and sat down.

Janet looked across the table at Michele and raised her glass, "Here's to Michele's miraculous recovery! Now I know why you suggested I come for a visit. You wanted me to know how she's doing, but weren't comfortable telling me over the phone, in case someone was listening in somehow."

"You were always quick," Cole said, hiding his smirk behind the big bowl of his glass. He noticed a manila folder on the table with *future story ideas* neatly written at the top in Michele's impeccable handwriting. Cole didn't do cursive anymore; he was a clumsy block letter kind of guy. A reporter's notebook lay open beside the folder, and Cole could see more of Michele's flowing script on the pages. "What's all this?" he asked, gesturing to the papers with his glass.

"That's my memory of the weeks before my attack," Michele said. "Or at least it's how Janet and I are trying to reconstruct it. It's frustrating, though."

"Don't say that," Janet said. "We've only been at this a few minutes, and what I see already is the research to support an amazing series on term limits."

"Maybe," Michele said, uncertainty tinging her words.

"Look," Janet said, sweeping strands of blonde hair away from her face and leaning across the table to be closer to Michele. "I know how this goes. Think about it. The moment you turned in the first draft of *The Killer Sermon*, you had time on your hands, right? Your editor took a few weeks before getting back to you with developmental edits. Based on what I see on the table here, you used that time to look into the next topics, the next projects you might want to take on. After you got your developmental edits back and made your revisions, you had to send them back to your publisher and wait some more before they sent you redline edits. Do you remember that? More time for you to look ahead and plan on what came next after the upcoming book tour."

Michele nodded. "I do remember some of that now."

"And when you came on my show, you were passionate about the issue of term limits. You jumped out of the television and into viewers' homes, a smart, likable, and persuasive force. I think you would be the worst nightmare for the powers that be that don't want to see their power diminished or threatened."

Cole could see confusion clouding Michele's face. He put his hand on her arm before turning to face Janet, "What I'm about to tell you is off the record and could make you as much of a target as Michele and I have been if the wrong people find out. I had a blunt conversation with Collin Jeffers last night, and I have his bootprints on my chest to prove it…"

"I hope you kicked his ass," the two women said together, then laughed.

"I'm proud to say that I got the best of him, but not too proud to admit that he got his licks in. He kicks like a mule. Anyway, he named the people who put him up to attacking Michele, and they're very, very powerful people."

The women waited a moment before Janet said, "Okay, you milked the suspense. Now spill it."

"The Speaker of the House, the Senate Majority Leader, and Roger Beneker the fifth."

"Well, shit," Janet said.

"What she said," Michele echoed. "I guess we should be glad the president herself isn't involved."

"I don't think that matters," Cole said. "From what I've experienced personally, the president will do pretty much whatever Beneker wants."

"What's next then?" Janet asked. "How do you take on three of the most powerful people on earth?"

Cole drained his glass and stood up to get another bottle of Cabernet. "That's what I plan to ask Gene Olson tomorrow morning. I texted him last night, and he agreed to meet me in Chicago."

Chapter Thirty-Six

Seventy-seven miles of interstate road separate the FBI office in St. Francis from Chicago's O'Hare International Airport. Cole, Li, and Lane made the drive in less than an hour and a half and were seated in a meeting room inside the airport well before their nine o'clock meeting time. It was no secret within the Bureau that Cole was one of Gene Olson's favorite agents, and he asked Gene to meet him in Chicago to throw off anyone who might have access to the deputy director's calendar or flight plan. The FBI's Chicago field office was one of the biggest in the country, housing three hundred and fifty agents. It wouldn't raise any eyebrows that the Bureau's second in command was making a stop in the windy city. Gene walked in at the top of the hour, and Cole got up and made introductions. Gene had never met Li or Lane in person before. Cole poured his boss a cup of coffee and refilled his own, and everyone sat down.

"Cole has spoken highly of the two of you," Gene opened. "Have either of you thought of making the move to D.C.? That's where the action is."

"Whoa! Whoa!" Cole protested. "Are you really going to start the meeting by trying to poach two of my best people? I thought you were here to help! And the reason I wanted to meet with you is because we've got all the action we need and then some!"

Gene chuckled.

"All I heard was, 'Two of my best people,'" Li said. "Don't think Lane and I won't use that when annual review time rolls around."

Cole leaned back in his chair and raised his hands in mock surrender. He looked at Gene, "And to think I asked you here for help." He pointed to Li and Lane, "And this, this is not helping! Not a bit."

Gene's laughter was loud and contagious, but when they calmed down, he grew serious, blowing out a sigh, "So what *can* I help you with? You and your team don't typically shoot up an S.O.S. flare like this."

"That's because we don't typically find ourselves up against not just Roger Beneker, but also the Speaker of the House and the Senate Majority Leader." Cole let his words sink in.

"What? Why would Beneker and the two biggest pols outside of the White House be out to get you?"

"It's kind of a long story," Cole said.

"For this, I will make the time."

Cole nodded and immediately started to explain their theory about the three powerful people and their interest in keeping Congressional term limits from being enacted. He started with Michele's appearance on Janet's television show, explained how they found out that agent Collin Jeffers had paid for the attack on Michele, and then finished by describing his fight with Jeffers and his confession about who was behind it. Li and Lane filled in some of the gaps in the story, and it took nearly forty-five minutes to tell it. Gene listened, occasionally raising a question.

When Cole finished, Gene said, "Collin Jeffers blames you for derailing his career even more than he blames me. How do you know this isn't just his sick way of getting back at you for that? How do you know he didn't act alone?"

"We don't. But I looked into his eyes when he told me who put him up to it. I don't think he was lying."

"Like you, he's been trained to pick up on cues to tell if someone is lying or telling the truth. He also knows how to mask his own tells."

"I get that, but I still think he was telling the truth. It's so absurd, so preposterous, that Collin would've never come up with such a story. He's not that creative, especially when he thinks his life is on the line."

Gene considered it, looked at the others, and shook his head. He stood up and walked to the large windows, just as a blue, yellow, and red Southwest jet rumbled down the runway and lifted into the clear skies. "That 737 that just took off has a maximum takeoff weight of more than one hundred and fifty-four thousand pounds. Seventy-seven tons and change. You ever wonder how the hell it even gets off the ground? I wonder it every time I sit my butt in a commercial airline seat." He turned to face his Milwaukee team, "But it's easier to get my head around that bit of aerodynamics than it is around how the hell we take down the three people who currently have you in their sights."

"If that's supposed to build our confidence, it's not working," Cole said. "At least not for me."

"Me neither," Li said. "No disrespect."

Before Lane could chime in, Gene continued, "I'm just saying that this is big, the biggest thing I've ever come across in my career. The normal rules don't apply to Beneker and the other two. We need to take our time to come up with a solid plan. And then we need to execute it flawlessly. Even then, the odds are against us. You know the saying, 'You come at the king, you best not miss.'" He paused before adding. "We miss this, get it wrong somehow, then we're all on the unemployment line. And that's best-case scenario. Worst case, we're six feet under."

Cole got up from the table to refill his coffee again, "You really do need to work on your pep talks."

"Just being real," Gene said.

After another moment of shared reflection, Cole said, "Gene's right about how big this is. If we've accurately described what's going on, then the best way to describe the magnitude of it is to say that, well, if you combined Watergate, Monica Lewinsky, Iran Contra, and the Teapot Dome scandal… this would make those look as sinister as an Easter egg hunt on the south lawn of the White House."

"The Easter egg hunt wouldn't be very sinister," Lane said.

Cole feigned taking a deep drag from an imaginary pipe, "Precisely my point, my dear Watson, er, Becwar."

"Do you even have any idea what the Teapot Dome scandal was about?" Li asked.

Cole shook his head, "Not a clue." Their laughter broke the tension.

Before leaving the group, Gene pledged his support, knowing he was likely putting both his career and life on the line. Cole appreciated his leadership and friendship even more because of it. It was up to him and his team to come up with the next steps in how to work the case, and Cole would have it no other way. But they had other business to attend to as well.

After Gene left to meet with the SAC of the Chicago field office, Cole said, "What do you say we get lunch and discuss where we're at in finding the missing women of the Good Earth Tribe?"

They had barely ordered their food and taken a bio break when a large cart filled with sandwiches, veggies, fruit, and cold beverages was wheeled in. The sandwiches were labeled, but Cole grabbed one without looking, along with a bottle of water. He took a bite of his sandwich and was getting ready to start the next phase of the meeting when he stopped abruptly. He quit chewing and ran his tongue inside his mouth before picking up his sandwich wrapper and reading the label for the first time: *Happy Hummus on Gluten-free Bread.* He discreetly spit the sandwich into his wrapper and threw it away. *Nothing remotely happy about it,* he thought, before carefully reviewing the other options. He grabbed two ham and cheddar sandwiches and took them back to the table. Li and Lane took it in and shook their heads in amusement.

"What?" Cole said. "That was inedible. The bread was dry, and the hummus stuff was slimy." He took a big bite of a ham and cheddar and smiled, holding up the remains of his sandwich. "This right here is all-American yummy goodness. That's what this is. Now, what've you got for us, Laney?"

"Some facts and an idea I want you two to consider."

"You've got my attention," Cole said, finishing his first sandwich and taking a bite of a granny smith apple.

"Slow down, fella. You inhaled that first sandwich. Literally," Li said. "Really, I don't think you chewed once."

"Hey! I had to get that other taste and texture out of my mouth. I'm good to go now. Carry on, Lane."

"Okay. Well, I contacted the tribe, and they quietly confirmed that the members are currently receiving roughly one hundred thousand dollars a year. Again, that can vary from year to year depending on the take from the casinos, but the number keeps edging up. I was hoping that they paid the money out once a month or so via paper check. Some tribes still do it that way, and it would've been a relatively simple thing for us to trace the checks to the addresses or PO boxes to which they're delivered. But the Good Earth Nation is more progressive than that. They make their payments the same way that the Bureau and most other employers pay their people today, electronically. When the girls came of age and had their high school degrees in hand, they signed up for their tribal payments. At that time, they submitted the account and routing numbers of their checking accounts to the tribe's business office, and they began receiving their first-of-the-month payments automatically. That continues until they die or they leave the tribe, and nobody voluntarily leaves the tribe."

"Why doesn't the tribe use checks?" Cole asked.

"The same reason almost all employers don't these days; it's more labor intensive and expensive than the electronic alternative. It's not cheap to print the special checks and statements, address individual envelopes, pay for postage, etc. And, just like employees, most tribal members prefer the electronic payments too. The money gets into their account quicker. And there's no more running to the bank to deposit the check. Or no more taking a photo of the check and texting it to your bank. The money just appears in your account the first of every month as if by magic."

"But we can trace the transfers to see what checking accounts the payments are being made to almost as easily as we could check the paper check trail, right?" Li asked.

"True," Lane said, stabbing a strawberry on the plate in front of him with a toothpick and eating it. "But we took the first step along that path, and it looks like it won't be that easy."

"It never is," Cole moaned. "What's the problem?"

"We've isolated the accounts of the four young women identified by the tribe's leaders. As soon as the payments hit those accounts, they're automatically rerouted to other accounts overseas, in places like the Cayman

Islands that make them hard to trace."

"Hard to trace? Or impossible?" Cole asked.

"Impossible, for now at least."

"Okay," Cole said, frustration rising in him like bile. "That means it's likely one group that took these women or that they're working together. Too much of a coincidence that the money from all four is bouncing to the Caymans and other places we can't easily penetrate. Also, they're a hell of a lot more sophisticated than the average thug." He blew out a long breath, "You said you had some facts to share and an idea. Enough with the facts. I'm more than ready to hear your idea now."

Lane smiled, "You ever see the movie *The Sting*?"

"Are you serious? Newman and Redford with Robert Shaw, in maybe his best performance outside of *Jaws*."

"That's the one," Lane said.

"You want to set them up in some kind of sting operation?" Li asked.

"I do. Because it's one of the things we in the FBI have a particular talent for. Remember ABSCAM?"

"Sure," Cole said. "Late 70s and into 1980. The FBI dangled bribes in front of politicians, supposedly from Arab countries that wanted favors. They caught six U.S. congressmen and a U.S. senator accepting bribes on tape and not only got them out of office but put them away for a while."

"I know the Bureau wasn't really keen on sting operations before then," Li said. "From what I recall, they were leery about being called on the carpet for entrapment. But it's a big part of our arsenal now."

"Right," Lane said. "My idea involves finding a way to get the women to come into the tribal offices to recertify their membership and their right to payments."

"We do that, and whoever took the four women will know that something's up," Li said.

"No, they wouldn't," Cole said, warming to the idea. "Not if we send the same message to every single adult member of the tribe who is currently eligible for payments."

"That's what I was thinking," Lane said. "We work with the tribal leaders, and they send out emails to all their members saying that they were hacked somehow, or they had a data breach, and they need everyone to come in person to the tribal offices to recertify their tribal membership. Their payments will stop until they come in."

"Pretty ingenious," Li said. "But I don't think the guys behind this are going to let our victims come in alone. They'll each likely have an *escort* who makes sure they don't do anything to call attention to themselves. And I doubt the women will all come in at the same time, either. We believe they're all controlled by the same group, and that means if and when we grab the first one, then that will tip off whoever traffics the women, and the other three will never come in. Maybe lost forever."

"What if we give everyone a piece of paper that they need to take to their bank to get the payments going again? Say it's 'authorization' from the tribe. We embed trackers on the four that we hand out to the missing women."

Cole nodded. "I like it. I like it a lot. We could have small teams of agents and MPD follow each of the letters and converge on them simultaneously once the fourth woman comes into the tribal offices. I'll call John Mishicot and get the tribal leadership's buy-in. You guys work directly with Ty and polish the plan. And do it quickly. I don't like to think about what a day in the life looks like for these women right now, but I gotta believe it looks a lot like hell itself."

Chapter Thirty-Seven

They hit traffic on the drive back from O'Hare, and Cole arrived at their St. Francis headquarters ten minutes late for a meeting. He heard laughter coming from his office as he walked down the hall, and wasn't surprised to see Ty, Jenny, and Gregory Acker, the District Attorney for Milwaukee County, when he entered and took off his suit jacket. "Good afternoon, all! Looks like everyone is getting along here. Sorry I'm late."

"No problem," Acker said. The D.A. was in his late sixties and wore his dyed black hair slicked back and stylishly long. He had been entrenched in his job for three decades and held an extremely high opinion of himself. He looked at Jenny, "Your assistant got us refreshments and helped us pass the time. I don't like to be kept waiting, but the time with Jenny was enjoyable. Thank you, my dear."

Cole noticed Jenny's cheeks redden slightly but wasn't sure if it was in modesty or anger at being called *dear*. He addressed her, "Thanks for taking care of these gentlemen, Jenny. You can step out now, and please pull the door shut behind you."

Jenny flashed the room with a smile as brilliant as the sunlight stealing indirectly through his southern windows before leaving, and Cole thought he saw Ty and the crusty D.A. blush a shade. It seemed no man was immune to her charms.

The three men were standing, and Cole gestured for his guests to take a seat at the table. He closed the blinds partway and joined them. The D.A. was less in the mood for small talk with Jenny out of the room, "Your assistant set this meeting up, presumably to talk about the attack on Michele Fields. I'm assuming the perpetrator is ready to forgo trial and plead guilty."

"Actually, I asked you both here to tell you that there is no case. Albert DeMario needs to be set free without a trial." Cole looked directly at Ty when he said the words, his face an apology, pissed at himself for not finding the time to give him a heads-up.

Acker stood up fast, knocking his chair over behind him. "What the hell nonsense is this? Have you offered him immunity for turning on the people who put him up to this? For heaven's sake, the man stabbed a Milwaukee resident. Bludgeoned her, too. Nearly killed her and left her in a vegetative state. I will not allow you to let him off!"

Cole thought the man's righteousness was mostly real, but he had been exposed to his bluster before and wouldn't be swayed by it. His voice was calm when he said, "What we have here is a victimless crime."

"The hell you say!" Acker ranted. "I've heard the rumors that you and the reporter were an item, and you may be abandoning her cause, but I shall not. She was viciously attacked in public, and today, she lies motionless in a hospital bed."

"No. She doesn't," Cole said. He got up and crossed the room, hitting the intercom button on his desk phone. "Please send her in."

The door opened, and Michele walked in wearing a stylish hat that hid her bald spot. She looked to be in perfect health outside the wrapping that peeked out from the left sleeve of her loose sweater. The D.A. was already standing, speechless for the moment, and Cole made quick introductions.

When everyone was seated again, Cole asked Michele if she planned to press charges against Albert DeMario. She shook her head. "No. I don't. I believe he is as much a victim in this case as I am."

"I don't understand," Acker said. "The man bashed your head into a podium and stabbed you brutally in the chest in front of hundreds of people. Don't you want to see justice served?"

"Of course. But taking a single father away from his sick daughter doesn't feel like justice to me. Powerful people made him choose between his daughter's life and mine, and he chose his daughter out of desperation and love. He's not a threat to society and will never harm another soul. I met with him face-to-face in prison, and I can tell you that he is remorseful. I want to see him reunited with his daughter and given a second chance."

Acker saw his high-profile, slam dunk case turning to dust and fought it. "You have all the right intentions, I'm sure, but I will not allow this man to go free. He is a public menace. He tried to kill you in a violent manner. Who knows what else he might do?"

"It's not your decision to make, Gregory," Cole said. "It's Michele's, and she's clearly made up her mind." He gestured to her, "And as you can see, she's of sound mind *and* body, a condition I'd ask that you keep to yourself for now."

Acker's complexion was darkened by anger and loss. He was used to winning and didn't want to give up. He turned to Ty, "Is MPD just going to roll over and accept this?"

Ty was still for a moment before finally nodding. "We will follow Michele's direction on this. She is an upstanding member of our community, and I know her personally to have sound judgment..." He paused another beat, turning his gaze to Cole, "Except possibly in her taste in men."

Cole and Michele laughed, but Acker turned a shade darker. "Is this all a joke to the three of you? I'll go to the press and paint a picture of MPD and the local FBI going soft on crime, letting dangerous criminals back on the streets."

Cole stood up and towered over the D.A., "I don't think that would be wise, because I'll paint my own picture, one of a vain district attorney who only wants the easy cases with lots of microphones and cameras on hand to capture his magnificence. Then I'll tell them that your hubris has put the very life of perhaps this city's favorite daughter in jeopardy." His voice softened. "And in the end, DeMario will be set free because, as I said earlier, the ultimate decision isn't yours, mine, or Ty's to make." He turned to Michele, "It's up to her. And I believe she's made her wishes clear."

Acker crossed his arms stubbornly in front of him. "I don't like it. This is a dark day indeed."

Cole looked at Michele, "Actually, I think it's a particularly nice day today."

Ty hung around a while after Acker left, catching up on Michele's recovery and listening to Cole's update on their evolving plan to try to find and free the missing women. Cole didn't bring up that morning's meeting with Gene Olson or anything about the people behind Michele's attack. It was clearly outside his friend's jurisdiction now, and Cole was sure his friend had more than enough on his plate without adding to his worries.

It was after four in the afternoon by the time Ty left, and Cole suggested that he and Michele take a walk. The St. Francis FBI offices stood just one hundred yards from the crashing waves of Lake Michigan, but he seldom took advantage of that fact, other than enjoying the views from his office. The former Director of the FBI had been on hand for the building's opening a few years earlier, and he had predicted the surrounding water, as well as running and biking trails, would provide great opportunities for agents and staff to heal. But it hadn't worked out that way for Cole and most of the others working in the building. *Too often, we become immune to the beauty and miracles that are closest to us, taking them for granted,* he thought. He looked at Michele... *No more.*

Chapter Thirty-Eight

Milwaukee County's Bay View Park abuts the FBI offices to the north, and the Oak Leaf Trail, one hundred and twenty-three miles of smooth, winding asphalt, runs right past the FBI's front doors. The Oak Leaf is the jewel in the crown of the county's extensive trail system, and nearly a quarter of it hugs the dramatic shores of Lake Michigan.

Cole and Michele followed the trail into the park. The waning sun was still warm, and the temperature was in the low sixties. Cole knew that it would get cool quickly when the sun finally set, but with winter closing in by the day, they needed to relish these moments while they could. This part of the trail offered panoramic views of both the lake and Milwaukee's evolving cityscape. It was breathtaking at times. Both Cole and Michele were proud of their adopted hometown, seeing it as a big city with a small-town feel. They took their time on the walk, soaking it in, stopping to sit on benches that offered spectacular views or a bit of solitude, before moving on. They walked the length of South Shore Park and past the South Shore Yacht Club before taking a seat again in tiny Cupertino Park, which offered possibly the best views of the city's skyline and the historic expanse of the Hoan Bridge.

They had talked little on the walk, each lost in their own thoughts. With the background noise of crashing waves, light traffic, and bird calls, it was a comfortable silence, broken only when one or the other would point out a particularly impressive scene. There had been no talk of the attack, the case, or the next steps, and Cole felt rejuvenated. But when he looked at Michele, he could see that she was tiring. They'd covered more than two miles of meandering trail with some changes in elevation, and she was still getting her stamina and balance back. Even with the intermittent stops, she had become winded. But he saw contentment in her, too, and knew that this had been as good for her as it had been for him. The life of a special agent and a reporter could be humdrum for long periods of time, until it wasn't. This was one of those times they both longed for the mundane.

The mood was broken when someone sat down on the bench next to Cole, causing him to scoot closer to Michele. He looked to his right and was surprised to see Collin Jeffers sitting next to him, dressed in jeans, running shoes, and a gray Harvard Law hoodie. He peered out at the lake from beneath the bill of a Washington Guardians cap.

Cole was wary, but knew the man could have killed both he and Michele already if that was his intention. "What do you want," Cole said, enjoying the symmetry of seeing Jeffers' bandaged right arm and Michele's left. It turned out his was more superficial, but it would still leave a scar.

"I came to tell you that I've been doing some thinking since you left my apartment and I, well, I want to change." Michele had noticed him and leaned forward to see him better. Jeffers kept looking out over the lake, but he could pick up on her anger in his peripheral vision. "I've been on the wrong side of things for a long time now. I don't know when it started or how, but somewhere along the line, I stopped caring about other people and focused only on myself. I saw the job not as a way to help others, but as a means to put the spotlight on me and to help my career." He willed himself to turn and look at Michele, to face her quiet rage head-on. "I'm sorry you were hurt and that I played a role in it. I've been a coward and listened to the wrong voices for so long now that I lost my way." He looked at Cole, "I don't believe that you had anything to do with the murder of the APAG CEO. I did when you were standing over me, but I told you I had time to think. I still believe you're a Boy Scout who doesn't color outside the lines. I'm going to help you, but not because I'm afraid you'll hurt me somehow; I'm going to help you because I've already hurt myself enough. If I don't turn things around now, I never will."

Cole looked at Jeffers closely before nodding. "I believe you, so I'm going to be perfectly honest with you. When this is all over, if we somehow take down the bad guys, you'll still likely have to pay a price for sending DeMario after Michele."

"And for sending the other two guys to your house," Jeffers admitted.

"Right, that too," Cole said.

Jeffers thought about it and knew that those crimes together would likely put him behind bars for life. He nodded anyway. "Understood." He held his hand out to Cole, and they shook. He held it out again to Michele, but she wouldn't take it, shaking her head instead. "Again, I'm sorry," Jeffers said before getting up and disappearing down the trail.

"You don't trust him, do you?" Michele said. "He tried to have both of us killed."

"Following someone else's orders," Cole said. "And he could've shot us both from behind right now without us even being aware. Besides, what choice do we have? Without someone on the inside, I'd say our chances of beating Beneker and company are next to none."

They sat soaking in the last of the day's sun when Cole had an idea, "Have you ever been to Three Brothers Restaurant?"

Michele shook her head, "Can't say as I have."

He helped her up. "Well, if you can make it another four or five blocks, I can steer us to some of the finest Serbian food this side of Belgrade. Three Brothers has been run by the Radicevic family since 1956."

"Seventy years?"

"That's right, my little math wiz. And it's been written up in *Bon Appetit* and *Gourmet* magazines. It's even earned a James Beard Award; they called it 'an American classic.' I guarantee you'll like it."

"Well, lead on then, my culinary tour guide," she said as they headed west toward the restaurant. "I hope they have burek on the menu."

"It happens to be one of Mama's specialties. Layers of paper-thin filo dough with spinach and cheese filling. Yum. That particular dish takes a while to prepare, though, so you'll have to sit across the table and stare into the deep blue pools of my eyes for a time."

Michele squeezed his hand, "I can put up with that."

"Good. Then I'll get the goulash, and we'll share. And we can talk about how we can best use the rehabilitating agent Collin Jeffers going forward."

Michele linked her arm in his as they walked and leaned into him, enjoying his warmth and the feeling of protection it gave her, "Sounds like a plan."

They strolled two blocks, still in no particular hurry, and turned onto Superior Street. Michele pulled Cole to a stop and pointed to her right. "Look at that historical monument. It's taller than a man and flanked by brick pillars. Must be something worth learning about. Let's see what it says."

Cole walked the short path with her to the monument, and together they read the raised lettering on the face of the marker. BAY VIEW'S ROLLING MILL stood out in all capital letters at the top. It told the story of the Milwaukee Iron Company, which built a rolling mill on the site back in1868, turning out iron products, including thousands of tons of rail for the railroad industry.

Michele read the next part of the inscription aloud slowly, "On May 5, 1886, the mill was the scene of a major labor disturbance. Nearly fifteen hundred strikers from around Milwaukee marched on the Bay View mill to dramatize their demand for an eight-hour workday. The local militia, called to the scene by Governor Jeremiah Rusk, fired on the crowd, killing seven people." She stopped and looked at Cole, "My God. Seven people, shot to death, all because they wanted to work eight hours a day and have some time to live and love. Talk about burying the lead! I never knew this story."

"I remember this now. Some people call it the Bay View Massacre. Others refer to it as the Bay View Tragedy. I guess it depends on your perspective." They turned and walked on toward the restaurant as Cole added, "It just shows that this whole abuse of power thing we're dealing with right now isn't anything new."

Chapter Thirty-Nine

Their meal at Three Brothers was a treat. The restaurant featured old-world comfort food served in a warm and cozy setting. They Ubered back to the FBI offices after dinner so Cole could pick up his car, and they arrived back home a little after eight. Cole hadn't looked at his phone since they'd started their walk four hours earlier, but he checked it when Michele went to take a shower. Two missed texts. *Lane Becwar. Gary Schettle.* Cole sighed. Since the advent of texts, emails, and cell phones, he was never truly off duty. And while he lamented that fact, he wasn't about to leave his analyst or his agent hanging. He called Lane.

"Hey, boss. Sorry to bother you. I sent my text some time ago. I feel a little silly breaking up your night for this."

"Not a problem, Laney. I'm just sitting here thinking about what a good day it's been, and what beer I might quietly celebrate with. What's up?"

"I was wondering...we worked all afternoon planning the sting operation that we hope will help us find the missing women and bring in the guys who snatched them. It feels like we need a name for this operation. What do you think?"

Cole smiled, "Your idea. Your plan. You should name it."

"I was hoping you'd say that. I'm thinking we call it 'Operation GE.' Obviously, it stands for the Good Earth Nation, but GE also has a huge presence in the area with its medical division. So, I think it's relevant, and it resonates."

"I like it," Cole agreed. "Whatever it might lack in flash, it more than makes up for in substance. Operation GE it is." When they ended the call, Cole thought about Lane. He teased him more than probably anyone else who worked for him, but it was because he liked him a great deal. He saw a little of his own early naivete in him, and he was proud of the strides he'd made since joining the Bureau. It probably wouldn't be long before he was poached by one of the bigger field offices in New York, LA, or the like. He'd be happy for him when the time came and enjoy the time he had with him now.

He went to the fridge and poured a hazy IPA into a stemmed glass, enjoying its meringue-like head and dense orange color. It was the first time he had tried the beer, and he looked at the can's almost psychedelic label. It was called Dare Mighty Things. *Don't mind if I do,* Cole thought, taking his first delicious sip. He noticed it was crafted by The Brewing Projekt in Eau Claire, the same city agent Schettle worked out of, and he wondered if he should pair his calls with brewery locations more often. While he waited for the agent to pick up, he remembered Schettle had earned a black eye while laying the groundwork for the poultry plant raid. He felt like he owed the man.

Schettle answered, "Hey, Cole! I texted you earlier to give you an update on what's been happening up here since we executed your warrant to search the Ladysmith plant. But it can wait until morning if you'd rather."

"No need, Gary. What have you got?"

"Do you remember a loudmouth who goes by the name of Ron Eager?"

"You are referring to the dishonorable sheriff of Rusk County, Wisconsin, of course."

"Now referred to as the former sheriff of Rusk County! He was in court today for his arraignment, and he was sporting a big, beautiful cast on his arm."

"Damn my clumsiness," Cole deadpanned.

"Right. Anyway, when the judge read off the charges spelled out against him in the indictment, it took a long time. Since the story of his arrest broke, the phones in both the prosecutor's office and ours have been ringing off the walls from all the businesses and individuals that Eager's been shaking down. It's been going on for years. The crook has several million dollars stashed in different accounts and owns nice homes in Arizona and Florida besides the palatial one he owns just outside Ladysmith. He's going to go down on dozens of counts of extortion."

"There's that abuse of power again," Cole said, mostly to himself.

"What?"

"Nothing. Sounds like we've done some good then."

"I believe we have, but there's a problem."

"Let me guess, all of Eager's deputies are dirty to some degree, and there is nobody left in the department to protect the good people of Rusk County."

"Damn. You are good. Now, having nobody is probably better than what they had, but what do they do about law enforcement in the county now?"

"I'm pretty sure the governor is going to have to name someone to fill the remainder of Eager's term, and then county residents will vote for his successor. Hopefully, their judgment will be a little better the next time around."

"Well, he had a lot more money to throw at his campaign than the average small county sheriff."

They were quiet for a moment before Schettle asked, "Remember Santos?"

"I sure do," Cole said. "He's been through an awful lot in the few years he's been on this planet."

"That's for sure," Schettle agreed. "Anyway, I talked to a guy I know who works for ICE, and he told me that they allowed Santos to go back to his uncle's home. He obviously won't be working in the plant anytime soon, if ever, but he can go to school, shovel snow, mow grass, etc. In other words, he is going to have a normal life."

Cole thought about that, "A normal life, but one without his mother or father." He sighed, "But he's got a chance. And I'll bet he makes the most of it. I only saw him for a few minutes, but you could see the determination in him. Thanks for sharing that with me, Gary."

They said their goodbyes and ended the call, and Cole remembered telling the D.A. earlier that it was a good day. *Turned out to be a pretty nice evening, too,* he mused, before getting up to see if there was anything Michele needed help with in the shower.

Chapter Forty

Operation GE went live four days later, the FBI teaming up with MPD and other resources brought to bear by the joint human trafficking task force. They would have liked to have taken more time to plan, but everyone involved knew that the missing women needed to be found sooner rather than later. They imagined the worst when they thought of the girls' lives since being taken, and they knew even then that they could be underestimating it to make it easier on themselves. Emails had gone out to all members of the Good Earth Tribe explaining the data breach and the need for each member to come in personally to re-register in order to continue receiving their monthly payments. The tribe had received several complaint calls, but most members were simply complying. The Bureau had set up in an empty downtown retail space and brought in three native American agents to work alongside members of the tribe's business office. Only two people in the Good Earth Nation knew that it was a sting operation, John Mishicot and his business office manager.

There was a small line outside when they opened the doors at eight a.m., and inside, several cameras connected to facial recognition software were hidden around the large, mostly open, space. Multiple photos of the four missing women taken from different angles had been fed into the software program, and Cole and others would be alerted immediately if one of the girls walked through the doors.

They got their first hit two hours later when a young woman walked in with a large gentleman holding her arm. She wore nothing on her head, and her face was clearly visible. She appeared nervous. The man accompanying her wore a tattered ballcap with a hoodie pulled over it, shrouding most of his face. His eyes were covered by large sunglasses, which he didn't bother removing, even after stepping inside and away from the morning glare.

Cole was watching on a large screen in a room a door away from the counter where the people were checking in. "Make sure the woman who just came in with the large guy in shades gets a golden ticket," he said into the microphone clipped to his collar. His agents out front had earbuds and their own hidden mics. One of them turned around to avoid being seen talking by the pair, "Consider it done," she said.

The young woman showed her driver's license and signed a form, and the man snatched the letter from the agent when she told them they had to take it to their bank before the payments could be restarted. When they walked outside, two unmarked units were prepared to take turns following them, one manned by agents of the FBI and the other by MPD officers. The plan was to repeat the process until they had eyes on the first three missing women, and the fourth showed up at the storefront to sign up. Then, they would snatch all four back along with the bad guys simultaneously. It was risky, but they saw no other way to get all of the women back safely.

Two more of the missing women came in over the next three hours, both of them accompanied by men Cole would best describe as thugs. They signed up and took their bank letters without incident. Joint FBI/MPD teams were now tracking the first three women while he, Ty, and others waited for the fourth to show. So far, Lane's plan was working to perfection. Later in the afternoon, with less than an hour before their operation was set to close for the day, Eve Keeshik walked into the space to show her ID and fill out the form that would allow her to keep her payments coming. At the same time, Cole received an call from one of the agents he had tracking the first missing woman. "Boss, this is special agent Flierl. The girl and the dude with her just pulled into the parking lot of the Brookfield branch of Associated Bank. They're likely going inside to hand in the form. We can still try to tail them without the tracker, but we'll have to stick to them a lot tighter than we have been. You said they're a pretty sophisticated group, and they might notice the tail. It wouldn't be that hard to lose us in that case.

What do you want us to do?"

Cole watched Eve Keeshik on the cameras while he thought. Her daughter could walk in at any moment, and they could reunite them. But if they waited for the daughter, they could lose the other three and maybe still not bring Ashlyn home to her mom. Ty was listening in, and he nodded at Cole; they both knew what had to be done. As hard as it was to do, it was an easy call, "Units one, two, and three, bring your women home with as little fuss as you can. We'll wait here to see if our fourth woman shows."

Cole and Ty heard their agents and officers acknowledge the command and hoped they would be able to grab the girls and take down their captors without incident. They were also hoping for a miracle that Ashlyn Keeshik would walk through the doors before anyone told her keeper that it was a trap.

Eve Keeshik reached the counter. She recognized a couple of the people from their business office, but not the agents. "New help?" she asked one of the Good Earth staff.

"The manager thought we might need some extra help, so he brought in some temps. It's been busy all day, so we appreciate the help."

Satisfied, Keeshik completed the form and put her license back in her purse. She turned around and saw a large man on his cell phone outside the plate glass windows. He looked annoyed. The man yanked on the arm of someone behind him and pulled her away from the store. Keeshik only caught a glimpse of the young woman, but she knew in her heart it was her daughter. She dropped her purse and screamed, "Ashlyn," and ran to the door to catch up to her.

Cole heard Eve scream her daughter's name, and he rushed into the open room and nearly beat her out the door. The facial recognition program hadn't pinged on her daughter, but maybe she saw her outside. Or maybe she imagined it in her grief. He ran hard, catching her, and yelled, "Where is she?" Eve was panting already and pointed. Cole looked ahead and saw a man dragging a girl behind him a half block ahead. He put on speed. The man turned and caught sight of Cole and pulled a handgun from his hoodie. Cole drew his Glock, but he couldn't shoot without risking hitting Ashlyn or even a bystander. He kept it pointed down and ahead of him regardless. "Let her go, and I'll let you walk," he shouted.

"Sure you will," the man shouted in return while he fast-walked backward, dragging the girl with him. "Stop there, or I'll start shooting. Who knows how many innocent people get hit in the crossfire? I don't give a shit, but I figure maybe you do."

Cole kept advancing, but slowly. He didn't want to set off a shootout on a busy street. *Why the hell didn't we set this sting up on a quiet street in a rural fucking setting,* he asked himself.

The gunman was at the corner and pulling the girl around it when he was knocked off his feet by someone. That someone tumbled to the ground with the kidnapper and the girl. Cole sprinted to close the distance and got there just as the bad guy recovered his weapon and turned it on Ty. Cole grabbed the man's gun hand before he could pull the trigger and bent his wrist so the muzzle was pointing to the ground. Then he stepped in close and headbutted him. Once. And again. The man's nose broke with the first blow, and he went to the ground unconscious with the next. Cole stood dazed, a trickle of his own blood running into his eyes, holding the kidnapper's gun. He reached down and helped up the young woman. "You must be Ashlyn," he said. "Your mom has told us all about you. You're safe now."

The woman was confused, unsure what to make of everything. But when her mom ran up and hugged her, she let go. She squeezed her mother tight while they both sobbed. Ty got up and brushed himself off, then cuffed the unconscious man.

"Where'd you come from?" Cole asked.

"I went out the back door and down the alley. I figured you had the front covered."

"Nice call. I can think of all kinds of bad ways that would have ended if you hadn't done what you did. I owe you."

"I don't see it that way," Ty said. "He had me in his sights after I took him down. He would have shot me if you hadn't grabbed his arm. I'd say we're even. But I didn't know you liked to headbutt so much. You made a mess of his face."

"Seemed like a good idea, in the moment," Cole said, wiping blood from his face. "I'm not so sure anymore. I feel a little loopy."

"Sounds like you're normal then," Ty laughed.

Cole patted down the trafficker and removed a knife from a sheath on his belt. It wasn't long before other MPD officers arrived on the scene and Ty directed two of them to read the now groggy suspect his Miranda rights and to take him to the nearest precinct to be booked. Then they helped Eve and Ashlyn back to the storefront, where John Mishicot stood waiting for them.

Mishicot hugged both Keeshik women. When Cole saw tears flowing freely down the stoic man's face, it caused his own eyes to well. "It's nice to know that we can make things better once in a while," Ty said. Cole turned to him and saw that his friend's eyes were leaking a little, too. It made him smile. "Jesus, we must be getting soft. C'mon," he said. "We've still got some work to do. He received his own hug from Eve and then pulled Mishicot into the back room with Ty. "Let's see how our team made out with the other three women."

When they were in the back room, Cole keyed his microphone. "Unit one. Report in."

"Unit one here. Special Agent Flierl reporting. We have the young woman with us, and we are en route to your location as we speak. She seems to be doing okay. We'll be there in ten."

"Great news," Cole said. "What about the dick she was with?"

"He's got a couple bumps and bruises. He tried to resist and went down hard on the lobby floor of the bank. Not sure if it was marble, terrazzo tile, or whatever, but I can tell you it didn't give. He gave out a little whelp when he thumped against it. Our MPD buddies read him his rights and took him into custody."

"Excellent. Unit two, report."

"SAC Huebsch, this is Special Agent Pinzer. Our woman is shaken up, but she's otherwise okay and looking forward to being reunited with her parents. We're on our way to you and maybe five minutes away. The bad guy has already been read his rights and booked by our MPD brethren."

"Nice work. Unit three? Tell me we're good!"

"Aces, boss. This is Special Agent Novey, and our girl is doing well, all things considered. We just pulled up in back of the building and will see you in a minute or two. MPD wrapped up our suspect and took him in already too."

"Great work all around," Cole said to his agents in the field and those standing around him.

Mishicot stepped forward and extended his hand to Cole; the two men shook. He did the same to Ty. "I don't know yet what happened to our young women, but I know that they are safe now and that they have a chance to live the lives they were meant to. Family and community mean the world to our people, and all of us felt a little lost, not quite whole, while these members of our tribe were away from us. You have found them and brought them back to us, and we are forever grateful."

Eve Keeshik had come into the room, her arm snugly around Ashlyn's shoulders. "Thank you, Agent Huebsch and Lieutenant Igou. I thank you as a member of the Good Earth leadership, and also as a mom who was desperate to find her daughter. Bless you both and the brave teams you work with!"

Chapter Forty-One

By eight that evening, Cole was seated at a long table at Faklandia Brewing, the whimsical St. Francis brew pub conveniently located just a half mile from the FBI offices. Gene Olson and another former mentor had taught Cole early in his leadership career to celebrate the victories; it helped carry a team through days of drudgery and the inevitable 'ones that got away.' Operation GE was turning out to be one of the biggest victories the Milwaukee office had ever had, with a far broader reach than they had imagined earlier that day. They interrogated the four kidnappers separately after taking them in, hoping at least one would crack under the threat of a long prison sentence. One did. And the tale he told got not only their full attention, but that of the top FBI brass in D. C. as well.

It turned out the Milwaukee trafficking operation was run by the owner of the seediest strip club in the area, a shady character who was working with several other loosely affiliated club owners throughout the Midwest. They operated like individual terrorist cells that cooperated but ran without common leadership. The Milwaukee group would snatch girls in Wisconsin and send them to clubs in Cleveland, Indy, Louisville, and other cities where they were forced to dance and turn tricks. The girls were far less likely to be recognized by friends or family in those cities, and they were far removed from their support systems and possible rescuers. In return for every girl the Milwaukee club snatched and sent, they would receive a young woman grabbed in one of those cities. Clubs in Minneapolis, Chicago, Cincinnati, and other cities were involved too. Cole's team used the informant's information to produce a warrant and had it signed by a magistrate within an hour of the successful interrogation. They immediately raided the local strip club and found five of their dancers had been kidnapped in other cities and were being held against their will. Similar raids were now going on across the Midwest, thanks to the work of his team. It was a proud moment.

Cole had invited the entire office to the brewpub and would foot the bill himself. Maybe thirty or so staff showed up when the party unofficially kicked off an hour earlier. Not a bad showing, given they had only received a short two-hours' notice about the impromptu celebration. He saw agents Flierl, Novey, and Pinzer laughing at the end of the table. Flierl was animated, and Cole was pretty sure he was reenacting his earlier takedown of his suspect. Cole waved his hand until he caught the attention of the three agents. He nodded to them and then raised his beer glass in a silent toast. They returned the sudsy salute.

Cole had ordered an array of appetizers earlier, including multiple orders of chicken nuggets, cheese curds, mozzarella sticks, jalapeno poppers, and haystack onions. All Wisconsin bar food essentials. Looking at the tables around him, he could see that the plates were mostly picked over and that the glasses of his staffers were running on empty. He knew his team would start streaming out soon, so he stood up and clinked his own glass with a fork. "Attention! Attention!"

His team quieted down immediately, and the people sitting nearby who were unaffiliated with them hushed, too, curious to hear what might be said. Cole looked around the room, his eyes catching those of every member of his group. "You guys did something pretty incredible today. You found missing women who were being held against their will, and you reunited them with their families. What you did here and what you touched off is freeing captive girls and women across the Midwest." He let the enormity of that sink in. "And you are also no doubt responsible for ensuring that other young women will not be ripped from their loving homes in the future, because today, you have put some of our nation's absolute worst scum behind bars. Thanks to each and every one of you." With that, he raised his glass to the team before taking a drink to raucous applause.

After a bit, the group realized Cole had something else to say, and they quieted again. "Thank you. I have just one more thing to say. This operation, Operation GE, was the brainchild of analyst Lane Becwar." Lane was seated next to Li and Jenny, and the group hooted and clapped for him. Li held up one of Lane's hands in victory, and Lane blushed a deep crimson. Cole continued, "Lane came up with the original idea for Operation GE. He also led the planning around it, and he even came up with the catchy name. And it could not have gone off more flawlessly, thanks to him and each of you. Great job, Lane! Great job, team!" Cole set his glass down and led another wave of applause. He was about to sit back down and finish his beer when someone touched him on the shoulder. He turned to find himself facing a young woman who he thought could be a year or two on either side of thirty. "Hi. I'm Monica Yohann. I'm a reporter with the *Milwaukee Journal Sentinel*. I was sitting at a table nearby and couldn't help hearing your toast. Pretty inspiring, I'd say. Would you mind if I ask you a few questions?"

Cole held up a finger, "Give me one minute." He stepped a few feet away from the reporter, pulled out his phone, and placed a call. Michele answered on the second ring. "Hey! What's up? You're not calling to scold me for missing the party, are you?"

"No. I'm calling with a quick question. There's a woman here by the name of Monica Yohann who claims to be a JS reporter. Can you describe her for me?"

When Michele did, he said, "Okay. I'm pretty sure it's her. What can you tell me about her in a nutshell?"

"In a nutshell? I'd say she's really talented and exactly where I was a year or so ago. We used to commiserate, and I know she wants to do bigger stories. I suppose every reporter does."

"Well, I've got a hell of a story here. Should I trust her with it?"

Michele thought about it. "If you talk to her now, some of the other media will be pissed that she got the story first, but it sounds like she came to you."

"That she did."

"Well, in that case, I would trust her with it. She'll do a nice job, and it could get picked up nationally."

"Thanks. I should be done here in an hour or so. See you soon," he said before ending the call. He turned to Yohann. "What have you decided?" she asked.

"We can share the story with you."

She reached into her purse and pulled out a reporter's notebook and a pen. *Do they all carry those damn things the way special agents carry a sidearm?* he wondered. "I'm ready," she said.

"Not with me. With him," Cole said, shaking his head and pointing to Lane's surprised face. "If you heard my little speech, then you heard that Operation GE was his baby. Talk to the proud father!"

He stepped away then, not wanting Lane to think he was listening in on the conversation. He took the time to check in with each of the small groups of his team members, giving each individual words of thanks or encouragement before heading up to the counter to settle the bill.

He was leaning on the bar with his back to his team, waiting to catch the eye of Nate, the owner, when he felt a warm presence at his side. He thought he might be losing it when he caught the scent of pumpkin pie and felt the stirrings of his arousal. He shook his head and turned around, only to find himself nearly nose-to-perfect nose with Jenny. She batted the long lashes that shielded her dark brown eyes and asked, "You're not planning on sneaking out on us, are you?" She pulled her hair away from her face, exposing her long, elegant neck.

Cole leaned back a little, the edge of the bar digging into his spine. A little pain might help him focus. He hadn't paid particular attention to Jenny during the evening, and he wondered if she had been drinking too much. He couldn't tell if her eyes were dreamy or glassy, but he didn't like the implications of either. He was glad that he'd limited himself to two beers, because he didn't want to think about what might happen if his inhibitions were lowered. He was in a committed relationship with Michele; hell, he loved her. It made him angry with himself that he was tempted at all by this younger woman. He held up the bill their waitress had given him earlier, "Sorry, I don't mean to be rude, but I need to pay this." He turned around then and called for Nate. The owner/brewer checked him out, and Cole headed home with only a quick wave to the remaining members of his team.

The next morning, he was showered and dressed by six-thirty. He stood in front of the full-length mirror in the bedroom he now shared with Michele, quietly perfecting the double Windsor knot in his tie.

"Aren't you the early bird," Michele said sleepily, head on her pillow. She still slept more than before the attack, but she was gaining strength every day.

Cole stopped preening and went around to her side of the bed. He leaned down and kissed her lips, "Good morning, sunshine. I'm sorry if I woke you."

"Not to worry. I can always just slip back off to dreamland while you slave away all day."

He smiled at her. "You're entitled for a while. But the day is coming when you'll have to make yourself available to all your swooning followers."

"Speaking of swooning, I remember you telling me that Annie was retiring, but I don't think you mentioned that you'd found a replacement already."

With great effort, Cole fought the urge to blush and sputter. *Jeez! Her Spidey sense must be tingling,* he thought. He was pretty sure this conversation was a road he didn't want to go down, a road filled with potholes. But it was too late to throw it in reverse now. "Yeah. You met her when you came to the office to meet with Ty and the D.A. the other day. I'm sorry I didn't get the chance to introduce you. She was handpicked by Annie, and I had Lane and Li interview the finalists for the job, too. They agreed Jenny was the best candidate available to us."

"I didn't spend much time with her, but she seemed very, um, what's the word I'm looking for…professional."

Cole could see her smirk in the room's semi-darkness and could tell she wasn't angry with him. She was toying with him. He leaned over her, "You wouldn't be teasing me, would you?" With that, he tickled her, and she giggled and screamed. He laughed, "Might be a little hard for sleeping beauty to fall back to sleep now!"

Chapter Forty-Two

Cole stood in front of the east-facing windows of his office a little before seven. The awakening sun was fighting through a mélange of wispy clouds, setting the sky ablaze with brilliant hues of oranges, pinks, violets, and reds. Sunrises and sunsets had always spoken to him somehow. They fascinated his father, and Cole thought maybe his own love for them came from him. It was a connection to a man whose face he sometimes now struggled to remember twenty-odd years after his passing. Cole best remembered days when he would encounter a soaring sunset while walking out of the woods after an afternoon small-game hunting with his dad. When that happened, his father would invariably say, "Let's take a minute," and they would sit together on the nearest log and watch the colors of the setting sun roil and shift until they would be looking at a completely different heavenscape just a few minutes later. The masterpieces of color and light touched his soul and made him feel closer to his Creator than at any other time. The chirping of his desk phone broke his mood, and he quickly lowered the blinds, temporarily blocking his beautiful view of the lake and the light. He stepped around his desk and plopped down in his chair as he hit the button to accept the call, "Special Agent Cole Huebsch here!"

"And this is your biggest fan!" Gene Olson said, nearly rattling the blinds with his booming voice. Cole tapped down the speaker's volume button. "It's eight a.m. Eastern time. Isn't that a little early for you Bureaucrat types in Washington to be up and about?"

"Ha! I've been up since the crack of dawn!"

"That's what I'm talking about," Cole said. "Dawn is cracking here as we speak. I just shut the blinds on an amazing sunrise over Lake Michigan to take this call."

"Well, I was just calling to congratulate you on the great sting operation your team pulled off yesterday. Operation GE will be part of FBI lore in the days ahead. The Cole Huebsch legend is burnished once again!"

"Burnished, huh? I'll assume that's a good thing. But it's more the beginnings of FBI analyst Lane Becwar's legend. You just met Lane in Chicago, and Operation GE was his idea, his plan, his name, his everything. I've been a little preoccupied trying to figure out a way to take down the biggest powerbrokers in the country."

"I read the reports last night. Sounds like you personally got into a scuffle with one of the bad guys. You and your buddy Ty saved the day and the daughter of one of the tribe's leaders. Nobody got hurt. Not even the traffickers. Eve Keeshik and John Mishicot have been reaching out to anybody and everybody in Washington D.C. to get you some kind of recognition."

"No need. I've had more than my share. But I was going to suggest some kind of commendation for Lane, and it would be nice to have Ty recognized, too. Ty literally took down the asshole who was holding Eve Keeshik's daughter. I believe he tore the pants on his uniform, making a textbook tackle. We should do something to make up for that."

"I'll see what I can do. Did you celebrate with your team last night?"

"Of course. I learned from the best. Too bad the Bureau doesn't reimburse for craft beer and fried foods."

"We could pick up the cost of the fried food, at least. And I'd be willing to cover the cost of the beer myself."

"No need. Already taken care of."

"Well then, how's your other plan coming along? You know, the one where we challenge the most powerful people on earth, risking life and limb to do so?"

"A little dramatic, aren't we?"

"Truthful, I'd say. And you didn't answer my question."

Cole took his time, picturing his friend sitting at his own desk at 935 Pennsylvania Avenue. He was likely looking at the same exact model desk phone and waiting for a reply that would give him a spark of hope. "Honestly, I don't have anything yet, other than to tell you that I think Collin Jeffers is solidly on our side. He visited me to tell me that he saw this as a way to turn his life around, make something of himself he could be proud of, and I believe him."

"I don't trust him at all," Gene said, anger tinging his voice. "I can still picture him berating you while you were in the hospital recuperating from being shot in the line of duty. Collin Jeffers thinks of one thing and one thing only, and that's himself."

"I felt the same way, but he convinced me he's different. And I told him that even if he helped us, he would likely have to pay for coordinating the attacks on Michele and on me. He understood and still wants to help. And let's face it. We will need someone on the inside or close to it to beat these guys."

"You're right about that."

"One other thing about Jeffers. I was taking a stroll along the lake with Michele when he came to town to see me. I might have been distracted a bit. He was able to get close enough to us to sit down on a park bench with Michele and me before I noticed he was even around. He could have just shot us and walked away. The fact he didn't speaks even louder to me than his words."

Cole looked up and noticed Jenny standing in the doorway. She appeared different somehow, pretty, to be sure, but maybe wearing less makeup and not trying as hard to look like a runway model. "Anything else, boss?" he asked Gene.

"I guess not. But do us both a favor and finalize your plan as soon as you can so that I can vet it with you and your team. I feel like this is hanging over our heads like a guillotine, and I want to get on with whatever it is we're going to do next. I don't want to rush, but I'm also getting sick and tired of waiting."

"I'm with you," Cole said before saying goodbye and hanging up the phone.

"May I come in?" Jenny asked.

Cole considered joining her at the table but instead pointed to one of the chairs across from his desk. He thought it might be a good idea to keep a little distance and a solid slab of timber between them. "Sure. Take a seat."

Jenny sat down with her hands in her lap. She had no notes and nothing to write with. She looked up at him, and Cole could see tears forming in her eyes. "I've got something to tell you, and it's not going to be easy."

Cole sat back in his chair, knowing immediately that she had come to see him to tell him she was resigning. Relief washed over him, and he let out a lung full of air. While she was efficient and professional, Jenny had somehow made him uncomfortable almost from the beginning. He was confident that he and his team could find a good replacement. But he was also curious as to why she was quitting so soon. "I take it you're resigning. Let me guess: you feel the job isn't a good fit. Or maybe you just don't like your boss. He's old and stiff and doesn't understand the younger generation. Something like that?"

Jenny's confusion was written clearly on her face. "What? No! That's not it. Not at all. Everyone's been great. You've been great, even though I knew I was clearly making you uncomfortable."

Now Cole was confused. "I don't understand."

Jenny put her hands on the desk and leaned forward. "I was sent here to get close to you. At a minimum, I was supposed to keep tabs on you, and the real hope was that I would compromise you."

Cole shook his head, "I still don't understand. What are you saying?"

Jenny's face was beat red, and tears began to trail down her cheeks. She caught some with a tissue, but others fell onto Cole's desk. She rushed the next words, "Have you ever heard of a honey trap?"

"Sure. It's a ploy the KGB used a lot. They would use attractive women to get romantically close to their enemies in order to compromise them somehow. Then they'd be able to control them. Does that sound about right?"

Jenny rolled her eyes. "You're soft-pedaling it. In a honey trap, an attractive woman has sex with the target. It's caught on tape, and then the tape is used to control that target. *You* were my target! I was supposed to get in bed with you, and then you'd be compromised. The people who sent me would then tell you who to go after and when to back off an investigation. They would own you."

"Why would the Russians care enough about me to want me compromised?"

Jenny shook her head. "Not the Russians, people in power in Washington D.C."

Cole sat back in his chair. Things were starting to make sense all of a sudden, pieces of a five-thousand-piece puzzle clicking into place. "Why are you telling me this? I thought you might be coming on to me a little, but I had no idea there was anything more to this than that. Why come forward now?"

"Because I like you and the team. I haven't been here long, but I've already seen how much good you do and how well you treat your people. It's like a family, and I feel like I've been trying to rot that family from the inside out. Unsuccessfully, I might add. I've tried to be a little subtle, but I've been practically throwing myself at you, and I just bounce off like a ball beaten against a backboard." She looked down at her hands. "I'm ashamed to say that I've done this, the honey trap thing, more than a few times. This is the first time I've failed. It's usually too easy. Even with guys in seemingly happy marriages." She looked at him with a feeble smile. "You're the first one who was impervious to my charms."

"I wouldn't say completely impervious. It was definitely messing with my head. So, what now?"

She paused, collecting her thoughts. "Well, I know I have no right to ask for this, but now I need your help."

"Explain. What do you need my help with?"

"I was put up to this by Roger Beneker, or at least people who work for him. He..."

"Roger Beneker!" Cole cut her off. "What does he have to do with this?"

"Everything!" Jenny said, sitting back in her chair and folding her hands in her lap again. She examined her nails briefly before looking at Cole again.

"Maybe I should back up. Would you be willing to listen to the story of how I came to be here? I'd like to start at the beginning."

Cole tamped down the anger that had flared within him at the mention of Beneker's name. He nodded, "Please, go ahead."

"My memory has faded over the years, but I remember growing up on an estate in Oaxaca, Mexico, a member of a loving family. We grew coffee and sold our beans throughout the world. We weren't rich, but we were well off for our country. My parents had three children. I was eleven when I was abducted by traffickers while walking home from school. My older brother, Santiago, was fifteen, and he was with me at the time. They beat him unconscious and took me. I also had a baby sister named Sophia. I have not seen any of my family since they grabbed me. Except in videos," she added after a pause.

"That's horrible," Cole said, involuntarily conjuring the image of Santos Garcia in his mind, another child who had his parents ripped out of his life at the same tender age. He shook the thought away and tried to concentrate. "Please know that I am not dismissing your story, but what does it have to do with Roger Beneker?"

Jenny's face went dark, and she looked away from him. "I was sold to him. Beneker bought me and had me smuggled into America. He kept me in the basement of his Georgetown home, a mansion, really. I was well-fed and clothed. I had tutors. And I had all the toys a young girl could want. But I was also raped several times a week...by Beneker and certain friends he wanted to impress. And then, on my fifteenth birthday, the rapes stopped." She shook her head and laughed harshly. "I guess I was too old for his particular tastes then."

"I'm sorry," Cole said, seething inside and knowing his words were inadequate.

"After that, Beneker sent me away to boarding school and then college. He and the people who work for him trained me to be a spy in the mold of the old KGB agents. I've been invaluable to him over the years. I live in relative luxury, but I am called to do despicable things like try to compromise you, and my life has never been my own to live."

"I don't understand. When you were away at boarding school or college, surely they couldn't monitor you at all times. Couldn't you have escaped? Gone to the authorities?"

Jenny looked down again, and the tears flowed more freely. "I told you earlier that I haven't seen my family since the day I was taken from them, except in videos. I've watched my siblings grow into adulthood and my parents age through these videos, but they've only been shown to me as what kidnappers refer to as 'proof of life.' It has been made clear to me from the day I was taken that if I ever step out of line, try to escape, or ignore a directive, my family will be slaughtered."

Cole considered this. "They could be bluffing."

She shook her head in slow certainty. "They murdered my best friend's family the day after I was kidnapped and videotaped it solely so they could imprint on my brain that they were able and willing to follow through on their threat. They said that I should feel lucky, that they would have kidnapped my friend, but they didn't consider her *pretty* enough to fetch them top dollar."

Cole stood up. He believed Jenny's story and its depravity and enormity had stirred different emotions inside him. They were swelling, twisting, and battling for control over him. He felt sick at the thought of the unthinkable things Jenny and no doubt other children had been forced to endure, and he was incensed at the thought of the people who inflicted their will on the children, Beneker in particular. Men who maimed children's spirits and flesh and ended their lives on a whim. Their whim. Their sick, perverted whim.

Cole crossed the room and went to the east-facing windows, raising the blinds and brightening the room. He turned to Jenny. "I will help you. We'll find a way to protect your family, but I'm also going to need you to be willing to help us."

"If you can ensure the safety of my family, I will do anything. I'd like nothing more than to take down Roger Beneker. I don't think I could kill anyone, but if he died, I wouldn't mourn the man."

"I don't think I'll need you to kill anyone, but having someone like you on the inside might even the odds for us a bit."

"Thank you, Cole." She got to her feet. "Anything else you need from me before I go back to my desk?"

"I can't think of anything right now. But my head is full, and it's spinning like a top. I might have more questions later."

"Okay then." She started to walk out of the office.

"Wait a second, Jenny. There's one more thing that's been nagging at me, and it's kind of a weird question," Cole said a little sheepishly. "But, were you wearing perfume last night that smelled like pumpkin pie?"

Jenny blushed, but a sly smile pulled at her lips. "Actually, yes. I read an article in *Cosmo* a few years ago that said pumpkin pie is one of the most effective scents a woman can use to attract a man. It's based on research that indicates the smell of that particular pie increases the blood flow in a lot of males."

"Blood flow?"

Jenny looked away from him but answered, "Yes, blood flow. You know, down there?"

Cole didn't get it right away, but when it finally dawned on him which blood flow she meant, it was his turn to redden. "Jesus! I guess that explains why Thanksgiving has always been my favorite holiday!" They both laughed.

Chapter Forty-Three

Cole reached out to Eric Rhodes. When he found out the senator was back home for the rest of the week, he asked him if he would be able to stop by the FBI offices later that day.

"Five o'clock work for you?"

"Perfect," Cole said.

"And what are you bringing me in for this time?"

"No crime that I know of," Cole said. "I'm working on that something big we discussed in your D.C. office last time I saw you. It's right in your wheelhouse, and I'm hoping you might be able to help us out."

"I'll see what I can do then."

After they hung up, Cole put his head down and did the dirty work his job demanded, slogging through emails and returning phone calls. Jenny came in after a couple of hours with a fresh cup of coffee and a copy of that morning's edition of the *Milwaukee Journal Sentinel*. "Sorry you're just seeing this now, but the delivery got delayed somehow this morning."

"No problem," Cole said, putting aside everything else and diving into the front-page article about Operation GE. The reporter had done a great job of telling the story, and it painted a glowing picture of the planning and execution of the sting by his office. It also praised the close collaboration with MPD and the Good Earth Nation. Finally, it tugged at the heartstrings, with individual words of gratitude expressed by the families of the young women rescued and by the tribal leaders.

Cole knew that the *Journal Sentinel* was part of the Gannett chain and its four hundred papers around the country. This story would likely be featured prominently in every one of them, and the career of local reporter, Monica Yohann, would get a nice lift. He was also confident it would be on the desk of everyone on the sixth floor of the J. Edgar Hoover building in D.C., the FBI's national headquarters. He was mulling that over when Lane knocked on his door frame.

"Well," Cole said dramatically, "It's the man of the hour." He held up a copy of the paper. "Seriously, nice interview. It was a helluva sting, and the story reflects that. Your stock has never been higher."

"That's nice, I guess."

Cole looked at his analyst more closely and noticed he seemed down. "What's up with you? You should be on top of the world today!"

Lane took a chair in front of Cole's desk, uninvited. He sat down and looked at Cole with sad eyes. "I'm over the excitement of the hunt now, and I'm way deep into the details of what was happening to these women. It's inhuman the way they were treated."

Cole thought about Jenny being ripped from her family when she was just eleven and Santos watching his parents murdered in front of him at the same age. He understood the depravity they dealt with, but usually, he was able to numb himself to it so that he could enjoy the world beyond his work. But it was obvious that Lane was mired in the muck of it. "What's going on?"

"We took the hard drives from the computers we found at the strip club and from the owner's house, a nice six-bedroom mansion in River Hills, by the way. The guy was kind enough to leave us a spreadsheet that listed all of his usernames and passwords to various accounts and sites. That led us to a shared site on the dark web where the strip club owners would put up photos and stats, things like height, age, weight, hair color, 'experience,' etc., of girls they had grabbed and who were available for trade."

Lane stopped and swallowed. Cole could tell he was trying to keep his emotions in check. "These guys acted like the owners of professional sports teams or something," Lane continued, shaking his head. "They would trade these young women back and forth, sometimes straight up, but other times with cash involved too. We found transactions that included three and four club trades, most intended to move the girls as far away from their homes as possible. Sometimes, it would be a simple cash purchase, almost like the old slave auctions."

Cole felt sickened as he thought of the inhumanity that Lane was describing. He understood now that his analyst had a heart and soul and couldn't bask in the glory while he was covered in slime.

"The other thing we're finding," Lane said, "is that this loose network was growing pretty fast. We've already linked it to clubs in the deep south and out east. We think there could be some out west, too. The Bureau has already set up a national team to follow up on all this. I've been asked to be part of it."

"I recommended you to Gene. I also told him you deserve a commendation."

Lane's smile was lame. "Are we really making a difference, or will a whole new mess of cockroaches come out of the woodwork when we stomp on this nest of them?"

"We're making a difference," Cole said as Lane got up and headed out of his office. But deep down, he knew he was trying to convince himself as much as he was his analyst.

Chapter Forty-Four

It was an eclectic group that gathered in the Milwaukee SAC's office at five p.m. Cole crowded around his small round table with Lane, Li, Jenny, and Senator Rhodes. Gene Olson and Collin Jeffers were together in a conference room inside the J. Edgar Hoover building in Washington, joining the meeting and appearing larger than life on the monitor in Cole's office.

After greetings were exchanged, Cole kicked off the meeting. "I want to start by thanking everyone for making time for this little gathering." He focused on the monitor. "We need to get moving, because it's already past six p.m. where our D. C. colleagues are sitting, and they're late for happy hour." The group chuckled at the remark, and Cole let things die down before turning serious. "We've been dealing with a lot lately. We've worked hard, had to think through a lot of difficult issues, and we've wrestled with emotional ones as well. Our team needs a break right now, *deserves* a break, but we don't have that luxury at this time. Right now, this evening, we're about to start what could be the most important planning meeting in any of our careers." He paused a moment. "I don't think I'm exaggerating about this. And because of that, I'm going to steal a page from the leadership book of Alan Anderson, a man I consider a friend and who has been a mentor to Eric for many years. Most of you know that Alan is a hospital administrator; he makes decisions that impact patients' lives every day. What you may not know is before any important meeting that Alan leads, he starts with a brief reflection. He tells me it helps pull his people away from the clamor and clutter of both their personal and professional lives, and it helps to center them. I called him earlier and asked him if he could email me a reflection for this meeting, and he sent this one by author Shannon Alder. I think it's perfect. So here goes..."

Cole read from the heart, *"I don't really care if people forget me. My legacy wasn't about me. It was about everything I could do for another. When that sinks in...well, you try a little harder. You dream a little broader. Your heart stretches a little farther and you find that you can't go back to the same place and make it fit. You become a person of ideas and seek out your own kind. And then it happens: One day you discover that staying the same is scary and changing has become your new home."*

He let the author's words sink in before continuing. "You guys all know that I like to have fun and keep things light when I can. I don't apologize for that. The world we work in can be a very dark place, and you can get lost in it if you're not careful. But this is our time to do something important for our country, and I'm not in a joking mood. When I first realized that we were up against Roger Beneker, the fifth, the Speaker of the House, and the Senate Majority Leader, I frankly didn't like our odds. Now, when I look around this room, I know we have more than just a fighting chance." He looked at Li and Lane. "I trust these two with my life. Both are smart and courageous in their own way." He looked at Jenny. "My assistant here has been working under the direction of Roger Beneker." Everyone turned to Jenny, and her face reddened before Cole quickly added, "But she was working for him under duress, under the constant threat by Beneker that he would massacre her family back home in Mexico if she didn't do exactly as ordered. She came to me this morning and volunteered this information, and she's willing to help us if we can guarantee the safety of her parents and siblings." Cole turned to Eric. "Our own U.S. senator has agreed to help us however he can, which at the very least will give us access to the Capitol Building. He may be a first-term senator, but he still has contacts that could help us out. And he's exactly the kind of elected official we all want, one who puts the needs of his constituents above his own. I don't need to tell you all how rare that is today.

"Gene will give us whatever discreet cover he can, and I'm hoping he might have some idea of how we can protect Jenny's family in Mexico while we take care of things on this side of the border. He's been my mentor for years, and I will charge any hill he tells me to."

Finally, he looked at Collin. Jeffers was fidgeting a little but caught himself and held Cole's eyes through the screen. Cole pointed to something behind his desk, "There's a hole in the drywall in my office here that serves as a reminder of bad leadership. It's one of the reasons why Agent Jeffers isn't a completely trusted member of this team yet. But as uncomfortable as it may make some of you, he holds the lives of all of us in his hands. If he wasn't on our side right now, I believe we would all likely be dead already. He told me he wants to change, and I want to believe him. I *need* to believe him. Because without his help the bridge before us would be a bridge too far." He let out a deep breath. "Enough of that. I want to go back to the basics, and I've asked Senator Rhodes to walk us through term limits at the national level and what's at stake."

Eric looked around the room and at the screen and could see that everyone was paying attention. Those listening wanted to better understand the issue and why their country's leaders were willing to kill over it. "Term limits have been vigorously debated in our nation since its very beginning," he said. "Some of our founders believed that without term limits for our presidents and members of Congress, we would evolve into something like an elected monarchy. But it wasn't until the twenty-second amendment to the U. S. Constitution was ratified in 1951 that we even had presidential term limits. Washington and Jefferson had set the precedent of limiting their terms to two voluntarily, but it wasn't until after FDR won four terms that Congress finally pushed through term limits for POTUS. But as Congress is often wont to do, they passed a law that affected someone else and not them. Sound familiar? So, our country's commander-in-chief is limited to two four-year terms while our senators and representatives can *serve,* and I use that term loosely, as long as they breathe. Robert Bird represented West Virginia in the Senate for more than fifty years, and John Dingell, Jr., of Michigan, was *in the House* just shy of sixty years."

"Holy shit," Lane said.

"More like unholy shit," Li replied.

Eric waited them out. When he was sure he had their attention again, he continued, "The reason the lack of term limits matters is because the longer you stick around as a senator or representative, the more money and power you amass. Your campaign war chest becomes so big nobody, no matter how good a candidate, stands a chance against you. Also, the most senior members of the House and Senate, those with the most tenure, get the plum committee assignments. The appropriations committee, for example, which writes the spending bills. Ways and Means. Energy and Commerce. You get the picture. Those are the committees that attract the biggest lobbyists with the biggest bags of money."

"But more than eighty to ninety percent of voters want Congressional term limits," Li said. "And that's not debatable; poll after poll show the same numbers, regardless of who's asking the question. The latest national poll I just saw regarding term limits showed that eighty-seven percent of Americans are in favor of them!"

Cole jumped in, "Yes. And that would mean something if our senators and representatives actually gave a shit about what the people who elected them want. They have zero interest in tearing up the rails on their own gravy train. Um, present company excepted, of course."

"Of course," Eric chuckled. "There was a lot of momentum on term limits a few decades ago. Between 1992 and 1994, seventeen states enacted term limits for their congressmen, bringing the total number of states with term limits for their U.S. senators and representatives to twenty-three, nearly half the states. And then in May of 1995, the Supreme Court ruled five to four in U.S. Term Limits, Inc. v Thornton, that individual states cannot impose term limits upon their elected federal officials."

"No kidding?" Gene said. "That wasn't all that long ago, and I don't remember that."

"Yeah. That close vote has been mostly forgotten. The four liberal justices at the time, Souter, Ginsburg, Breyer, and Stevens voted to make it illegal for states to limit the terms of their U.S. senators and reps, and they were joined in that decision by Anthony Kennedy, a Reagan appointee. The conservatives on that court, Chief Rehnquist, O'Connor, Scalia, and Thomas, all dissented."

Eric took a sip of water. "Sorry about that. Almost done with the free history lesson." He looked at Cole. "You might have to order in pizza, if we're going to be here for a while. I can let Karri know I'll be later than expected."

Cole pulled out his phone, "I'm on it." He looked up at the monitor on his wall before placing an order, knowing Gene and Collins' stomachs were an hour ahead of his, "Not sure we've got the technology yet to feed you guys from here."

"Not a problem," Gene's voice boomed. "We may not have term limits beyond the presidency yet in our nation's capital, but we can goddamn well get pizza delivered." He muted himself and phoned in their order.

"Moving on," Eric continued. "Back in 1994, the year before the Supreme's Thornton decision, the House of Representatives voted on a proposal to limit U.S. senators to two six-year terms and U.S. representatives to six two-year terms. The bill won a majority vote, two hundred twenty-seven to two hundred and four. But it was well short of the two hundred and ninety votes needed to hit the two-thirds threshold of a constitutional amendment. No Senate vote has won so much as a simple majority, including a vote in 1995. That's the last time either house in Congress allowed a vote on term limits. The majority of my party has sided with mostly long-in-the-tooth Republicans to keep it from happening. It's a high hurdle. Putting congressional term limits in place requires a bill winning two-thirds majority votes in both the House and Senate, and then it needs to be ratified by thirty-five states."

"And neither Republicans nor Democrats want term limits," Gene added. "That's patently obvious. Because both parties have controlled the House, the Senate, and the Presidency all at once at one time or another since the early nineties, and neither has even brought congressional term limits back up for a vote. That says something to me: that they're obviously colluding to keep things status quo."

"They'll hike the retirement age for social security and gut Medicare and social programs before they give up their power willingly," Li added.

"So now we know what they're trying to preserve, and we know they're willing to kill people to make that happen. What can you tell us about the Speaker and the Senate Majority Leader, Eric?" Cole asked.

"Robert Wacouta is a Republican and the Senate Majority Leader. He's a Texan serving his seventh term in the Senate, more than forty-plus years in all. He served in the House two terms before that. He's in his late eighties, on the shorter side, and, well, beefy."

"Rotund in the rotunda!" Cole quipped.

"What?" Eric asked.

"Sorry," Cole said, "It took longer for you to explain term limits than I expected. That tells me you picked a good profession, though, because if you taught history, they'd call you Professor Snoozenheimer."

Eric scowled at him.

Cole shrugged, "Sorry. I can only be quiet and serious for so long. Plus, my stomach is empty, and I'm thinking of the pizza now."

Gene and Collin already had their pizza. Gene held a gooey slice up in front of his camera, and it loomed large on the screen in Cole's office. He made a point of licking his lips. "They made this in the commissary here special for us and just brought it up. It's really good. Sorry for the interruption, Senator Rhodes. Carry on."

Eric shook his head before continuing. "I should've also mentioned that Bob Wacouta is also known as a lech. He tends to hire almost exclusively attractive young female aides, and he churns through them at a rate that's hard to dismiss. But if anything has gotten to the ethics committee, it hasn't seen the light of day beyond it. Of course, Wacouta decides who chairs and sits on that committee and likely supports them with his war chest when they run for reelection. If an aide filed a complaint or went to the media, Wacouta would make sure the woman never worked in Washington again.

"Gloria Brisbois was elected Speaker of the House five years ago, and she rules her kingdom with an iron fist. She's represented the state of New York as a house democrat for the past forty-five years. Being on the Senate side of things figuratively and literally, I don't interact with her much, so there's not a lot more I can add."

"It's said she's had more work done on her face than all four presidents on Mount Rushmore," Li said, and while Eric looked exasperated, Cole reached across the table to fist-bump her.

A knock on the door broke up their laughter, and a security guard walked in carrying three large boxes of pizza. He set them on the table along with plates, forks, and napkins. He smiled at Cole and said, "Not sure this is in my job description."

Cole nodded, "Just take the top pizza down to the crew and carry on. No further lip required, Andy."

When everyone had what they wanted, Cole asked Collin to fill them in on what he knew about the politicians and Beneker.

"I attended Yale University for my undergraduate degree, and Roger Beneker, the fifth, was my roommate throughout those four years. I wasn't a bad student in high school, but Yale was out of my league academically. My dad's money and reputation got me into the school, but Roger kept me there. He wrote some of my papers or found someone else to write them for me. He had access to test answers. Everything I needed to get a diploma. But in the end, it came with strings attached. He wanted me to go into the FBI. He said it would look good when I ended up running for public office down the road. He and his dad called in a couple of favors to get me into the Bureau and to move my career along a little faster than it otherwise would have until I got too full of myself, and Gene here knocked me down a peg. Anyway, in return for the Benekers' help, I got them inside information from time to time." He looked away from Gene when he said this.

Collin looked back at the camera. "A few weeks ago, Roger somehow got me pulled back to D.C., and he invited me to attend a meeting with him at an exclusive club in the city. That was the first time I met Senator Wacouta and Speaker Brisbois. The three of them call themselves the Trinity. Sometime after that, we met again at the U.S. Capitol, and at that meeting, I saw that each of them carried large leather binders. Three-ring binders. I was sitting a distance away, but it was clear from the conversation I overheard that those binders held specific information on senators, representatives, others serving in high-elected offices, and even key Bureaucrats. It's damning information that the Trinity uses to ensure that the votes go their way on the issues that matter to them. They use the dirt that's there already, affairs their colleagues have had, bribes they've taken, hidden family scandals, whatever. Where there is no dirt, they create it. Through honey traps or even the threat of violence. They didn't say it, but I believe that Roger has even had key colleagues and others killed who wouldn't bend to the will of the Trinity."

"Why would they keep that kind of incriminating information in a three-ring binder, for Christ's sake?" Cole asked. "Why not have it on some secure site? It seems old-school, even to me."

"I asked Roger about that," Collin said, "and he told me that the Trinity has been doing this for decades. His grandfather led the Trinity back in the day and neither he nor his father trusted computers when they came along. Roger doesn't trust them either, and he carried on the tradition of recording everything in the leather binders. He told me that older binders were destroyed when they were no longer relevant or useful."

"So, this is about more than simply keeping term limits from happening. It's also about ensuring that the interests of big pharma, the health insurance industry, and their other huge donors are served, regardless of the cost to the nation," Cole said.

"I haven't been in the swamp long," Eric said, "but even I've heard vague rumors about this kind of thing. Veiled references to the deep state or shadow government. I never believed it, though. I never *wanted* to believe it. The sons of bitches are willing to kill programs like Medicare and social security in order to serve their special interests and line their own pockets. They're goddamn parasites, sucking the life from our nation!"

"I'd say more like big, slimy anacondas squeezing the life out of it, but we're mostly in agreement on your assessment," Cole said. "Now, the question is, what do we do about it?" He looked around the room. "On the plus side, we now have two different operators on the inside: Jenny and Collin. We also have a U.S. senator who works in the same building as two-thirds of this unholy Trinity. We have assets. We just need to deploy them wisely."

The room was quiet for a moment, before Jenny offered, "I can get us one of those binders." She turned to Eric. "If you can get me in Senator

Wacouta's office, I can get you a binder."

"What are you thinking?" Cole asked.

"Roger Beneker knows me, of course, and Gloria Brisbois will be immune to my particular charms. But it seems likely Robert Wacouta won't be."

"I could get you into his office," Eric said quickly, catching on. "You could go to the capitol with me, and I could send you to his office. You could say that you're my new aide and that you have a message for the senator's ears and nobody else's. His aides will likely protest, but if Wacouta gets one look at you, he'll take the meeting. Guaranteed."

"I'll take that as a compliment," Jenny said.

"That part sounds simple and straightforward enough, but how do we know he'll have the leather binder with him?" Cole asked.

"We ensure it," Collin said. The St. Francis group turned as one to the screen. "We need them to convene a meeting of the Trinity, which they seem to do whenever one or more of them sees a threat. What we need to do is make them feel threatened somehow. Maybe we let them know that Michele Fields is better and that she's going to start hitting the bookstore and media circuit to talk about her current book and upcoming projects. If they hear that, they'll schedule a meeting of the Trinity, and they'll bring their binders to that meeting."

"No," Cole said, a little too loud and harsh. "I'm not going to set her up as a target or bait. With the power behind this Trinity, nothing we do can guarantee her safety. I'm not taking that chance. There has to be another way."

"I could do it," Eric said. "What if I went to Senator Wacouta's office myself and told him my constituents are demanding that congressional term limits be enacted? I could demand that he bring the measure to the floor of the Senate for a vote. He'll deny me that opportunity, but then I'll tell him that I'm going to call a press conference instead. I'll say that I'm sick and tired of turning my back on the wishes of the people I serve and that I'm fed up with our either ineffective or corrupt Senate leadership. It's the truth, so it wouldn't be hard for me to sound convincing."

"That would sure as hell poke the bear," Li said.

"The portly bear," Lane added.

"So, Eric threatens Wacouta that he's going to the media to rail for term limits and against the ineffectual leadership in Washington," Cole said. "That gets the Texan's dander up enough that he calls the other members of the Trinity to the table. If they work the way they have been lately, Collin, as their henchman, will get a call to attend that meeting; he can alert this team."

"And then between the time the meeting gets set and is actually held, Eric sends me to Senator Wacouta's office to grab the binder," Jenny said.

Cole nodded to the group. "This could work. We get that binder, make some copies, and we should be able to almost dictate to the Trinity where things move from there." He thought things through, "So, how do we safeguard Jenny's family?"

Gene wiped grease from his fingers with a napkin. "I think I can arrange that," he said. "Teddy Beaumont is the current CIA Director. He uses me as a backchannel into the Bureau. We communicate at least every other week because he doesn't have a lot of use for Jim Trudell. Also, since Director Trudell personally pulled the strings to bring Collin back to D.C., we have to assume that he could be compromised himself or he's just too power hungry to be trusted. Regardless, Teddy is a good man, he's got plenty of assets in Mexico, and I think he'll help us. Cole told me how Beneker sends proof of life videos of her family to Jenny every few weeks. That doesn't mean the family is under constant surveillance..." Jenny started to interrupt, and Gene put up his hand and continued, "But we will assume that they are. I'm going to ask Teddy to have a team of his set up in Oaxaca and to be prepared to enter Jenny's family's home secretly in the darkest hours of the morning and then take the family to a safe place until things settle here. Hopefully, they can leave a few agents at the house to surprise the kidnappers if they stop by to check up on the family at some point. I'll let Teddy know what we're up against and that it includes corrupt elements of our own government who could try to take the family back or worse. I'll make sure they don't give the family up under any circumstances until they hear back from me, and I'll ask him to use his most trusted team and to treat the family like his own."

"With a little luck or some help from above," Cole said, looking at Jenny, "you can be reunited with your family when this is all over." She bit her lip, but nodded slightly, and the team knew that she was on board.

Chapter Forty-Five

Michele hadn't been outside the house since leaving the hospital, except for the meeting with the District Attorney in Cole's office. As she healed and grew stronger and more confident, she was also going stir crazy. The FBI agent assigned to protect her took his job seriously and didn't waste many words. He wasn't rude, but Michele wondered if he was worried about being seen as too chummy with the SAC's girlfriend. *Is that what I am*, she wondered? *Significant other, maybe?* They'd never really talked about it. Cole had texted to let her know he was on his way home, and she met him at the door when she heard his key working the deadbolt. Cole thanked the agent who had stayed with Michele and sent him on his way, and he took the glass of Cabernet she offered him.

"Long day?" she said as they walked down the hall to their bedroom. "Did you get anything for dinner?"

Cole told her about the meeting with Gene, Collin, and his local team as he changed into jeans and his favorite Marquette Wrestling sweatshirt. He considered the blue and gold pullover vintage, since he pilfered it the day after his school announced it was terminating the wrestling program he'd captained. Hard to believe that was more than two decades ago now. Cole could tell Michele was looking for conversation, so he suggested they take their wine and sit by the fire in the library.

Cole started a fire, and they snuggled close under a blanket on a loveseat facing the hearth. The flames were small at first but grew larger and friskier as the moments passed. The wood was well seasoned, but escaping steam still caused it to pop and crackle from time to time, as if it had a life of its own. The warmth of the fire and from each other was comforting, and it was Cole who broke the spell, "I thought you wanted to talk?"

"And I thought you needed this," Michele said, nodding toward the fire. "A little peace and quiet does a body good. And I like your body to be good."

He laughed. His arm was around her shoulder, and he pulled her even closer. "What I need is you."

They were quiet a little longer before Michele said, "I'm starting to go a little crazy holed up in this house. I know it's beautiful and all, but I think I'm about ready to resume my book tour. I want to get out in the world and tell my story."

Cole considered that. "I don't want to keep you locked away. I stayed late tonight working with Li, Lane, Ty, Jenny, Gene, and Collin on a plan that we hope will end this thing one way or another. We'll either go back to living our old lives, or we maybe won't be alive at all anymore."

"Aren't you being a little melodramatic?"

He looked at her and then kissed her softly on the lips, before pulling back, "No. I don't think I am."

"Well, in that case, tell me about this plan. Maybe I can help."

Michele was an incredible listener, and she had helped him work through cases since the day they first met. She had a great mind and solved riddles as well as anyone he'd ever worked with. He told her everything now, including about how Jenny had been working for Roger Beneker, sent to catch him in a honey trap.

"So, my man resisted Jenny, even though she threw herself at him repeatedly?"

"I'd say that's a pretty apt description," Cole said, proud of himself, before feeling Michele straighten a little.

"Funny, I don't remember you confiding in me that Jenny was flirting with you so indiscreetly…"

Cole heard a hissing sound from the fireplace and thought the split wood should've been too dry for that. It hissed again. "Well, it was covert flirting, you know? Like, she would stand a little too close, where I could feel her warmth and smell her perfume."

"Feel her warmth?" Michele pulled away from him a little.

Cole was getting flustered. "Did I tell you she wore pumpkin pie perfume to try to entice me?"

Michele laughed out loud. "Pumpkin pie?" She pulled him tight. "I'm just teasing you. If she was doing her best to get you in bed and you resisted her, then you, sir, are my hero."

"No more teasing me!" Cole said, before telling her more about the meeting.

Michele stopped him when he described Collin Jeffers' input. "You telling me that Jeffers had someone help him through college and up the Bureau ladder isn't surprising. What *is* surprising is that you're going to use him to help try to take down his old roommate. I'm not sure that's wise, especially since he leaked Bureau secrets over the years and tried to get you and me killed recently."

"I don't disagree. And I think there are still other members of the team who are unconvinced as well. But I really don't see a way our plan works without his involvement. In Collin and Jenny, we have two insiders working with us. I think that could be the key to David beating Goliath's ass in this fight."

Cole added a few more lengths of birch to the fire, and they settled into a comfortable silence for a while. Cole watched the flames leap and dance and began to grow drowsy until he felt Michele's hand migrate below his waist. Suddenly, he was wide awake. He turned to her, and her eyes reflected a heat that wasn't coming from the fireplace. "I told you I was feeling stronger," she whispered hungrily in his ear. "There must be some way I can reward you for ignoring young Jenny's bold advances, especially at a time when I was unavailable to take care of you in, um, the manner you've grown accustomed to."

Cole kissed her, a deep, lingering kiss. When they came up for air, he said, "I'm sure we can work something out."

Chapter Forty-Six

Jenny was already seated at her desk when Cole arrived at his office three mornings later. He didn't have to look at his skittish wall clock to know that it wasn't yet seven a.m. Milwaukee was an hour ahead of Oaxaca, Mexico, and both he and Jenny knew that her family should be in protective custody by now. CIA Director Teddy Beaumont had agreed to help, and the plan was for a small, elite team to sneak into the Contreras home at three a.m. Oaxaca time, four a.m. Milwaukee time. Beaumont's men would explain the situation to Jenny's mother and father and her sister, Sophia, and the family would then be quietly taken to a safe house that only Beaumont knew about. They would be released upon Beaumont's direct order only. Jenny's brother, Santiago, taught architecture at the private university in Monterrey, eight hundred fifty miles north of his family's estate. He had been approached at the university late the day before and was already at the safe house.

Jenny came into Cole's office. She looked tired, and he could only imagine how restless her night must have been. He hadn't slept well either. "Any word from Director Beaumont yet?" she asked.

Cole shook his head. "Nothing yet. I checked the weather in Oaxaca on my phone late last night, and it was supposed to be overcast for the next twelve hours, with a little rain mixed in. That would've provided perfect cover for the team on the ground. I don't see any reason they would have scrubbed the mission. But keep in mind that this was a delicate operation with a lot of moving parts. The team would have to enter your family home without being seen and then wake up your parents and Sophia without raising an alarm. Then they would have to tell them a convincing story about how the little girl they thought they'd lost more than a decade ago is alive and needs their cooperation. Imagine that! It would be traumatic, to say the least. And if all that goes smoothly and your family agrees, they would need to be moved to a safe house some distance away. There's no way Beaumont would put them up somewhere else in Oaxaca. It's not a small city by any means, but it's also not large. The whole operation would take some time. We just need to be patient."

Jenny nodded. She understood the logistics in her head, but her body betrayed her. For someone who was typically calm, cool, and collected, he could tell that she was barely holding it together. She went to Cole's window and looked out over the big lake and the low-hanging clouds that shrouded the sunrise. Brilliant rays of light pierced the gray swirls in places, like the sparks of hope she felt but didn't trust. She turned to Cole to ask another question when his desk phone chirped. Cole held up a finger and stabbed his phone's speaker button. "Huebsch here!"

"Cole, this is Teddy Beaumont. We have Jenny's family. They're all together and safe."

"That's fantastic," Cole said as Jenny's hands flew to her face, and she teared up. The dam she had built over the years to hold in her pain and sorrow was close to bursting.

"I have Jenny's family on a conference line," Beaumont said. "They want to speak to her. I'll patch them in now."

"Juana? Juana? Are you really there, child?" Jenny's mom's halting question was a mix of disbelief and hope. Her voice softened and quavered, "Juana?"

Cole looked at Jenny. He assumed 'Juana' was a pet name used by the family. Jenny's face was red, and she held her hands clasped over her heart while tears streamed down her face. She tried to answer but couldn't find either the breath or the words.

"Mrs. Contreras, this is FBI special agent Cole Huebsch. Jenny is right here with me. This is very emotional for her, as I'm sure you can imagine."

"I understand," she said, struggling to find the right words. "Juana, te amamos cariño!" *We love you, Darling!*

Jenny shook her head, tears raining down on the carpet, before crying out, "*Mamá! Mamá!*"

Six hours later, Cole and Jenny were seated in Eric's private office inside the U.S. Capitol. Jenny had been exhausted from lack of sleep and the heart-wrenching phone call with her family, and she slept the entire flight from Milwaukee's Mitchell Field to Ronald Reagan International Airport in Arlington, Virginia. Eric had just left to execute the next phase of their plan, to confront Senator Wacouta, and they were alone in the solemn room with their thoughts.

Cole looked at Jenny and noticed her head was bowed and her eyes were closed. Her lips were moving almost imperceptibly as she offered up a silent prayer. He knew that she had lived some hard years and done some despicable things during that time, but when he watched her now, he saw that not all of her softness, her innocence, had been stolen from her. She made the sign of the cross and looked his way, catching him watching her. She smiled at him, and he smiled back. He saw her now not as a temptress, but more as a loving daughter. He knew she had given up everything, especially her freedom, to safeguard her family all those years ago. He saw a strength in her, too.

"I never asked you before, but why did your mother call you Juana?"

Her smile grew, "That's my name. It's Spanish for Joan or Jane. 'Jenny' was given to me by Beneker."

"I noticed you said a prayer. I've been trying to get closer to God myself lately," Cole said. He thought about it more, and another idea struck him. "You know, you reminded me of someone, just before, when you were praying. You made me think of Joan of Arc. She was a young woman, too, and it's been said that she prayed in a little chapel before leading French troops into battle against the English. That chapel is in Milwaukee, and it's named after her."

Jenny's brows knitted in confusion. "Why would this young French woman pray in a chapel in Milwaukee before going to battle against the English?"

Cole laughed. "No! No! I'm sorry. This took place back in the early 1400s in a little chapel in a town just south of Lyon, France. That simple but perfect chapel was taken apart centuries later and moved to New York and then to Milwaukee. It was rebuilt at my alma mater, Marquette University, in 1966. I was just there not too long ago, trying to get a little closer to God."

Jenny was interested. "You say I remind you of Joan of Arc and the way she prayed before her battle against the English. How did that turn out for her? Were her prayers answered?"

He stalled for a moment, considering his words, "She led the French army to a decisive and improbable victory on the battlefield."

Jenny could sense that he wasn't telling her the whole story. "Did this Juana live happily ever after?"

"No," Cole admitted. 'She died a martyr at a young age. But she was a hero and became a saint."

"So she's got that going for her, which is nice," Jenny said in her best Bill Murray, Carl Spackler impression.

Cole laughed, "I wouldn't have taken you for a *Caddyshack* aficionado."

"Beneker had his people teach me golf," she said, sobering again. "He thought it would be an important skill that could help me get closer to some affluent men. He wasn't wrong about that." She looked at Cole more closely, her eyes welling. "I'm no saint, you know. I have lain with men and stolen their secrets. Maybe their souls. I ruined lives for sure. All to satisfy the devil."

"You did what you did to save your family." He thought about Al DeMario and his daughter. "Seems to be a lot of that going around lately."

At about that time, elsewhere in the same building, Eric was finally called into the Senate Majority Leader's private office. He'd been cooling his heels in the man's outer office for fifteen minutes. Wacouta didn't get up as the junior senator strode into his office and closed the door behind him. "What do you need, Senator Rhodes? What brings you barreling into my offices without the courtesy of an appointment?"

"I'd like to say that I'm sorry for disturbing you, but that would be a damn lie," Eric came out swinging. "I'm here to demand that you bring a vote on setting Congressional term limits before the full Senate. And do it now!

The latest polls are showing that almost nine out of every ten voters across both parties want term limits for their U.S. senators and representatives." He was carrying a sheaf of papers, and he removed the paperclip from them; he tossed them on Wacouta's desk and watched them spill onto his lap and the floor. "These are just a few of the emails I've received from constituents recently. For each of those, I've probably got another thirty or fifty I could have thrown at you. But I don't want to bury you in paper. I'm tired of ignoring the people of Wisconsin and across this great nation. The Senate hasn't held a vote on term limits since 1995, and it's time we did something about it."

Eric kept his eyes on Senator Wacouta during his fiery speech and worried he might have pushed him too hard. He saw the man's face darken and the lines around his eyes and mouth grow deeper. He could almost see smoke puffing from the Texan's ears. He wanted to push him to the breaking point, but not give him a coronary.

Wacouta sputtered as he rose from his creaky leather chair. "How dare you talk to me like that? You really think you can come in here and *demand* any goddamn thing you want? No! You can come in my office on your knees and *beg* for something, but you don't come in here huffing and puffing and telling me what the hell to goddamn do. Understood?"

Eric shook his head and sneered at Wacouta. He had to make sure he rattled the old crook. "I understand that's the way you want it, but I'm not playing your game anymore. Are you going to bring term limits to the floor of the Senate for a vote or not?"

"The answer is, 'Not.' No fucking way!" Wacouta sneered back.

Eric nodded, his smile now more of a snarl. "Good. I prefer it this way. Now, I can take this to the press and directly to the people. I picked up millions of followers on social media after I spoke at my party's national convention. And I'm kind of a media darling these days, too. So, I'll bring my demand for congressional term limits directly to the American people, and I'll start with a press conference on the steps of this building tomorrow. You can rest assured that I'll hammer home the fact that eighty-seven percent of the voters want term limits, that it is the will of the people, and that you are *personally* standing in the way of seeing them enacted. I'll paint you as either ignorant or shady, and you'll get a chance to explain to the people which one you actually are." He leaned toward the older man. "Between ignorant or shady, if I were you, I'd choose all of the above."

Eric turned on his heels and strode out of the room while Wacouta sputtered. The older man's vile shouts faded into the background as Eric walked down the wide hall on his way back to his office. He was nervous but also excited. The fuse on the bomb they'd planted was lit. A big smile spread across his face. He had poked the bear, and he had poked him hard!

Chapter Forty-Seven

Eric was ensconced in his private office with Jenny and Cole fifteen minutes later, and he had just finished regaling the two with the story of how he had challenged the Speaker. "Man, by the time I left his office, he was livid. I've never even heard of some of the cuss words that he let loose at me when I turned my back on him and walked out. When I leave the Senate, I can move to Hollywood, because that was an Oscar-worthy performance!"

Cole was about to ask a question when his phone chimed. He picked up when he saw the caller. "Hey, Collin. I've got you on speaker here with Eric and Jenny. Go ahead."

"I just got off the phone with Roger. The Trinity is meeting tonight at seven at the Cosmopolitan Club. I don't know what Eric said to Wacouta, but it must have been pretty convincing. The old windbag told Roger he wants Eric killed."

"Makes me both proud and scared shitless, truth be told," Eric said.

"You've only got a few hours before that seven p.m. meeting," Collin said. "If Jenny's going to try to grab Wacouta's leather binder, she's going to have to do it soon. He usually gets to the club early and has a belt or two of insanely expensive bourbon before he heads to the meeting room."

Jenny stood up and straightened her red dress. It was a little shorter and showed more cleavage than the typical female Senate aide wore, but it didn't cross the line into scandalous. It was her stunning face and figure that attracted attention more than the amount of skin she exposed. She picked up a large leather cognac-colored tote bag and slung it over her shoulder.

Watching her, Cole envisioned a young soldier slinging her rifle over her shoulder before heading into battle. Or a young woman heading out to lead her French troops against the English long ago. She showed no fear or hesitation, only a belief in herself and her cause. "I'm ready."

Wacouta's offices resembled a hornet's nest that had recently been hit with a stick when Jenny walked in minutes later. The door to the senator's private office was open, and aides were buzzing in and out as he bellowed orders from somewhere inside. A young woman sitting at the desk nearest the door stopped Jenny as soon as she stepped through the threshold from the hallway. She looked to be still in college, maybe interning, and her face was bright red. She was obviously flustered. She didn't ask what Jenny wanted, saying instead, "You might want to leave and come back some other time. The senator has a lot going on right now."

An even louder shout came from Wacouta's inner office, and the young receptionist's cheeks glowed.

"I'm from Senator Eric Rhodes' office," Jenny said, reaching into her tote and pulling out two pages stapled together. "He asked me to hand-deliver this press release to Senator Wacouta."

"Leave them and run," the young woman said. But Jenny shook her head stubbornly. "I can't do that. Senator Rhodes was very specific. I'm supposed to deliver this press release to Senator Wacouta personally and not leave until I'm sure he's reviewed it." She stuffed the papers back into the satchel.

A grumpy-looking but sharp-dressed woman in her sixties stepped forward. "I'm Cassandra Owens, senior aide to the Majority Leader, and you've got some nerve coming in here making demands of my staff!" She had borne the brunt of Wacouta's anger since Senator Rhodes had stormed out of the offices earlier, and she believed in the old adage, *Shit rolls downhill*.

Jenny kept her composure, however, flashing her best smile at Owens while clutching the bag to her side. "I'm sorry if my timing is inconvenient, but Senator Rhodes will be delivering these remarks here on the Capitol steps tomorrow, and he's sure that the majority leader will want to review them before then." She stood waiting patiently.

Jenny's calm pushed Owens' buttons, and she screamed, "Get the hell out of this office! Now!"

Jenny stood, unflustered, her smile widening if anything until Wacouta stuck his head out of his room like a tortoise sticking his neck out of his shell. He was curious to see who had the gall to scream even louder than he was. When he saw the attractive young woman standing in front of his aides, he called out, "What's going on here?" The bustle ceased immediately.

Owens glared at Jenny, not even bothering to turn around as she answered her boss, "This impudent young lady is an aide to Senator Rhodes. A flunky! She says he sent her here with implicit instructions to hand-deliver a press release to you and to stay here while you read it. I told her politely to fuck the hell off!" She screamed the last bit.

Wacouta licked his lips obscenely, "Nonsense. Send her back. I'd like to see what my esteemed colleague has to say."

Jenny stepped around Owens and marched straight back to Wacouta's private office with her head held high and her eyes straight ahead. She followed the senator into his lair, feeling several sets of eyes bore into her back until he shut the door behind them. They were alone. She immediately scanned the room and saw the leather binder on a shelf behind the senator's enormous desk. She walked around the desk, pulled the press release from her tote, and set it on the blotter. She stood next to the desk chair, inviting Wacouta to come sit down. He did, the chair creaking as he settled in, his eyes level with Jenny's breasts and mere inches away. He breathed a lusty breath.

Jenny said softly, "If you'll just take a look at the, um, press release, I can assure Senator Rhodes that you've read it and let you get back to your busy schedule."

Wacouta willed his gaze upward and looked into Jenny's dark brown eyes. They pulled him in. Jenny had employed these skills more times in the past than she wanted to remember, but she was sure that Wacouta's face was the most disgusting, the vilest, she had ever stared at. But instead of revulsion, her eyes hinted at the opposite, and Wacouta licked his lips involuntarily again. *He looks like the effing illegitimate offspring of a donkey and a toad,* she thought, while forcing herself to lean against the man's shoulder.

Wacouta turned and scanned the document on his desk, anxious to return his attention to the young aide. He felt his blood start to boil as he read the junior senator's words. He forced his anger down, knowing he would get his revenge on Rhodes soon enough. While he was reading, he didn't notice Jenny's slender arm reach behind them and slide the binder into her tote. When he finished reviewing the release, he looked up, and Jenny stepped away from him and toward the door. The senator looked surprised, "Where the hell do you think you're going in such a hurry?"

"Sorry, senator," she said, opening the door and pausing before leaving, "But I've got to go. Big plans for the night and all that!" She left Wacouta's offices and took the first public exit out of the building. Eric and Cole were waiting for her there in a dark SUV, and they took off as soon as she got in. The Senate Majority Leader noticed his binder missing ten minutes later, but by the time he arrived at Eric's office flanked by four members of the Capitol Police force, the offices were locked, with a hastily written sign on the door that read, *Closed for the Day. Enjoy your Evening!*

When Senator Wacouta read the words on Eric's door, his rage turned to panic. At the same time, Cole and the rest of the SUV's occupants were riding an elevator in the FBI's headquarters in the J. Edgar Hoover building a mile west of the Capitol Building. Gene had met them at the door and took them to the building's print shop. He badged them in and nodded at the receptionist. "Hey, Carl!" Then, he led them directly to a copier the size of a small car. "This baby's one of the baddest printers on the planet," he said. "It spits out nearly one hundred pages a minute."

Eric undid the clasp and opened the binder. He popped open the three rings and handed the pages to Gene. He knew a ream of typing paper was five hundred pages, and he guessed there were at least three hundred or so that he handed over to the deputy director. Gene set them in the machine, punched a couple of buttons, and the copier came alive, shivering as it made two copies of each original in little more than a second.

Cole ended up holding the empty binder, "Wow! When I heard three-ring binder, I pictured something cheap. But this leather's awesome. I think it might be Italian." The only thing on the binder cover was an embossed

Trinity symbol that represented the cycle of life, and Cole traced it with a finger. "Seriously, this is really cool. You gotta let me have this when it's all said and done, Gene."

Gene just shook his head. He had asked Carl for privacy, and the area near them had been cleared of staff, but the four of them still stood in a tight circle as the mechanical beast did its work. The rapid *pht, pht, pht, pht* noise would also shield their conversation. "We have to figure out what we do with the copies once we get done here," Gene said.

"Take them up to the director's office and bring him up to speed?" Cole asked, but with more doubt than conviction.

"Maybe," Gene said. "But let's take a look at what's in there first. Trudell's never been a guy to cause a ruckus, and if this stuff is as explosive as we think it is, it'll do just that."

"Yeah," Cole chuckled. "Like the first test of the atomic bomb in Los Alamos caused a ruckus."

"Holy shit, I remember reading about that," Eric said, "The code name for that test was 'Trinity.'"

"So, we'll call this little operation 'Trinity' then," Cole said, "because if we screw it up it'll cause a big bang heard around the world."

Eric said, "What if Gene keeps the original, and we give one copy to Fox News and one to the *New York Times*? One conservative media outlet and one liberal. At some point, Fox will likely share the dirt with the *Times*' more conservative print competition, and the *Times* will share it with the more liberal television media. We let the jackals off their leashes, and the cow chips fall where they may. Between them, they'll rip into every one of the indiscretions outlined in these pages and expose the truth."

"I don't know," Cole said. "From what Collin overheard, there are at least one hundred senators and representatives and other high-level politicians whose careers will end if and when the news comes out. Think about what would happen to Congress if they had dozens and dozens of their ranks walk the plank at the same time."

Eric thought about it. "I see what you're saying. Our government could limp along, but a lot of people across the country would lack representation for a period of time. I believe in all but four states, the governors would pick someone to fill out the term of the ousted senators and representatives, or until a vote could be held. That's not the will of the people; that's the will of one man or woman who each has their own priorities and prejudices."

They mulled that over before Eric said. "Let's face it, the people of this country don't trust Congress today." He pointed to the copier, "If we release these documents to the press, set off that bomb, then I don't know how the people will ever trust their elected officials again. Not in our lifetimes. Maybe not in two or three lifetimes."

Jenny had been quiet, but she couldn't hold her tongue anymore. "It sounds like you guys are considering just walking away from this whole thing now. After the Trinity has undermined the country for decades and attacked some of us and those we love personally."

"There could be another way out of this," Cole said, "I think it would end in a better result, but it's not going to be perfect."

Eric and Gene had been pulling the copies as they'd been coming off the press and skimming them. Before Cole could describe his plan, they made eye contact and said together, "We need to get the hell out of here now!"

Chapter Forty-Eight

Roger Beneker seethed as he sat in the same intimate private dining room inside the Cosmopolitan Club where the Trinity had met weeks earlier. A fire roared in the hearth, but Beneker burned hotter. Representative Gloria Brisbois sat next to him at the table, swiping through her phone, while Beneker's lapdog, Special Agent Collin Jeffers, sat on an overstuffed chair near the fireplace. Jeffers was to be seen but not heard. Senator Wacouta was twenty minutes late for their meeting, and the kingmaker wasn't used to being kept waiting. He swirled a rare twenty-five-year-old bourbon in a cut crystal glass and wasn't sure if the fire caught by the amber liquid was reflected from the hearth or his own eyes. He said to no one in particular, "Where is that tired old fuck?"

Brisbois looked up from her phone, "With any luck, he's had a heart attack and died a gruesome death." She raised her wine glass, "To his wondrous but untimely passing!"

The door burst open at that moment, and Senator Wacouta stumbled in as if on cue, pulling the door closed behind him before the club's staff could do the honors. "Well, there's another sweet dream dashed," Brisbois said, downing the rest of her wine in one gulp.

All eyes in the room were on Wacouta, and it was obvious he was out of breath. He took in big gulps of air as he mopped his brow with a napkin. Beneker was about to yell at the old fool when he noticed the man's pale complexion and the fat beads of sweat collecting on his forehead. Wacouta's tie was loosened, and his top shirt button undone, as if he'd been choking. "Where the hell have you been?" Beneker asked, his voice low but threatening.

"You asked for this meeting to discuss a press conference on term limits that Senator Rhodes is holding tomorrow. Is it really that difficult for you to keep your people in line?"

Wacouta waved the air in front of him absently. "I've, I've…I'm afraid I've misplaced my leather binder." He slumped into his chair, looking down at his hands.

Beneker squinted at him. "What? How the hell could that happen? Do you have any idea what will ensue if that binder ends up in the wrong hands? How do you 'misplace' something that important?"

Wacouta's face mottled, shifting chameleon-like from clammy to ashen. "I don't know for certain, but I, I'm afraid that an aide from Senator Rhodes' office took it."

"Let me guess, and this is just wild speculation on my part," Brisbois spat, "The aide was *young* and *female*." She drew the words out, and when Wacouta averted her gaze, she added, "How fucking pathetic!"

Beneker held a concealed carry permit and didn't go many places without his Sig Sauer pistol snugged inside his shoulder holster. He wanted nothing more right now than to pull the Sig and put two rounds through the senator's thick and apparently empty skull. He was picturing that image when the door opened again, and Eric Rhodes walked in with Cole Huebsch. The two men went directly to the table and sat down as if they had been invited.

"Sorry we're so late to the party, guys," Cole said. "We didn't want to keep you waiting. But we had copies to make. Speed reading to do. You get the picture."

"That's one hell of a good read, Roger," Eric said, pointing to the binder in front of Beneker. "We think it has the potential to be best-seller material. It's got everything a good thriller needs, including murder, mayhem, and villains galore. The only thing missing is a hero. But Cole and I are here to rectify that."

An open bottle of Chateau Petrus sat next to Representative Brisbois' empty wine glass. Cole picked up her glass,poured a generous amount of the Bordeaux, and swirled it around the bowl before taking a healthy gulp. "I hope you don't mind, Gloria, but I couldn't help myself. I don't often get the chance to drink wine this exquisite." He set the glass back down and smacked his lips. "I just hope to God I don't catch your cooties!"

Brisbois started to complain, but Cole shut her down, talking over her, "There's been a slight change in the agenda for tonight's meeting. After reviewing the binder, we actually see a way out of this for the two of you," he said, looking from Brisbois to Wacouta. "A happy ending, actually. Instead of Eric holding a press conference tomorrow to tell the public about the critical need for term limits, you two will hold it jointly."

When the two members of Congress began their protests, Cole cut them off. Steel replaced his nonchalance. "This isn't negotiable. You not only tell the public that you've heard them and will call a vote on term limits within a week, but you're also going to tell them that you'll be stepping down, vacating your seats as soon as the measure passes."

Wacouta stood up abruptly, "If you think we're going to just walk away after all our years serving this country, then you're out of your goddamn mind!"

"Sit down, senator," Cole said coldly, waiting until he complied before continuing. "All your years of self-service aside, your only other option is to go to jail for murder, blackmail, and fraud. Multiple counts of each. And thank you for keeping such meticulous notes, by the way. So, instead of enjoying your ill-begotten gains, you'll rot in a federal penitentiary or be put to death for treason."

"If anyone asks me, I think you two should be put to death for treason," Eric said. "I'm a bit of a history buff, and I don't believe this great country of ours has executed anybody for treason since 1953. In that case, Julius and Ethel Rosenberg were convicted of passing nuclear secrets to the Soviets during the Cold War. I believe what the pair of you have been up to these last few decades is even worse than the Rosenbergs' sins. And they both got the chair. Old sparky. I guess Julius died pretty easy, but Ethel was one tough bird. She had to be shocked five times, and it's said there was smoke coming from her head before her heart finally stopped beating!"

Cole looked back and forth between the two legislators as he let that sink in, "Can you believe that shit?" He took another sip of the wine. "If you two are honest with yourselves, you know you don't have a whole lot of good years left regardless of what happens. If you do this the way we're describing, you'll go out as patriots. Rich patriots at that. But if you decide to turn down our offer, then we'll share the contents of the binder with the media, and you'll go out in disgrace." He finished the wine, "Seems like a fairly easy decision to me."

Beneker could see the other two-thirds of the Trinity breaking. They were caving and would take the deal. In a few short minutes, they had morphed from the biggest, baddest bullies into sniveling cowards. He loathed them more than ever. "And why would you offer them this deal if it was so great? Why not just turn them in and have them pay for their crimes?" he asked Cole with distaste. "Let me guess, you admire them too much."

"No," Cole said. "That's not it. In my opinion, they're two of the lowest life forms to ever crawl the face of planet Earth. Just above you, but well below cockroaches and the larvae that live in cow shit, in fact. But the thing is, I love my country. And if these two and half the House and Senate all go to jail at the same time, well, chaos would rain down on our heads. The voters don't trust Congress now, and if all this goes public, they never will again. If the good senator and representative here announce that they're moving ahead on term limits and they resign together to show that it's time to let others step up and lead, it sends a very different and more positive message."

"And what about me?" Beneker asked.

"You resign from your firm and shutter it. Close the doors and walk away. You can sell the building, the furniture, and any incidentals, but not your client list or anything else."

"I took everything I learned from four generations of Benekers before me and built Capitol Gains from the ground up. I have no intention of giving it up so easily." With that, he pulled his Sig and leveled it at Cole. "I could just shoot you with this handgun that I legally carry and be done with it. But let me paint another scenario instead. You've been under a lot of stress lately. You and people you care about have been violently attacked. Something inside you snapped, and you broke into this meeting deranged, threatening two of our leading legislators and a junior senator. FBI Special Agent Collin Jeffers heroically stopped what will be described as an assassination attempt by shooting you, and, unfortunately, Senator Rhodes was caught in the crossfire." He nodded toward Collin without taking his eyes off Cole. "Agent Jeffers, this is where you spring into action."

Jeffers slowly reached inside his jacket and pulled out his handgun, pointing it at Cole. Cole had faced Collin on the FBI shooting range before and knew the agent was an expert marksman. He wouldn't miss from across the table. His hold was steady on Cole's center mass, and Cole knew that if he went for his gun, he would be shot dead long before he could pull his Glock. He second-guessed himself for trusting Collin but knew that without his inside help, they would've had no chance to bring down the Trinity. He thought to himself, *I can live with death* and smiled at the absurdity of it all. But regret quickly enveloped him as he realized that his naivety would cause him to not only forfeit his own life but that of Senator Rhodes, an amazing friend, family man, and one of the few politicians left in the world who was actually worth a damn. And he would never see Michele again, never hear her voice, see her face, or feel her touch. All these feelings and thoughts swirled through him in a moment's time, and a resigned sadness settled over him like an uncomfortable weight.

But instead of shooting Cole, Collin nodded slightly toward him and then turned his gun on Beneker. "Sorry, Roger, but you've steered me down the wrong road for more than half my life, and I'm getting off right here. Put the gun down, and we'll all walk away from this alive." He patted the outer breast pocket of his suit jacket. "I've been recording this meeting the whole time in case we needed additional evidence. It's overkill, I know."

Beneker's eyes flicked back and forth between Cole and Collin, "You ungrateful shit!" he said to Jeffers. He started gesturing wildly with his gun hand. "I can't believe you don't have my back after all my family and I have done for you!" Without aiming, he snapped off two shots, the first one hitting Collin in the shoulder and the second missing low, Cole thought, as he pulled his Glock from his hip holster and put three bullets into Beneker's center mass before Beneker could turn fully on him.

Beneker dropped to the floor immediately, and Cole knew he was dead. His pistol tumbled from his hand and onto the table, where it banged loudly before spinning idly between Brisbois and Wacouta. Both of their hands were on the table, within easy reach of the Sig. Cole was already moving to help Collin when he saw the crooked senator and representative exchange a confused look. "Just give me a chance to kill you two," Cole said over his shoulder, and Brisbois and Wacouta both pulled their hands into their laps like they'd been singed. Cole knelt by Collin, who was slumped in his chair. "Don't worry about the shoulder," he said, grabbing a clean white cloth napkin and putting pressure on the wound. "I took one in almost the exact same spot a while back, and it wasn't that bad. I mean, it was a pain and all. Don't get me wrong. But nothing you can't live with."

He thought his fellow agent might smile a little, even through the pain. Instead, he looked down, and Cole noticed blood pumping freely from his groin area. "Aw shit," Cole said, trying to slow the blood loss. It didn't take a physician to tell that the second bullet had hit an artery, and there was no way Collin would survive much longer.

Collin looked at Cole, "I should've put him down. I can't believe he got the better of me." His breathing was ragged, and his body convulsed. Cole pressed the napkin to his groin, knowing it was hopeless.

"Beneker wasn't better than you in any way," Cole said. "And you just took a bullet, two actually, for us. That's hero shit. And everybody likes a story of redemption, of the comeback guy. That's you."

He finally saw the smile of acknowledgment he was looking for in Collin's eyes, right before they blinked for the last time.

When two members of the club's security staff burst through the doors, Eric told them to call an ambulance. Cole stood up and showed them his FBI credentials, and told them to leave. By the time the EMTs and the D.C. cops showed up, the four surviving members of that meeting had their stories straight. Roger Beneker, the fifth, had gone crazy this evening and had tried to shoot two senators and a member of the House of Representatives. FBI Special Agent Collin Jeffers pulled his gun to stop Beneker but was shot twice in defense of the legislators. He died on the scene, in the line of duty, and his brave actions gave Special Agent Cole Huebsch the time he needed to pull his service weapon and put down Beneker.

Miraculously, the story held up, and the next afternoon, Cole stood on the steps of the Capitol with Eric and watched the historic Brisbois/Wacouta press conference. It was a mob scene, with every national media outlet represented. They were joined by thousands of other curious onlookers, both tourists and D.C. residents alike, who were drawn to the circus-like atmosphere. The two legislators hadn't leaked the content of their speeches, but the press knew that the two old political warriors never agreed on anything, and they had fought each other publicly for decades. The joint press conference was unprecedented and would be newsworthy regardless of the content. But nobody anticipated it would knock the national news cycle off its axis for the better part of the next year.

Wacouta stood shoulder to shoulder at the podium with Brisbois, and Cole thought they both looked younger somehow and, for lack of a better word, more dignified. He hoped it was because they were on the right side again after being on the wrong side for so long. "Good afternoon. Thank you all for coming," the senator began, "We're here today because the two of us had a close call last night. The speaker and I faced death up close and personal, and it caused us to think long and hard about how we are living our lives and how we are conducting the business of this great nation of ours."

Representative Brisbois leaned into the microphone. "For too long, both democrats and republicans have been at each other's throats. Instead of looking for ways to help our fellow countrymen, we've looked for ways to shame or dishonor our political opponents. We talk nonstop about how we will *fight* for our constituents and our beliefs, instead of talking about how we will *work* together for the betterment of mankind." She looked at the senator, "Today, Senator Wacouta and I want to put an end to partisanship in the extreme, and with our combined strength to push the pendulum back to where it's on the side of cooperation."

Wacouta leaned toward the mic again, and though it had been choreographed to the second, the back and forth between the two seemed natural.

"Gloria and I are committing that one week from today, we will bring to a vote in both houses of Congress a bill on term limits for U.S. senators and representatives. We will propose a maximum of two six-year terms for senators and four two-year terms for our representatives...and we will win the two-thirds majority we need to carry the day!"

The throng of reporters erupted with questions, but the questions were drowned out by the loud and spontaneous applause of the other people on hand. Brisbois shouted into the microphone, "Please! Please! We're almost through here, and we've got something else we'd like to say!" When the crowd quieted, she continued, "There has not been a vote on congressional term limits in either House of Congress in thirty years, even though we've known throughout that whole time that this is the desire of our nation's residents." She pointed to the massive domed Capitol behind her, "We know that nearly nine out of ten voters across the country want to see term limits enacted for those of us elected to serve in this hallowed building, and the senator and I are tired of subverting the will of the people." When the crowd broke out in applause again, she raised both hands over her head and brought them back to attention. "We know that this measure will not be popular with all of our colleagues in Congress. Everyone serving has worked hard to get to where they're at, and many will likely not want to give it up. Because of this, Robert and I have decided to set an example."

She turned to Wacouta, and he said, "Gloria and I have decided that one week from now, after passing the historic congressional term limit vote in both Houses by the required supermajority, that we will resign from not just our leadership positions, but our legislative seats. If that kind of personal sacrifice and servant leadership doesn't sway our fellow senators and representatives, I don't know what will!" As he finished those words, a super formation of twelve performance fighter jets, six from the Navy's Blue Angels and six from the Air Force's Thunderbirds, almost clipped the top of the bronze Statue of Freedom atop the Capitol as they screamed low over the heads of the gathering.

The crowd's roar equaled that of the jets' engines, and the reporters could only read Wacouta's lips when he announced they would take no questions before he linked arms with Brisbois and turned and walked into the Capitol building.

"Sweet Jesus!" Cole yelled. "Those flyovers make the hairs stand up on the back of my neck every time!"

Eric couldn't hear his friend over all the noise, but he knew what he was feeling. He stood on the steps, the afternoon sun warming him, basking in the glow of something even deeper. He turned to Cole with a smile on his lips and nodded toward the jets as they faded into the distance, "It pays to have friends on the Armed Services Committee."

"That it does," Cole agreed. "And I have to say, it almost seemed like those two old curmudgeons believed the words that were coming out of their mouths. That was one hell of a kick-ass speech. Historic even!"

Eric laughed. "You're only saying that because I wrote the damn thing!"

Chapter Forty-Nine

Gene Olson had watched the press conference alongside FBI Director Jim Trudell. The windows of Trudell's office shook as the fighter jets raced by, signaling its end.

"Holy shit!" Trudell said. "I don't think anybody saw that coming. That'll cause more turbulence around here than those super hornets and fighting falcons combined!"

"You couldn't be more right about that," Gene said, and something in his tone caused Trudell to turn to him. "And the next bit of it is going to be your resignation." Before Trudell could protest in earnest, Gene shared a few of the indiscretions that the Trinity binders held on the director and told him there were even more that he didn't want to get into. "If you want to avoid being convicted of treason, you'll resign and recommend to the president that I succeed you."

"So, it's blackmail then, is it? This is just a power play."

"Think what you want, but there were a couple of other Bureau names in the binder, and someone is going to have to do the house cleaning around here that you didn't have the guts to. Or maybe you were just too dirty yourself to clean up other messes. Either way, resign however you want. Tell the president you want to enjoy retirement, or say you've got health issues you need to deal with. I don't care, other than that you do it now, or the information I just shared will be leaked to the national media, and the jackals will be on you before you know it. All I can say is, that won't end well."

Trudell apparently agreed, because before the day was out, he sent both his resignation and his recommendation of Gene as his successor over to the White House. They hadn't found any evidence in the binder that the Executive Branch was involved in the scandal. President Charla E. Howard had won as another businessperson promising to "drain the swamp," and she would never know how much dredging Gene, Cole, Eric, and the team had accomplished toward that end in just a few days' work.

Over the course of the next six days, Cole, Eric, and Gene worked with Senator Wacouta and Representative Brisbois. They started early in the morning and ended late at night, meeting individually with the one hundred thirty-six members of Congress whose names and indiscretions appeared in the pages of the binders. The most egregious offenders were given the choice of resigning or having their sins made public. Whether through cowardice or a change of heart, all twenty-eight in that category agreed to resign. To a person, they understood that it was clearly better to keep their pensions and benefits than to forfeit them and likely end up in jail. As Cole put it, "Would you rather share a ten by twelve-foot cell with a stinky roomie, or enjoy your money and your freedom in the place of your choosing?" Unsurprisingly, each and every one of them ended up choosing option two.

The other legislators who ended up in the binders had mostly been victims of entrapment themselves. They'd been caught in honey traps like the ones Jenny set, or they'd been set up to take a bribe. These politicians were told that if they voted for term limits and used their influence to help get their colleagues to vote the same, they would be given a clean slate. A mulligan. And any evidence of their misconduct would be destroyed. Again, they had a one hundred percent acceptance rate.

With their work finished, Cole, Eric, and Gene met together in Eric's office. "Any chance Brisbois and Wacouta back out at the last minute? Pull some kind of fast one?" Cole asked.

"I don't think so," Eric said. "The two of them are rotten bastards, but they've gotten a taste for what it's like to really lead these past few days, to be admired for doing something good, and I think they actually like the feeling."

"I suppose it would feel good not to look in the mirror every morning and despise yourself," Cole said.

Gene and Cole shook Eric's hand, before leaving his office, thanking him for putting his neck on the line to help them. Eric pulled Cole in for a man hug, and Cole hugged him back tightly. It had been a hell of a few weeks.

As they walked to Gene's waiting SUV, Gene asked Cole if he would consider joining him in Washington. "Maybe take my old spot. More than ever, I could use someone beside me who I know has the best interests of his country at heart. Someone who has my back at the same time."

"I'll always have your back, Gene. But I think more than ever, there's no place like home."

Epilogue

"Growth and comfort do not coexist." – Ginni Rometty

Cole sat at the table in his office the next day with Li and Lane, cradling his mug of hot coffee and watching C-Span as the U.S. Senate began its historic vote on term limits. The House had passed what was now called the Brisbois/Wacouta amendment overwhelmingly earlier that morning, carrying the day with four hundred and two yeas against just twenty-nine nays. They were anxious to see Eric's name called and to hear his loud 'yea' for Wisconsin.

Lane reached for the empty leather Trinity binder Cole had left in the middle of the table as a souvenir of sorts. He traced his fingers along the Trinity logo and felt the fine leather. "This is awesome. Reminds me of the distressed leather you might find on a nice saddle."

"And without the smell of horse poop," Li added.

Before Cole could add to the banter, his cell phone vibrated. He checked it and saw that Jenny was FaceTiming him. He swiped to answer, and her smiling face filled his screen. "Hey!" he said. "I'm assuming you're back home with your family!"

"I am. Thanks to you and the CIA Director."

Cole heard laughter and the loud back and forth of a joyous family and watched as Jenny stepped out onto a porch awash in dappled sunshine in order to hear him better.

"Is everything good?" Cole asked.

She nodded, "Better than good. A few bad guys entered my parents' home after the family was moved to the safe house. The men were watching the house and hadn't seen any activity for a couple of days, so they checked it out. Beaumont's men took them down and interrogated them. It turns out they were members of a local cartel. Director Beaumont leveraged the hostages to set up a meeting with the leader of the cartel and had his men explain the situation to him. They told *el jefe* that the man who had been paying the cartel to keep an eye on the Contreras family was dead and that no more payments would be made. And they told him that if any harm befell my family that the Director of the CIA himself would hold them directly responsible. I don't think my parents will have any further trouble."

Cole smiled, thinking that the director had paraphrased John Wayne's Big Jake character himself. He thought it would likely work just as effectively for Teddy Beaumont as it had for the Duke and for him when he'd used it with Collin. "I'm glad everything turned out."

"Thank you, again."

"No problem," Cole said, sensing Jenny had something else on her mind.

"I was wondering," she said. "Oaxaca hasn't been my home since I was a little girl. I want to spend time getting to know my family again, and I'll never want to be away from them for long, but..."

When she didn't finish, Cole asked, "What is it, Jenny? Go ahead."

"I'm wondering if there's any way that I could still work with you and the team there," she blurted. "If you could trust me, that is. And if Gene Olson would even allow it."

Cole thought about how to express his next thought, and Jenny misinterpreted the pause, "It's okay. I understand," she said.

"No, you don't. I was just trying to choose the right words. I was about to say, '*Mi familia es tu familia!*' My family is your family. You risked everything to help us, and you've earned our trust. You can come back whenever you're ready."

Cole filled Li and Lane in on his call with Jenny and had just told them she would be rejoining the team when Senator Rhodes' name was called by the legislative clerk. The camera showed a closeup of Eric, and Cole couldn't help but notice how earnest and dignified his friend looked. He was proud of him, and the three-person audience in his office cheered out loud when he declared his "Yea" with surety.

The final Senate tally was even more one-sided than the House vote, with the yeas outnumbering the nays ninety-eight to two. It wouldn't be official until seventy-five percent of the state legislatures voted in favor of the bill, but that was a formality. State senators and representatives had nothing to lose by voting for term limits for their federal counterparts, and they liked trying to be seen as leading a bill with so much support from their own voters. Across the country, state politicians were fighting each other to get the votes scheduled. Cole turned off the screen, and Li and Lane left to work on other cases. Just another day at the office.

Cole went over to his desk and settled into his chair. He thought about everything they'd been through the past few weeks and let out a sigh. He wondered if he would be able to focus on the other tasks his teams were working on and contemplated leaving early to be with Michele. He hadn't spent much time with her lately, and she would soon be off traveling the country on her belated book tour. Maybe he could swing by the little chapel on the Marquette campus on his way home; he had a lot to be grateful for and felt ready to express his thanks. He downed the rest of his coffee and stood up to leave when his desk phone chirped. He hit the button to take the call, and Gene came on. At least, he thought it was Gene, but instead of loud and brash, his voice was subdued.

"Hey, Cole."

"Hey yourself!"

There was a pause, and Cole could sense his mentor stalling, "I'm calling to tell you that Collin Jeffers will be added to the Wall of Honor here two weeks from today. I didn't want you to hear about it from someone else."

Cole was silent, and Gene added, "We need to do this. He died in the line of duty. If we don't, it'll raise questions and draw attention we don't want. Listen, I know he attacked Michele and tried to have you killed on behalf of Beneker and the Trinity, but..."

"No buts! Just stop, please," Cole said. "It's okay, Gene. You're taking my silence for something it's not, but I've gotten that more than once today. I think Collin *should* be on the Wall of Honor. He saved Eric and me and died in the process. In fact, I'd like to be present for the ceremony. If Collins' parents are there, it will give me the chance to tell them what their son did and how grateful I am."

Gene considered that. "I appreciate that, Cole. If you'd like, I'll include you in the ceremony, and you can say a few words. If memory serves, the two of you entered the Bureau at the same time and went through training together."

"That's right," Cole remembered. "It would be an honor to be part of the ceremony."

When the call ended, Cole leaned back in his chair and felt both drained and content. He knew that congressional term limits wouldn't fix everything that was wrong with his country's government. It was no magic pill that would cure all its ills. But it was a step in the right direction, finally, and a big step, at that. He looked up at the wall near his desk and smelled the faint odor of fresh paint. If he squinted slightly, he could just make out the patch job it covered, but only because he knew where to look. Earlier, he had removed the silver frame and the small "leadership" tape that mocked Special Agent Collin Jeffers. He thought about how Collin had only changed when that change was forced upon him and how both Brisbois and Wacouta had done the same. But all three had acted admirably from that point on. He could dismiss their actions, but instead, he'd rather celebrate them. *The world really does love a comeback story,* he thought, and he was glad to be part of that world.

With that, he walked to the door, shut off his office light, and headed home to the woman he loved.

A Note from the Author

Writers write to be read, and our readers make us or break us. If you like *The Killers' Terms*, I hope you will give the other novels (*The Killer Sermon* and *The Killer Speech*) in my Cole Huebsch series a try. And please consider writing a short review on Amazon, Goodreads, and/or Barnes and Noble. If you want to learn more about me, this book or upcoming author events and news, please visit my website—kevinkluesner.net. You can contact me from there and I will personally answer any questions you have. Thanks for joining me on this author journey!

Acknowledgements

Thanks first to my readers. The warm reception and encouragement I receive from you through library talks, book clubs, and my website (kevinkluesner.net) provide the energy to make future books possible. I'm especially grateful to all those who've left positive reviews of my earlier novels, *The Killer Sermon* and *The Killer Speech,* on Amazon, Barnes and Noble, Goodreads, and other popular book sites. Established authors tell me more reviews stimulate more buzz and more readers, so I'm unabashedly asking you to please take the time to review *The Killers' Terms.* And reach out to me on my website. I promise to respond to every email. Thanks to my family and early readers, especially Karri Adamson, Janet Kluesner, Paul McInerny, Mike Murphy, and Ty Kluesner. You all gave me encouragement and found things in this book that eventually made it better. Thanks to Cole Kluesner for putting his BA in Fine Arts from the U of Iowa to use in creating and designing the book cover for The Killers' Terms. This collaboration is becoming a habit and one I'm rather fond of. Finally, thanks to the "Dames of Detection" at my publisher, Level Best Books, for making my author dreams come true!

About the Author

Kevin Kluesner holds a BA in journalism and an MBA from Marquette University. He's worked as the outdoor writer for a daily newspaper, taught at the undergraduate and graduate level, and served as a chief administrator of an urban safety net hospital and a mental health emergency center. A Wisconsin native, *The Killers' Terms* is his third novel set in Wisconsin. When not reading thrillers after bedtime, he enjoys spending time with his wife Janet, finding wonder in nature, and golfing.

AUTHOR WEBSITE:
kevinkluesner.net

SOCIAL MEDIA HANDLES:
FaceBook: Kevin Kluesner
LinkedIn: Kevin Kluesner
Instagram: Kevin Kluesner

Also by Kevin Kluesner

The Killer Sermon

The Killer Speech

Printed in the USA
CPSIA information can be obtained
at www.ICGtesting.com
CBHW031435201024
16110CB00005B/12